Praise for Curse of the Midnight King

Curse of the Midnight King is perfect for readers looking for a haunting and evocative story that draws from familiar fairy tales but has enough of its own unique magic and mystery to keep you guessing with every page.

~Jenni Sauer

Author of The Evraft Novels

Magical and mesmerizing! Goldsberry elegantly weaves together two classic fairytales with an enchanting setting and altogether unique cast of characters. Prepare to be swept away in the first novel of what will undoubtedly be a dazzling series!

~Tara K. Ross

Award-winning YA author of *Fade to White*

Goldsberry takes familiar threads from a number of classic tales and expertly weaves them into an entirely new story as complex as it is captivating. Faye's inner struggle demonstrates how the lies we believe about ourselves can prove every bit as dangerous as curses or enemy kings, and her moving journey offers hope to anyone who has ever felt crushed by the weight of past mistakes. *Curse of the Midnight King*'s blend of danger, mystery, magic, and romance will keep fantasy fans eagerly turning pages and anticipating the next book!

~Laura Lucking

Award-winning author of The Tales of the Mystics

Curse of the Midnight King

Book One of the Tales of Faerie Land

To: Madison

Yakira Goldsberry

Yakira Goldsberry

Illuminate YA Fiction is an imprint of LPCBooks
a division of Iron Stream Media
100 Missionary Ridge, Birmingham, AL 35242
ShopLPC.com

Cover design by Elaina Lee

Library of Congress Control Number: 2021945489

ISBN-13: 978-1-64526-330-2
eBook ISBN: 978-1-64526-331-9

To Mom.

Thank you for instilling the love of stories in me and believing in me when I didn't believe in myself.

And to all the girls who have ever felt unworthy of love. God sees you and He loves you, no matter what.

Character Glossary

Revayr

Raoul de la Rou – Human King of Revayr
Nimue – Queen of Revayr, Titanian Faerie
Colette – Eldest Daughter of Raoul and Nimue
Desideria (Desi) – Second Eldest Daughter of Raoul and Nimue
Adalie – Daughter of Raoul and Nimue, Twin of Faye
Faye – Daughter of Raoul and Nimue, Twin of Adalie
Estelle – Daughter of Raoul and Nimue
Genevieve – Daughter of Raoul and Nimue
Kamille – Daughter of Raoul and Nimue
Linette – Daughter of Raoul and Nimue
Helaine – Princess of Revayr Daughter of Raoul and Nimue
Jenine – Princess of Revayr Daughter of Raoul and Nimue
Margaux – Princess of Revayr Daughter of Raoul and Nimue, twin of Belle
Belle – Princess of Revayr, youngest daughter of Raoul and Nimue, twin of Margaux

Madame Aurore Leroux – Former Countess of Avonlea, Wife of Gabriel
Delphine – Daughter of Gabriel and Aurore
Bonnie – Daughter of Gabriel and Aurore

Eura

Richard ap Owen – King of Eura, father of Lionheart
Lionheart (Leo) ap Owen – Prince of Eura, son of King Richard and Queen Cordelia
Cordelia – Former Queen of Eura, deceased
Jack – Leo's guard

Underworld/Everland

Athena – Previous White Lady of Everland
Cassiopeia – Daughter of the White Lady
Sirius – The self-proclaimed previous Midnight King
Andromeda – Wife of Sirius, the self-proclaimed Night Woman
Nosos – Sirius and Andromeda's eldest son
Ekidikeo – Sirius and Andromeda's second eldest son
Phagos – Sirius and Andromeda's son, twin of Pathos
Pathos – Sirius and Andromeda's son, the current Midnight King of the Underworld, Phagos's twin
Poneros – Sirius and Andromeda's second youngest son
Daimon – Sirius and Andromeda's youngest son

Prologue – Sirius

Everland was once beautiful. Thriving. A safe haven for Enchanters and one of the last islands untouched by those filthy creatures called Humans. It was a place where Sirius could work, creating an elixir that granted his fellow Enchanters immortality. Until the White Lady caught wind of his doings.

She stopped his experiments. She destroyed his laboratory. She stole his Human slaves he'd spent decades capturing. She even had the gall to set them loose, allowing these base creatures to call themselves citizens. Then, these Humans she rescued, coddled, and cared for turned on her. On him. On all of their kind.

They stole their dangerous potions of enchantment and brandished iron weapons. And although Sirius had made himself and his family immune to iron's effects, the others weren't so lucky. They fell to their deaths because they believed in a world of equality.

Wielding weapons long forgotten in Enchanter lore, he did what no one else could. He fought back, hunting the Humans one by one. When the others saw his courage, they joined him in his fight. Rising as one, they stood together to remove this plague of Humankind from sacred Enchanter soil.

But, one by one, the Enchanters fell. Each loss more bitter than the last. Until Sirius, his wife, and his sons were the only ones left.

And the White Lady.

For years, he had hunted the White Lady down to mete out her punishment. And after twenty years he found her here, in the Field of Sacrament, alone. Abandoned. Sirius curled his lip in disgust. She looked so frail amongst the bodies of the dead Humans she fought so hard to protect. They lay strewn across the muddied ground like forgotten toys, cast aside with their iron trappings.

Spread amongst them were the Enchanters. Those who had died fighting for the freedom to live without the Humans invading their land. The truth that Sirius had told them. But Sirius fought for another truth, a deeper truth. The truth of immortality. The very reason why the White Lady had turned on them.

Sirius would not let her take away his immortality. The White Lady began this war. And Sirius intended to end it.

Pain filled every bone, every muscle, every vein of Sirius' body. He gasped for breath, the air thick with ash and smoke. Digging his boots into the blood-soaked soil, he gathered the power within. Only, when he reached down into his core, he found nothing. No wild rush of energy that filled him like the swell of ocean waves. No burning taste of steel on his tongue. He was empty.

To his right, his beloved stood, her raven hair juxtaposed against the white ash covering the ground like snow.

She was stunning, even with the muddied ash and blood caking her face. Andromeda, the Night Woman, his wife. Her veins glowed a brilliant red as she gathered her energy for one final blast. How ironic that they were the last of their kind, on the verge of extinction. Here, they would die, on the very grounds that served as the birthing place of the very first Enchanters. When her ebony eyes met his, there was no doubt. If they went down, they would go down together.

But, as she spun, snapping her fingers, the White Lady swept in like a wave, knocking her down with a single strike of white light.

His beloved fell. Struggled to breathe. And grew still.

Seconds passed. Hours it seemed. But she did not rise. Rage, pure and unbridled rage burned in his chest, eating him from the inside out. How dare she betray her own kind!

On Sirius's other side, his son Pathos let out a wild scream. "Mother!"

Pathos burst into a run. Sirius held out his arm to keep him back. Pathos slammed into his arm; the boy's face twisted in agony.

Sirius glared up at the White Lady, who loomed over him on the top of the hill, sweat plastering her silver-white hair to her wrinkled forehead. She was old, almost as ancient as the grounds beneath his feet, but still the most powerful Enchantress to ever walk the earth. The first to ever achieve immorality.

She had been his tutor, teaching him everything he knew. He had even dared to call her friend. But now she was their murderer.

Pathos' cries rang through the heavy silence. Sirius pulled him close, trapping the boy against him. The White Lady's chin trembled. She looked on Pathos with sympathy, her shoulders slumped with weariness. Or was it regret?

Still, she lifted a steady hand. Light filled her palm. Sirius shoved Pathos behind him. A cloud of ash rose as Pathos stumbled. Sirius coughed and his lungs seized in protest.

"So," he rasped, "this is how it ends for us? An Enchanter dying at the hands of his queen?" He spat blood. "And for what? So you could protect your little pets? Your *Humans*? The same creatures you once so eagerly drained for immortality?"

She stood firm, her jaw clenched, white eyes hard. "That was before I knew the price we would have to pay."

"You were the one who started this sixty years ago. One of the first to steal the years of life from the creatures you now fight so hard to protect." Sirius unleashed a laugh as he collapsed to the earth.

Pathos broke free and ran to his mother. The White Lady didn't take her eyes from Sirius. He plunged his hand into the ash, searching for his dagger. He had lost his sword long ago.

"Had you been wiser, perhaps you would have refrained from teaching your dark arts to a willing student."

"I will no longer sacrifice mortals just so I can live!"

"And that, my *lady*, is what makes you weak," Sirius growled, stalling her for as long as he could. "A few lives taken won't change the balance of the world. And goodness knows the Humans benefit from the occasional culling. The filth reproduce like rats."

The White Lady shook her head, her face streaked with tears. Her arms trembled—her skin now pockmarked from years of endless battle. She carried the weakness of age, and yet she still managed to keep death at bay. It was infuriating.

"You are wrong. What if the mortal you killed was meant to fulfill a prophecy? What then? The fate of everything changes. And *you* are the one to blame," she bit out, her tone accusatory. Her hands glowed brighter and she took a step closer.

Sirius felt something hot beneath his fingers. He grabbed it tight. "I care not for prophecies and fate. I care only for the future. *My* future."

With those words, he shoved to his feet. The White Lady raised a hand, the clouded sky pierced by skeleton trees as her backdrop. Pale light spilled from her fingers. He had only seconds to reach her before she would burn him from the inside out.

Shoving forward on his toes, Sirius surged up the hill.

"Father!" Pathos called but Sirius ignored him.

The White Lady cupped her hands together. The light in her palms grew brighter. Sirius lunged. His dagger connected with her chest. But it was the wrong side. He had pierced her lung, not her heart.

Letting loose a wild cry, the White Lady shoved Sirius with her shoulder. They both tumbled down the hill and Sirius slammed into the trunk of a burnt tree. Pain shot through his side. He coughed and heaved in a wild breath.

Beside him, the White Lady staggered to her feet, the dagger still embedded in her chest. She lifted her arms and a brilliant white light flashed. Sirius covered his eyes, but it still spilled through his fingers and turned the world red.

The ground shook. It was just a tremor at first, then strengthened, until everything vibrated with power. A loud cracking filled the air and Sirius struggled to rise. What was the White Lady doing? Tearing Everland in half?

"Haven't you destroyed enough of our land already?" he shouted, voice rasping in his throat.

The sun's pale light dimmed. To the west, the walls of the sea rose up, hovering over his castle in the distance. His breath caught in his throat. Horror gripped him in its icy claws, and he leaned heavily against the tree. The bark dug into his skin. He had never seen this kind of magic before. He knew that the White Lady was powerful but not this. Not this.

Pathos ran to Sirius's side, terror in his eyes. Sirius clutched his son close.

"Father, what's happening?"

"I don't know but stand strong. She hasn't defeated us yet."

Pathos' thin shoulders straightened, and he pulled his own golden dagger from his belt. Though fear made his hand shake, he stood firm. His son's innocent courage brought an ounce of determination back into Sirius's bones.

Today, he would show his son the true meaning of courage. So that he would grow to become an unstoppable Enchanter. Sirius' heart pinched. That is, if they didn't both die today.

The White Lady remained standing, unshakable. She dragged her hands down and coughed, blood spurting from her lips. The ground shook again, harder. The sea rose higher but did not crash onto land. As far as Sirius knew, she could only manipulate light and land. Not water. That gift had only been bestowed to himself. She couldn't—

Impossible. She was pulling Everland underground.

"No!"

Sirius lifted his own arms and gripped the ocean. The water roiled at his touch and he pulled downward. A funnel formed, the water folding in on itself. It spilled down into the hole the White Lady had created. He could feel the coldness of it, the frigid water crashing and filling.

Dropping one hand, the White Lady flicked her fingers. A ripple of light slammed into his chest. Searing pain flared, burning, eating away at his nerves, his skin. He fell back, hitting the ground as he lost his hold. Sirius reached out once more but his magic slammed into a barrier. Waves of light rippled around him. He was trapped.

Fear, cold and empty, snagged at Sirius' heart. He stared at the castle out of reach, where Nosos, his oldest son, had taken his brothers. Had they made it? Were they crying, scared and alone? Tomorrow was to be the spring of Daimon's immortality, sealed with the light of the rising sun. An ancient ritual that would grant his youngest son a life three times as long as that of a mortal's. But as the walls of the sea rose higher and higher, Sirius realized it was too late. They would be trapped underground until their last dying breaths.

Sirius pounded on the barrier. His fists sent up brilliant white sparks that rained down on Andromeda's body and Pathos' head. His heart squeezed in his chest. Was he to lose both his sons and his wife to a madwoman?

"You can't take this from me, from us!" Sirius roared. "Die already!"

The White Lady looked at him, her triumphant grin stained red. "Never fear, dear Sirius," she shouted over the rumbling ground. "Your sons will be granted immortality. But it shall only be a half-life. Cursed forever as one of the Undead."

"No!"

With one last punch, he broke through her light. The taste of steel touched his tongue as he drew on his power. The wild rush of magic filled his bones, and elation set his nerves tingling. He reached for the dagger in her chest. Maybe he couldn't save them. But he could certainly kill the traitor queen.

He jerked his hand back and the dagger flew from her chest. The hot metal connected with his skin and he tightened his fingers around the hilt. The White Lady gasped and fell to her knees. Still, the sea rose.

Only, it wasn't the sea anymore. Darkness covered the land as earthen walls rose all around. Roots and rocks, brown soil and red clay. The ground was eating them alive. It arched over their heads, closing in, knitting itself together even as they continued to descend.

Sirius fell to his knees.

"Never shall Everland see the light again. This place shall be cursed! An underworld of suffering and pain."

"You cannot do this!" Sirius spun toward her.

He reached out with his magic and threw the dagger. It grazed by the White Lady, sliding into the ash.

The White Lady coughed, blood spilling from her lips to stain her white dress. The soil turned to stone. Deep, grey stone lit only by the light shining from her skin. With a clap of her hands, the rumbling slowed. The ground jerked, then stilled. Above, a crunching crackle sounded as the rock twisted into a tight spiral. With one last crack, everything grew still.

Sirius steadied himself, then summoned the dagger back to his hand. It landed in his palm. He gripped it tight and staggered to his feet. His ears rang in the silence. The White Lady's gurgling breaths grew loud.

"How could you?" His voice was just a whisper.

He couldn't make the words come any louder. But he needed to know. He needed to know why she would side with the Humans. With the vermin. So what if he had been rounding them up and stealing their years? They were expendable creatures, like mice to feed the cat's belly. It didn't give her any excuse to destroy this ancient land and mow down her own people like wheat. To curse his sons.

The White Lady ignored him. She lowered her hands. Her shoulders sagged and her hair fell before her face, shielding her expression. With a sigh, she crumpled. Ash billowed around her like embers from a fire.

Struggling to breathe, she coughed and then spoke. "I didn't want this. I didn't want to destroy our land. But you forced my hand."

"I forced nothing." He stalked closer, his grip so tight around the dagger that it trembled.

"Hear my words, Sirius." The White Lady pushed her long hair away from her face. "This is the curse I lay upon you and your family until you learn to treat others with respect.

"If your sons can lay aside selfishness and prejudice, and find the true meaning of love, they will break free of the curse. Only then will they be able to live the lives of Enchanters and build a new Everland."

Sirius growled as he gripped her hair and jerked her head up. He placed the knife against her throat. If he stopped her from finishing the curse, it would be void, as the laws of Everland stated. He pressed the blade into her aged skin.

"You shall be immortal, Midnight King." She grinned, even as the blood dripped down her throat. "And the only thing that can kill you now is gold."

Pain lanced through Sirius's hand. His fingers seized and he dropped the blade. The gold of the hilt winked up at him in the twilight. Anger surged through his veins. With gold containing the most potent magic, she had just wrested away his sons' only means of protection.

If only he could squeeze the life out of her. Drain her soul and revive his magic. Then maybe, just maybe, he could reverse this whole mess. Instead, he fell to his knees, his energy spent. Sorrow, sharp and swift, pricked his heart.

"Are you finished?" he growled. "Or do I have to break your neck and silence your tongue?"

She blinked, the movement slow. "I wasn't the one who did this to you. You are. You have terrorized the mortal world enough, Midnight King. Now, you can only be a terror to yourself."

Quick as lighting, she gripped the dagger and drove it into Sirius's chest. Sirius let out a roar and knocked her to the side.

She fell to the ground, her white eyes sightless, her chest still. Sirius let loose a wild yell that echoed in the stillness. She was wrong. The White Lady had to be wrong. *He* hadn't brought this upon himself and his people. He had only wanted what was best. Immortality, without fear of death.

He only wanted to live in freedom. Able to do anything he wished. Free to wipe the existence of the disgusting Humans off the face of the earth, to make it safe for his family to live in. For all Enchanters.

Turning, he crawled through the ash toward Andromeda, sending up clouds of white. Sirius brushed the hair from her forehead. He would take his revenge. Bring down the walls of her curse for Andromeda's sake. For his sons'.

Pathos gripped his mother's shoulders and shook her.

"Mother," he whimpered. "Mother, wake up!"

Sirius leaned closer, heart pounding. He pressed his ear to her chest. Her steady heartbeat thrummed in time with his own. Relief loosened the muscles in his shoulders and filled the growing hole in his heart. Death had not robbed him of her yet.

Pathos's eyes widened as he turned to Sirius. "Father, you're bleeding!"

Sirius looked down. Blood soaked the front of his embroidered grey tunic. He fought for breath. Panic seized him. He couldn't die. He couldn't leave his sons alone. Trembling, he gripped Pathos's shoulder.

"Listen to me, son. Look after your brothers. Keep them safe."

"But Father, Nosos is the oldest. He—"

"I know!" Sirius crouched and warm blood filled his mouth. "But I'm bestowing my powers to you. You will become the new Midnight King."

Pathos's beautiful black eyes, so much like his mother's, widened and he nodded. His jaw clenched. "I'll try, Father. I'll try to protect them."

"You must find … find a half-blood Fae from Revayr. You must find them and make them dance to break the seal. Only an In-Between is strong enough."

"But how do I do that?"

"You'll—" Sirius coughed again. He collapsed into the ash. Pathos released a cry and tightened his grip on Sirius' arms. Sirius reached up and gripped the back of Pathos' neck. "You'll be able to visit the upper world. My death will weaken the curse just enough. You won't be in your physical body, but you can do it."

"Father, don't leave me," Pathos whimpered. Tears ran down his cheeks.

"The only way for the seal to fully break is if an Enchanter descended from the White Lady uses their magic. The combination of Fae and Enchanter magic will destroy any remnants of the curse. The In-Between will be drawn to the Enchanter's magic. You *must* find this Enchanter. Do this, and you and your brothers will be free. Do you understand?"

"Father, you're not making any sense."

Sirius lunged forward and gripped Pathos' shoulders.

"You *have* to understand! Tell me! Do you understand?"

Pathos nodded, face twisted in pain.

Sirius could feel his life nearing its end. He pulled Pathos into a tight hug and kissed his hair.

"Promise me," he rasped. "Promise me."

"I promise, Father. I'll save us."

Sirius closed his eyes. There was nothing more he could do for his sons. He just hoped that they would fight for their freedom and renew the war against Humans. The White Lady was dead. But this was only just the beginning.

Chapter One – Faye

"Do you think it's all true, Faye? About the princesses? The ones who went missing?"

Faye dropped a clothespin, cursing her clumsiness.

"They say it's just an old story, *petit papillon*," Faye said as she carefully tucked the bloomers under her arm and stooped to scoop up the clothespin.

Squeezing her way between rows of squash and tomatoes, Faye returned to the clothesline.

A few feet away, just beyond the low picket fence, Bonnie Leroux lay on her stomach beneath the shade of an ancient willow tree. Blond curls haloed around her soft round face, contrasting beautifully against her golden-brown skin. With tiny fingers she idly plucked off the heads of daisies blooming in the tall grass.

"Yes, but what about *you*?" Bonnie waved a daisy in the air as if to emphasize her point. "Do you believe?"

Faye paused, unsure of how to answer. In the Human world, fantastical tales involving Fae magic had always been reduced to myths and bedtime stories. And here, in Eura, those stories were just that—stories. But still, the memories of her home called to her, echoing in every inch of her being. It was becoming harder every day not to share stories of her homeland, of her sisters. Especially with little Bonnie. It helped ease the homesickness and, for a little while, helped her forget the curse.

But, it was dangerous to speak of the truth here. King Richard ap Owen would behead anyone who revealed themselves as Fae or magicfolk. Just last week a Draconian woman was hanged for crossing the border and her body was sent back to Draconia with a warning.

1

And then there were the wings. Faye bit her lip. She shoved the image from her mind. Bonnie had done nothing wrong by expressing curiosity. Perhaps it wouldn't hurt to treat the stories as myth and leave it at that.

But she couldn't bring herself to lie.

Just one small truth. That's all, she told herself.

"Yes, I do believe in them," Faye replied, giving Bonnie a gentle smile.

Bonnie nodded, humming a tune from an old nursery rhyme.

Pinning up the bloomers, Faye let her fingers run along the thick cord. At least she seemed satisfied, for now.

As Faye continued to hang up laundry, she made sure to keep Bonnie within sight. The little girl was prone to darting off after squirrels and rabbits, and the last thing Faye needed was another scolding from Madame Leroux for letting her precious little cherub get muddy.

Lifting one of Bonnie's petticoats from the basket, Faye sighed. The once flawless cream fabric was now permanently marred by a brown stain. Red clay. Another outfit ruined. Biting her lip, Faye set the petticoat aside. It looked like she'd be taking Bonnie to the tailor again sooner than she thought.

As Faye neared the bottom of the basket, she heard Bonnie pipe up once more, "But *why* do you believe?"

There was no avoiding it now.

"Because," Faye murmured, dreading the lecture from Madame that would follow. "I knew them."

Bonnie gasped and clutched her cheeks. "You *knew* the princesses? Really, truly knew?"

Smiling, Faye nodded, though underneath, she shuddered. Never before had she dared whisper this truth to Bonnie, or even to Madame Leroux. It was a truth she couldn't bear to face in the daylight. If they found out who she was, what would they say? What would they do?

Most believed the tale of the twelve disappearing princesses was Naught more than a myth. Others believed it to be the work of witches. Madame Leroux had forbidden all speech of myths and tales for their safety. Faye wasn't sure just how much more she could share.

"They were lovely," she said finally, keeping her tone light. "Just like you."

Bonnie beamed and bounced in the grass. "Ooh, what were they like?"

"Well—"

"Bonnie!" Madame Leroux's silken voice floated across the garden. "Bonnie dear, come inside!"

Relief flooded through Faye, even as Bonnie's countenance fell. With a heavy sigh, Bonnie clambered to her feet, her toes snagging on the hem of her dress. She fell backwards and burst into giggles. Faye couldn't help but smile. This time as Bonnie stood, she pulled her skirts up to her knees.

She looked back at the house, then to Faye.

"Mama is calling me." She pouted, sticking out her bottom lip.

Faye gestured toward the house. "Then you'd best run off."

"I know." Bonnie dragged the toe of her pristine white shoe in the grass.

Then, with a shy smile, she dashed forward and threw her arms around Faye's waist. Faye ran the back of her hand down the girl's soft cheek.

"Run along now. You don't want to keep her waiting."

Bonnie skipped off across the lawn. Delphine, Madame's eldest daughter, appeared at the corner of the house and held out her hand. Bonnie took it and together they disappeared.

The sight filled Faye's chest with an odd ache. While the family had welcomed her as part of their household, she never felt like she belonged. And she would never presume she was accepted that way. It was too brash a thought. But it made her long for her own family even more.

For three years Faye had been living with them. She paused at the thought. Three years ago, her life was wrenched from her grasp. No title. No kingdom to call her home. Nothing but a pair of slippers tying her to her wretched mistake.

When Madame Leroux found Faye that day, it was the morning after she and her sisters had been dragged down into the Underworld. Faye had wandered the streets of this strange country, unsure of how she had arrived in Eura from Revayr. Cold, hungry, and desperate, Faye wasn't sure if she would ever recover from the nightmare.

But then Madame Leroux had come along. Faye had been huddled in the corner of an alley, too afraid to move, when a woman leaning on a gilded cane hobbled up and asked her if she was alright. Too frightened to reply, Faye only shook her head. Madame then reached down and beckoned her to come.

Keeping at a distance, Faye had followed Madame home and was greeted by her two daughters with mild curiosity. They gave her a warm supper, and an invitation to stay as long as she needed. Faye had lived with them ever since, unsure if she could even go home. The ever-looming threat of being swallowed by the Underworld had her hesitating. Faye shuddered and wrapped her arms around herself. Cold crept through her limbs.

Closing her eyes, Faye tilted her face to the sun. She imagined its brightness shining down on her home castle. The brilliant white turrets and the red-and-blue flag of Revayr. The abundance of fish and snail for supper and the marzipan for dessert. The wild swans that would nest on the shores of the lake. The beautiful, round language.

Faye reached back into the basket and shook out a bodice. Her home was known as the kingdom of dance, and for good reason. Every year they held a celebration that lasted a whole week, a week of dancing and feasting and basking in the freedom it gave. The thought constricted her throat.

She paused as longing overwhelmed her. She longed to hear her mother whisper her name. To feel the warmth of her father's hugs. To listen to the stories Mama always told of her homeland of Titania, the world of Fae inside Eura. She longed to stay up late whispering with her sisters of pretty dresses and princes and nonsense.

Faye bit her lip hard as her eyes grew hot and stung with tears. She pinned more clothing onto the line with a sort of aggressive ferocity. She couldn't think about them. She couldn't think about that last night they had been together, *really* together and not separated by distance across a shadowy ballroom. Of that time when they prepared for an evening of dancing. Dancing on a stage to music and the applause of the crowd. Waiting to start the midnight performance.

Only they never did.

Faye shook her head and the skirt she held slipped from her shaking fingers. No. She couldn't think on that either. Not again. If she did, she would scream.

I'm sorry. The thought echoed in her mind, over and over. Faye wiped at the tear on her cheek and sucked in a breath. *I'm so, so sorry.*

Her silent apology hung in the air like an empty promise. There was nothing she could do to change what she had done. Wishing away guilt would get her nowhere. Emptiness, cold and hard, coiled in her chest. It weighed heavy, pulling her down.

Pushing back tears, Faye picked up the skirt and shook the dirt and grass from it. She pinned it to the line.

"Faye!"

Madame Leroux. Faye's heart skipped a beat as Bonnie's question returned to mind. Had she told Madame about the story? What if Madame connected the pieces together? If she figured out that Faye was not only half Faerie but also one of the missing princesses …

Faye pushed aside her worries. Madame was from Revayr, just as she was. Madame wouldn't turn her over to the king just for being a half-blood.

Would she?

"You're being such a goosecap," Faye whispered to herself. Madame couldn't glean her identity just from a few innocent questions.

"Faye!"

Brushing her hands on her skirt, Faye tried to calm her racing heart. Everything would be fine. Just fine.

"Coming, Madame!" she called back.

Picking up the basket, she carried it across the garden, past the looming sunflowers, to the back door. She gripped the wooden handle and pulled, but the door wouldn't budge. A sigh escaped her lips. Stuck again.

Making her way through the trellis, she walked down the tiny path to the front of the house. The bustle of the street grew louder as she approached the front gate. A horse and cart passed by; the driver slouched in his seat. Beyond, a boy and a girl raced each other across the cobblestones. A woman across the street chased a goose from her cottage. Faye took a small step backwards at the sight. A small shiver ran across her skin. While she loved swans, she had never been particularly friendly with geese.

The sound of hoofbeats on stone announced the coming of a group of riders. Tall, sleek horses festooned in the royal colors of red and gold stepped in time. Each carried a rider decked out in royal livery.

Faye inched closer. They were guards, either on their rounds or escorting some Eurish noble. The sight of them always brought on a mix of odd emotions. Grief. Terror. Longing. They represented riders of doom for magicfolk, and yet Faye couldn't help but think of her own kingdom. A cruel reminder that she was here, and not home.

When her gaze settled on the central rider, she gasped, and the laundry basket slipped from her fingers.

It was Prince Lionheart ap Owen of Eura, surrounded by guards dressed in stiff red coats with golden embroidery. He sat tall in the saddle, lips stretched in a wide, jovial smile. He was laughing, posture relaxed. Lifting a hand, he brushed it across his tousled red locks that gleamed a fiery orange in the sunlight. Embarrassment, or maybe the heat, brought a scarlet blush to his pale cheeks.

But there was something else about him. Something Faye could never quite put her finger on. It drew the eye and if she weren't looking directly at him, Leo almost seemed to *glow*, as if his happiness could be seen on his skin. If Faye were foolish enough, she'd call it magic. But Leo wasn't magic. He was a Human, through and through.

He turned his head, bright grey eyes latching onto hers.

Faye sucked in a gasp. He was here. On the street. Next to Madame's house. And he was looking right at her. Fear coiled in her stomach and she froze. Would he recognize her? It had been three years since they had seen each other, but despite the fact, he hadn't changed much at all. So, he must recognize her. Would he call out to her?

Oh no. She couldn't have that. She couldn't let him see her. No. What if he sided with his father? His father, King Richard, had a hatred for Fae that knew no bounds. And half-bloods were despised even more. While Leo hadn't been averse to her before, three years could change a person's mind.

Something silver flashed in the crowd. Faye's heart jumped into her throat. Something tracking Leo.

In between the horses she caught a glimpse. A gray wolf head. Everything inside Faye froze. Her muscles stiffened and the urge to run flooded her.

That wasn't just any wolf head.

Whirling around, she darted inside, bolting the door shut behind her. It couldn't have been Pathos. It couldn't have. Pathos would never dare to show his face in sunlight.

Chapter Two – Leo

Prince Lionheart "Leo" the Second of Eura sat tall on his grey charger as he rode through the capital city of Brighthaven. The day was bright, the trees lining the streets were all in bloom, and the people bustled with life. Just the whole busyness and fascination of it all brought a smile to Leo's lips. It was certainly a wonderful day.

"You seem very exuberant today, Your Highness," Jack, the captain of Leo's guard, called out from atop his monstrous bay mount.

Leo twisted in his saddle toward the large man. Jack and his horse were very much alike—both of a coppery color, well-muscled from hard work, and both blessed with an unflappable disposition. Jack's steadiness and stability were just what Leo needed, or so his father said, to keep his *unchecked behavior* at bay. Father just didn't know how to have any fun.

"Indeed I am, Jack! As exuberant as a man can be when he has escaped a madman with a paintbrush who insisted I *sit still*. Heavens above, what a dull and tedious task sitting still is!"

Jack laughed and shook his head. "Indeed, sitting still for a portrait that just might help a woefully hideous prince get married is such a daunting task."

While Leo knew Jack was jesting, he couldn't have spoken a better truth. "I'm afraid you may be right. However, while you may be inclined to the idea of marriage, I am still but a young man who has yet to see all corners of the world. Not being tied down to a woman of Father's choosing and being free from the abhorrent task of running a kingdom is all that I could ever ask."

He reached up and brushed at his hair, nervous energy surging through him. The idea of marrying a woman he knew he couldn't love, or would never love him in return, was unthinkable. Before Mother had died, Leo knew hers and Father's relationship had been strained at best.

Glancing to the side, he caught sight of a young woman holding a basket, watching as he rode by. Her hair was long and rippled with waves and shone like melted caramel. A dreamy look filled her dark eyes. Leo shifted, uncomfortable. He received many dreamy looks from maidens both young and old, simply because he was a prince, and not because he was handsome.

Leo narrowed his eyes. Something about her seemed familiar. She looked almost like …

But no. It couldn't be.

The girl's expression changed from dreamy to frightened. Twisting about, she fled down the gravel path and into the house, leaving the basket behind. Leo gripped his horse's mane and twisted back to look until his knees protested.

Not the common reaction he was used to. Usually, women fawned over him with concealed—or unconcealed—greed. Leo liked to think it was because of his rugged good looks, but he knew the truth. Unfortunately, he hadn't inherited his father's kingly looks—the square jaw and steely eyes—but instead inherited his mother's soft oblong face, making him look more like a sad aquatic creature and less like a prince.

Jack's voice drew Leo's attention once more.

"There was a time, Your Highness, when marriage was the only thought on your mind. The only thing poor you could think of was that pretty little princess, Faye de la Rou of Revayr."

Leo's smile slipped and he cleared his throat. His jovial mood faded. *Blast it all.* Couldn't Jack leave it be? It had been three long years since Faye and her sisters had disappeared. And ever since then, Revayr had fallen into ruin. With twelve half-Fae princesses and a Faerie queen missing, the Fae had grown enraged, engaging the Humans in a tiresome battle. They blamed the Humans for their disappearance while the Humans blamed the Fae for the same thing. All the while King Raoul tried to keep the peace in his crumbling land.

It took Leo only a few months of watching the chaos engulf the once beautiful land, before he decided to join the search for the princesses and queen. However, the task proved difficult, as King Richard, Leo's father, held no love for Fae kind. He saw them as a plague to be eradicated and had even passed an edict stating that all those of Fae blood were to be exiled to the Blackwood.

If things continued the way they were, Leo was afraid the Fae of Eura would start a revolt.

Jack cleared his throat. "Forgive me, Your Highness. It was insensitive of me to bring up the princess."

Leo swallowed back a sarcastic reply. It had been three years. Jack should know better by now not to bring up Faye.

"No matter. What's done is done. No need to dwell on the past."

Still, he couldn't blame his guard for his skepticism and jokes. Jack, like many others, had never stepped foot on Revayr's shores. No one except Leo, his father, and a few select servants even knew Leo had gone to Revayr as a child.

King Raoul's weapons master was renowned in all the five kingdoms. Father had wanted only the best for Leo. Master Pierre was barking mad, but he knew his craft and Leo strove to be the best student he could. It quickly became the best few years of Leo's life.

However, because of Eura's animosity against Fae, Revayr suddenly became a myth among his people and their royalty characters of legend. It was disheartening, seeing the wonderful family Leo had spent his summers with reduced to nothing but fables—the princesses even labeled as monsters.

"The sooner we get this whole marriage thing over, the better. I'm absolutely tired of these portraits and proposals," Leo said at last.

"That's the spirit!"

"Not helping."

"Forgive me, my lord, but with the rumors of the Enchanters …"

"What?" Leo asked, jolting up in his saddle.

"It's nothing, my lord." Jack shifted his weight and cleared his throat. "Just a slip of the tongue."

"Jack, tell me now," Leo demanded. "What's this about the Enchanters? Father decreed they went extinct years ago!"

Again, Jack cleared his throat. His neck turned red. "You see, well, your father expressly forbade me from telling you …"

"If I'm to be your king, I would find out eventually."

"Very true, my lord. It's just, after what happened to Faye and the others, we were afraid how you would … take the news."

"What news?"

Jack grew quiet a moment. He looked away. Leo held up his hand and the procession came to a stop. He steered his horse to the right so that it blocked Jack's horse. Jack sighed and rubbed his neck.

"It seems one of the princesses is dead."

"Who?" Leo asked, his heart racing.

"According to the letter, Princess Colette. But all that was sent was a box, a note, and … it's horrible, I can't—"

"Tell me." Leo gripped his reins so tight his knuckles popped.

"And one of her fingers." Disgust filled his words.

Colette. She was the eldest of Raoul's daughters. Cold and distant, she'd never attempted to befriend Leo. But this news was still a blow to the gut.

12

"The note stated that if the king continued his crusade against magicfolk, they'd send up the next princess' head."

The world swam before Leo's eyes. He sat back in his saddle as a crushing weight pressed against his lungs. Colette. Dead. Murdered by the monsters locked in the dark. That could only mean ... He shuddered and bile rose in his throat. There was something more going on here. Something he could see taking shape in his mind.

"That ... that is ... is ..." He struggled to find words to name this monstrosity.

Jack nodded. "The White Lady should have just killed them all."

The Enchanters were a plague and a menace, stealing Humans and using them for their own twisted gain. Leo's gut twisted. Because of it, his own father had turned to punishing magicfolk.

"Father won't do anything about it, will he?" It was more a statement than a question. He knew his father. His cruelty toward magicfolk would never be swayed by the potential of mending the rift between Eura and Revayr. Father was too proud for that.

Still, ostracizing those with magic just because of the wickedness of a handful of Fae had torn Revayr apart. Leo didn't want the same happening in Eura. Although, he couldn't deny that it had already begun. After all, even admitting sympathies for the Fae was social suicide, something that Leo, as a prince, couldn't risk.

The only way to stop both kingdoms from falling into ruin was to mend the rift. And the only way to mend it was to find twelve princesses and a queen who could all very well be dead.

Chapter Three – Faye

The little clock above the hearth chimed twelve. Magic, sharp and bitter, tugged at Faye's mind like tiny, grasping claws. Faye groaned. If only she could sleep just a little bit longer.

The plush couch was comfortable, begging her to go back to sleep. Her thick blanket kept the chill at bay and weighed her down. She snuggled deeper, too tired to move. The infernal magic tugged again. Grumbling, she stood and leaned against the fireplace, blinking hard.

Fatigue still weighed on her, both from chasing after Bonnie all afternoon and helping a distraught Delphine find the right shade of purple for her latest embroidery project. Then, that evening, Madame Leroux took her daughters to the graveyard to honor their dead father and brother. Faye had tagged along, too afraid to stay home alone.

Everywhere she saw the silver wolf mask. But when she blinked, it was gone. Remnants of fear clung to her sleep-addled mind.

Everything was dark. The fire burned out hours ago. From the window, the full moon's weak light outlined the sitting room's few occupants: a large family portrait that hung over the fireplace next to the clock, the small round table that held Madame's herbs, and the pile of books balanced on the windowsill.

Something glinted next to the books. Faye jumped and bit back a gasp. The moonlight played along the lip of Delphine's teacup she'd left on the sill. Faye placed a hand on her chest to calm her racing heart. She was just being silly. Pathos would never come into Madame's home.

The house was a sanctuary, protected by its sleeping occupants. At least, that was what she told herself every night. This house was safe. As long as she stayed away from the door and windows, she was safe.

"Not tonight," she whispered to herself, the fear sinking its claws back into her.

The magic yanked at her again, as if there were a string tied about her heart and some cruel boy was pulling on the other end. She stumbled forward and growled as the fear spiked. She would not let Pathos control her emotions.

Crouching down, Faye tossed her long hair over her shoulder and pulled a brick from the center of the outer hearth. Reaching inside, she removed a pair of glass slippers.

Cut from wyvern-forged glass made by the Draconians of the far northern highlands, they were delicately crafted with a scrollwork heel and pattern of pointed leaves cut along the edges. And they were severely uncomfortable.

Faye and her sisters each received a pair of the horrid things on their first night in the Underworld. And every night since, Faye's feet suffered perpetual blisters and bruises. That was the curse of delicate Faerie skin. It always took much longer to heal.

The magic tugged again.

"I'm coming, you impatient monster," she mumbled.

She slipped the shoes over her bare feet and crawled into the fireplace, the coals hot beneath her palms. Reaching out, she pressed her fingers against the back wall of the fireplace. It released a loud scraping sound and slid open like a door. There was a time when Faye worried that the others in the house would be awakened, but they slumbered on as if in an enchanted sleep, deaf to every sound she made. It was not a comforting thought.

Once she entered the tunnel, the back of the fireplace swung shut behind her, leaving her in total darkness. Faye waited, her breath the only sound. A light sprang up beside her, forcing her to squeeze her eyes shut. It spilled through her eyelids, turning her vision red. When she opened her eyes, tiny spheres of light hovered in the air, glowing a soft gold, illuminating the murals on the walls.

Faye crawled forward a short way. The tunnel was more like a long doorway, lasting only the length of Madame's fireplace floor. Beyond, the ceiling rose sharply into darkness. Faye stood upright and the lights rose with her. They danced and flitted like the pixies of the obsidian forest. Paintings of silver, gold, and diamond trees covered every inch of the smooth stone walls. Really, if this weren't the path to her nightly nightmare, she would have admired the paintings. Like she did the first time.

Her heart sped up its tempo and her throat tightened as slowly her soot-stained nightgown cinched tight until it felt like it had melded with her skin. When Faye felt she could no longer breathe, the nightgown changed. Color bled into the ragged skirt, a deep and rich gold. Flaring out, layers of fabric formed underneath, and glimmering threads wove through the outer skirt along the hem, forming the silhouettes of gold-trees, razor-edged leaves dropping from the branches. The fabric was as smooth as silk yet rippled like liquid glass.

Faye sucked in a breath as her top twisted, the loose fabric curling and hardening into a corset. Embroidery ran up the boning and around, curling into hundreds of small branches, each tipped with tiny diamonds that winked in the enchanted light. The neckline folded and became square, lined with delicate white lace.

A golden fan appeared in her hand and her hair was tugged back. That blasted comb Pathos had given her the day they had first met scraped her scalp, settling over her right ear.

Faye paused as the tunnel sloped down into a curving staircase. She leaned against the wall and sucked in deep breaths.

Pathos. That monstrous demon who stared at her with hunger in his eyes, just waiting for the day when he could fully claim her as his own. She shuddered and for a moment, tears stung her eyes. She pushed them back. It was no use crying. This was her fate. Her just punishment for pulling her sisters down with her into the dark. She deserved every hurt she received.

If only her sisters didn't have to suffer with her.

Straightening her shoulders, Faye placed her foot on the first step. The walls fell away and, in their place, grew a forest. Golden trees with golden leaves stretched across soft ground as far as the eye could see. A perpetual twilight hung over the branches, bathing them in the soft kiss of pale incandescence.

Faye kept her eyes ahead as she descended the steps carved from loamy earth. They twisted down in a spiral, and the forest twisted with them. Slowly, the gold-trees thinned and were replaced by skinny, silver-trunked trees with silver needles.

Faye paused before the very last gold-tree. She held out her hand and waited. Bending forward, the gold-tree shed a handful of teardrop-shaped leaves into her palm. The leaves melted into a puddle of gold, then twisted and turned until a colombina mask rested in her hand. The edges were gilded with lace-like patterns of swirling gold. A giant, gilded butterfly wing swooped around and out from the right eye. It seemed to glow in the light, beautiful and pristine.

The mask weighed cold and heavy in her hand. The urge to throw it into a raging fire and watch it melt away swelled within her and her fingers twitched. She could do it. She could destroy the mask, destroy the slippers, and never see this place again.

Instead, she held it up to her face. The mask melded to her skin so tight that no amount of dancing would make it fall off. Then, lifting her chin and pushing back the dark thoughts, she pressed on.

Beyond the silver-trees was a forest of squat, translucent trees made of diamond. Their shape reminded Faye of holly bushes, complete with spiny leaves. When she reached the bottom of the staircase the diamond trees ended abruptly, growing right up against a cliff face. Faye stepped into another solid stone tunnel, her glass shoes clinking delicately against the floor. The tunnel was short, and it opened to a twilit world.

Above, the sky was dark, with no stars peeking out of the black canvas. Deep green grass stretched out before her in a field dotted by tiny blue flowers. The grass faded into the glistening white shore of a large black lake. The sand looked so innocent, but Faye knew it was ground glass. Belle had tried to scoop up handfuls of it once and her hands had been scraped badly. It had taken Faye and Colette hours to remove the glass. *After* their night of dancing.

Five boats made of the finest obsidian floated near the shore, bobbing in the gentle breeze. In the bow of the closest boat stood a cloaked figure. He wore a mask in the form of a red wyvern's head, the horns curling up in loose spirals beyond the hood. Nosos, eldest of the five brothers to the Midnight King. His presence always sent a chill down Faye's spine. Thankfully, he wasn't violent like Phagos, Pathos's twin. But he still had an aura about him that spoke of danger. Of death.

In the next stood Ekidikeo, his orange-and-black tiger mask almost snarling in the twilight. He watched as she passed, head swiveling in time with her movements.

Phagos loomed in the prow of the third boat, wearing a bright yellow bull mask with short, blunt horns. Faye fought the anger that threatened to rise. His mask was fitting. Phagos always mistreated Adalie when they were together. Faye could only imagine what he did to her when they weren't dancing.

In the fourth boat lounged Poneros. His mask was a deep green and sculpted into the head of a rat, complete with wire whiskers. Of the five, Faye found him hardest to read, as he always seemed to bow to Pathos's wishes without complaint. However, as far as Faye knew, Poneros never spoke a word.

The last boat held Daimon. Large, green eyes were painted over the eye holes of his deep-blue mask that twisted into a hissing snake. Daimon's violent and unpredictable nature scared Faye the most. It chilled her to the bone whenever he came anywhere near Estelle. He would mete out his punishments swiftly, with no warning. Unlike Phagos, who bellowed and roared before his attacks.

Faye dropped her fan into her dress pocket, then clutched her skirts in her trembling fists as she inched toward the boats. Step by aching step she moved across the sand, her stomach twisting.

Just one more step, she told herself. *Just one more step.*

The scent of rusted steel filled Faye's nostrils. She turned in time to see tunnels open in the cliff face behind her. Out of each stepped her sisters, all dressed in clothing fit for queens. Her heart leapt into her throat as she counted them. Ten. No telltale red dress appeared. She narrowed her eyes and counted again. Where was Colette?

Faye hurried toward the nearest boat. She spied Desideria holding her hand out to Ekidikeo, waiting for him to help her step inside.

Stopping beside her, Faye grabbed the sleeve of her pastel orange dress. "Desi," she gasped.

Desi pushed Faye away, her brown eyes wide behind her tiger-striped mask. "Faye. You should be getting into your boat."

"Where is Colette?" Faye whispered.

Faye searched the boats and her gaze fell on her twin, dressed in pale yellow. Her heart skipped a beat. Adalie was on the other side of Desi, climbing into her boat.

"I don't know," Desi said, her voice strained. "Get back to your boat!"

Ekidikeo, marched toward them and grabbed Desi's arm. He jerked her toward him and shoved Faye's shoulder. Faye scrambled to catch her footing. A gasp escaped her throat as her feet caught on the hem of her skirt and she fell into the sand. Tiny pieces of glass dug into the heels of her palms. She bit back a cry, yanking her hands out of the sand.

"Get back to Poneros," Ekidikeo growled before spinning on his heel and jerking on Desi's arm, leading her away.

Helaine hurried across the shore and knelt at Faye's side. She gripped Faye's wrists—her grey eyes downcast.

"Does it hurt?" The words escaped her lips in a barely audible whisper. She hunched her shoulders. They looked so small inside her oversized silver ball gown. While only twelve, Helaine looked much, much older from the fatigue that pinched her eyes.

"No, I'm alright." Faye's voice shook and she bit her lip.

Fear had her trembling, something she hated to do in front of her younger sisters. She had to be brave for them, to show them that there was nothing to fear.

Helaine helped her to her feet and they made their way to the fourth boat.

As soon as they were settled in opposite ends, Faye began picking at the glass embedded in her skin. She focused on the pain, on the way the glass shimmered. On the way her heart pulsed like a wild thing in her chest, each beat sending a fresh wave of pain.

She blocked out the smooth black water and the voice of Ekidikeo rising over the lake, hot and angry. Her fingers shook but still she worked. When she had picked out as much as she could, she pulled an old handkerchief from her pocket and tore it into strips. It was much harder to wrap her hand than she thought it would be, but Helaine leaned over to help. Their foreheads touched and Helaine's warm breath brushed across Faye's arm.

"He shouldn't yell at her like that," Faye whispered.

Helaine glanced toward the other boats and tucked a strand of blond hair behind her ear. She nodded. It was small, almost imperceptible, but Faye had seen it. Something warm tugged at Faye's heart. At least she had her sisters.

Poneros plunged his pole into the water, pushing them across the lake with swift, jerky movements. Anger seemed to pour from his skin like tar. Hot and binding. Faye flinched. Poneros and Ekidikeo would tell Pathos what she had done. Desi would be punished. And Faye would have to live knowing that she could have prevented this, if only she had listened.

Biting her lip hard, Faye curled her fingers and rested her forehead against them. She shouldn't have spoken to her. She shouldn't have reached out. Colette was most likely already at the castle, safe and well. Unharmed.

Throughout the rest of the boat ride, she continued to tell herself the lie. It was much better than facing the truth.

∽

The ballroom was resplendent, with shimmering chandeliers dripping candles, a grand staircase, a huge iron throne sitting atop a dais, and murals of dancers painted on the domed ceiling. Gold-plated statues of Enchanters surrounded the ballroom, each perched atop a pedestal near the ceiling.

Faye hated the statues the most. Poised in elegant but impossible positions, bodies contorted in exaggeration of ballet, Revayr's most prized form of dance. Each one graceful and beautiful. Each one a reminder of what she had to face every night.

Guests made of shadows lined the walls, floating and whispering among themselves.

A horn blast, wild and haunting, filled the air to announce the arrival of the princesses. Faye held back a snort. To whom were they announcing to? The gargoyles? Whoever those shadowy people were—whether conjured or fellow prisoners—they cared not for the fate of the de la Rou girls.

Helaine looped her arm around Faye's as they made their way down the stairs and into the ballroom. Her grip was tight, and Faye felt her trembling. Helaine kept her eyes locked on the dark blue marble floor, her feet tapping out a rapid rhythm. Urgency hung thick and sticky in the air. Her sister's fingers were cold as she gripped them in what she hoped was a comforting gesture.

Together, she and Helaine made their way to the center of the ballroom where they lined up with their already waiting sisters. Faye once more looked for Colette. No sign of her. She bit her lip and risked a glance at Desi. Desi shrank behind Ekidikeo, pressing a finger to her lips. Nodding, Faye lowered her gaze to the golden veins that threaded their way through the marble.

Fear coiled around her lungs, cinching tight. Colette was gone because of her. That had to be it. Pathos must have seen her staring at Leo like an addled, empty-headed fool. He'd been there; he'd seen her. And now he'd see to it that not only would Desi face punishment for Faye's actions, but Colette as well.

The silence swelled until Faye felt she would drown in it.

Then, the master of the ball arrived.

There was no trumpet to announce his arrival. No form of fanfare or proclamation. Only the cold chill that gripped Faye's bones until they ached, as if on the verge of cracking. Smoke floated from the side of the dais where a hidden door lay, rolling out like black fog. It coalesced in the center, forming the shape of a man.

From the fog he stepped, a black iron crown of wicked spikes on his head. Covering his face was a silver mask formed in the shape of a wolf head.

"All hail the Midnight King!" Nosos crowed from the foot of the dais.

Helaine released Faye and dropped into a curtsy. Faye gripped her heavy gold skirts with aching fingers and curtsied low. She fought to keep her breathing even as panic set in. Breathe. In, out. She swayed, suddenly lightheaded.

If Faye had seen this side of Pathos, if she had known what he was, she never would have followed him into the dark.

It had started when they were children. Whenever Faye ran off alone in the garden to get away from her sisters, Pathos would be there, a boy in a silver mask, watching. He would tell her stories of his homeland, a magic place where they could dance all night without getting tired. A world with shining black lakes that held the light of the stars and shores of crushed diamonds.

A world where Faye wouldn't have to be afraid of her Faerie blood.

Pathos's stories filled Faye's head every night when she gazed out at the stars. It had all sounded like a dream, like it couldn't have been real.

But it was more real than she had ever wanted it to be.

The memory burned through her mind and she clenched her jaw so hard she was afraid she might crack a tooth.

If not for him, her sisters wouldn't be trapped in the first place.

If not for her selfish wants, her sisters would be free and living in the light of the sun. Faye pulled in a deep, determined breath. Maybe if she was good, if she was perfect tonight, Pathos might tell her what happened to Colette. She would have to work extra hard to keep her sisters safe.

Beside her, Helaine straightened, and so Faye also rose from her curtsy. The Midnight King lowered himself onto his throne.

From the side door came a flash of red. Faye stared in shock. Colette inched her way onto the dais. Though her eyes were shadowed by her mask, Faye could see the way her mouth was pinched and her movements stiff. Pain. What happened to her? What did Pathos do? Faye searched her sister for some form of injury. A bandage covered Colette's left hand. The urge to run to her sister gripped Faye, but she fought it back.

Perfect. She had to be perfect tonight.

"Welcome back, dear sisters." Pathos's voice boomed through the room, a shout, then a whisper. He raised his staff. "Begin."

Soft music drifted down from above. Pathos reached up and removed the crown from his head. The darkness dissipated and he placed the crown on the seat of his throne. His boots clacked a sharp rhythm as he descended the steps and stood before Faye.

Pathos bowed. "My lady," he murmured.

Faye lowered her head. "My king."

He took her hand and led her to the middle of the ballroom. Sweat slicked her palms and for a moment she was grateful Pathos wore gloves. Faye looked back at Colette once more. She was a scarlet flame up there beside the shadowy throne, her dress a resplendent design that reflected the beauty of the phoenix.

Tonight was the last night of the full moon. Which meant Faye had only hours to discover the truth. She glanced up at Pathos. Exactly how she would get him to talk was the problem.

Pathos released her hand and they separated, he and his brothers forming a line, and Faye taking her place among her sisters. The youngest sisters paired up, so that they faced each other for the dance. Kneeling, Pathos touched his fingers to the floor. His brothers did the same. The golden veins lit up with a soft glow and the music swelled.

Faye lowered herself into a deep curtsy as Pathos bowed. She glanced at Adalie, who stood beside her. Her twin kept her face forward, not even bothering to try and communicate. Regret tugged at her heart.

She gathered her skirt in one hand and stepped forward to meet Pathos. She then stepped back and walked slowly around Adalie, into the space Desi left. With each touch of her glass slipper on the floor, a ripple spread out across the marble, as if she were dancing on the surface of the lake.

The ripples overlapped and the center of the floor glowed, forming tiny waves of sparkling light, and a symbol starting to take shape.

"Adalie," she whispered.

For months now, she hadn't dared speak to her twin. Not after the last time she had tried, and Phagos had left a permanent scar over Adalie's left eye.

Adalie stiffened. "Faye," she whispered, longing filling her voice.

Faye's nerves tingled at her sister's voice. It was wonderful to hear even one word. She longed to hug Adalie, to grab her hand and drag her from the ballroom, far, far away from the castle and its monsters. The longing grew so sharp that Faye nearly gasped from the pain of it. All her sisters deserved the chance to escape. If only she could give it to them.

The dance continued, and as time ticked by, Faye's shoes rubbed against her feet, the glass chafing. She winced as she twirled beneath Pathos' arm and slipped. He caught her smoothly and held her tight, bringing them close. Faye fought the urge to pull back and let him sweep her into another spin.

He leaned close and his mask brushed her cheek. "You're welcome."

"I never said thank you."

26

His grip tightened on her hand, but not enough to hurt. "You don't have to. I know you're grateful."

Faye closed her eyes for a moment, not wanting to see the silver wolf that served as his face. That was the thing about Pathos. When he was Pathos, and not the Midnight King, he never, not once, lifted a finger to harm her. Always he was gentle. Always he was kind. No matter how much she hated his brothers, she could never hate Pathos. She could hate only herself for giving in.

She spun away from him, trading places with Adalie. Phagos took Faye's hand and they stepped together toward the dais, Adalie and Pathos before them. She glared at Pathos' back. If only he would yell at her. Call her names. Anything to give her an excuse to hate him. Instead, he remained a stalwart gentleman.

The night wore on with more and more dances, some fast, some slow. With each shift in the music, the color of the ripples changed. With each change of the dance, the symbol in the center of the floor faded and was replaced by a new one. The symbols pulsed with life, shifting, twisting, forming letters Faye couldn't understand. She could only guess that they were binding symbols, meant to keep them locked in the Underworld for however long Pathos wished.

As each dance continued, Faye's feet grew more and more chafed within the shoes. Pain lanced through her feet. She tried not to make a sound, but as she spun on her toe, she tipped over and fell. Pathos caught her again and brought her around to step beside him.

"Why are you so clumsy tonight, my lady?" A hint of fear laced his voice.

Faye lowered herself to the floor and lifted her skirts. She bit back a cry. Her clear, beautiful glass slippers were stained red with blood. Pathos released a curse and hauled her to her feet, his grip tight.

Clutching her elbow, he led her through a series of quick steps, almost lifting her off her feet. Desperation filled his voice. "You must keep dancing."

Faye held back the tears that clogged her throat. The shoes had never chafed so much before. It must be punishment for talking to her sisters.

"Pathos, I can't!" She didn't try to keep the desperation from her voice. "Please, I can't."

"You must!" He dragged her across the floor in the dance, his breathing quick and shallow. "Please, you must, for Adalie's sake. I can't stop him, Faye."

"But you're the king."

"In title only. I can't make my brothers serve me."

Faye glanced at her sister, at the jagged scar half hidden by her mask. He was right. If she disobeyed, if she stopped for one moment, Adalie would pay for it in some form of pain.

"Dance, Faye. Dance for Adalie."

She would rather die.

Instead, she placed her hand on his shoulder, and danced.

Chapter Four – Faye

Faye pushed the fireplace open and crawled through the ashes. She sat and yanked off her slippers. Blood dripped onto the hearth and she fought the urge to break the slippers right there. She squeezed them so tight she could feel the engraved leaves digging into her skin. But if she broke them, she would be severed from her sisters forever. They would be locked in the Underworld, unable to see the sun, unable to breathe the fresh air. The thought gripped her so tight she couldn't breathe.

She dug her knuckles into her forehead. No. She had to keep going for them. She needed her sisters more than she needed freedom. And they needed her.

Tears stung Faye's eyes, but she pushed them back. There was no use crying. She shoved the slippers into their hole in the hearth and dropped the brick back in place.

The sun was just coming up now, making everything in the house iron gray and heavy. Or maybe it was just her body that felt that way. Faye crawled across the floor toward the kitchen, her feet throbbing.

It took her several tries before she was able to wrap her feet in clean bandaging. She bit her lip. Blisters that formed along her heels had burst. Thankfully, it wasn't as bad as it had looked.

The stains on the cloth reminded her of Colette's brilliant red dress. Like a coward, she'd forgotten to ask why Colette was no longer dancing. Had she given in? Was she now on the side of the Midnight King? Faye's mind spun at the thought and she drove the heel of her hand into her forehead. She needed answers.

Tears splashed the floor. It served her right, getting those blisters. They were just another part of the punishment she deserved. Angry, she scrubbed the tears from her cheeks. There was no use crying over it.

Her head pounded and her eyes felt gritty as she stumbled back into the sitting room. She fell toward the couch but landed on the floor. Pain ricocheted through her body. She needed to climb onto the couch, to crawl back under the covers …

∞

"Wake up!"

Faye jerked awake as someone shook her shoulder.

"Faye, what are you doing on the floor? Wake up!"

Sitting up, she rubbed at her heavy eyes. Blinding sunlight cut through the sitting room and she groaned. Beside her, Delphine stood, an apron over her dress and her black curls pulled back in a messy braid. Madame's eldest daughter looked very much like her mother, with the same glowing green eyes and deep midnight skin.

"Are you alright? I found blood on the floor." Her eyes flicked down to Faye's feet.

Faye pushed herself up off the hard floor, heat rushing to her cheeks. "I'm well. Just stepped on some glass."

Delphine hurried into the kitchen as she called, "Can you walk? Do you need a doctor?"

"No, no doctors. It's fine. I can walk." She took a few steps to test her theory. Her ankles throbbed, but her feet felt like they were on the mend. Hopefully Jane would have salve for her this afternoon.

"Oh, good. I need you to go to the market, get more eggs. We've run out and Mama wants her breakfast."

Faye blinked hard as her eyes watered in the bright light. She fumbled with her soft leather shoes, slipping them on over the bulky bandages.

"Wh-what time is it?" she asked as she snagged her clothes from the day before off the couch and quickly put them on.

"It's almost eight. You've been sleeping the morning away." Delphine peered around the kitchen doorframe, brows wrinkled. "Are you sure you're feeling fine?"

Faye gaped. Almost eight? Had she really slept that long? Guilt curled in her stomach. She'd never been this weak after dancing before. Faye shook her head. It was her own fault, giving in to the rest. She was better than this. Stronger.

Faye grabbed the basket that sat next to the couch and bolted for the door.

"I'll be back soon, I promise!" she shouted.

The last thing she needed was to burden Madame Leroux with her tardiness. Not when the poor woman suffered from migraines every day.

The streets were already filled with bustling people, mostly servants hurrying toward the market. Bright-colored clothes hung on lines strung between the cottages and a woman's soft voice rose over the noise, singing an old love ballad. A man's voice clashed with hers, belting out a jaunty tune accompanied by a citole.

Clopping hooves and clacking wheels preceded carts and carriages, and Faye jumped aside in time to stay clear of the wheels. A little boy carrying a rat cage tipped his hat to her as she walked by. Faye gave him a smile and a small curtsy. His cheeks turned bright red and he dashed away.

Wincing with each wobbly step she took, Faye followed the long line of iron fences toward the market. The sun beat down on her neck, heating her hair that hung in limp waves about her shoulders. A thousand thoughts swam through her mind. She'd seen Leo for the first time yesterday. But that moment had been shadowed by Pathos.

31

Faye's stomach churned. It always led back to Pathos. There had to be something more going on. Colette would never stop dancing. As the eldest, she was their leader. She took pride in being strong. Distant. But this ... It wasn't her.

Her thoughts circled back to Leo, but Faye pushed them aside. She couldn't allow herself to think of him. Not now.

Jane, the maid who worked at the house across the street, hurried to Faye's side, her nose smudged with soot and her smile wide. She cocked her head and gave a small skip in her worn boots, kicking up the skirts of her pale green frock. Two years younger than Faye, Jane was always full of energy that rivaled the sun.

"It's the best bloomin' sunshine we've had in weeks," Jane said cheerfully. "Though I don't mind a dark cloud or two. Rain's good for the ground, ya know." Her thin lips stretched in a wide smile.

Faye tried to smile back. Her joy brought more memories of Leo to the surface. Faye swore on the Blackwood that nothing could ever dampen Leo's spirits. Not rain, not hardship, not even embarrassment.

Again, she shoved the thoughts aside, chastising herself. Why couldn't she just put him in the past where he belonged?

Jane raised a brow. "I'd say good mornin', but it looks like it's right foul from your standin'." She picked at her teeth with a fingernail as she strolled at an easy pace.

Faye smiled at her friend's words. "I was only thinking is all. It is a good morning."

Jane reached in her pocket and pulled out something wrapped in cloth. "Saw the full moon last night. Figgered you'd be out with blistered tootsies again."

"Thank you, Jane." Faye took the bundle and sniffed it. Just as she thought. It was Jane's favorite salve, a mixture of pungent herbs and honey.

Jane shrugged. "Not a problem." She looked at Faye askance. "I likes runnin' round under the full moon same as any young'un, but if I were you, I'd keep it down. Half the folks here think yer a werewolf or somethin'."

"You can't be serious." Faye's heart skipped a beat.

"Nah, don't worry your little fancy head." Jane shoved Faye's shoulder with her own. "Besides, ol' King Richard exiled witches 'bout fifteen years ago. If anything, they all thinks you're crazy, and they're right goosecaps they are."

Faye gave Jane a smile. "Thank you for believing in me."

Quirking a grin of her own, Jane nodded.

"Did ya hear, Mrs. Haversham over in the northwest corner had her baby last week. And can ya believe it, it weren't one wee babe but two!"

Faye listened to Jane's story as they continued through the market, even though the words escaped her mind. Still, it was better than listening to her thoughts that begged for her attention. The anxious beating of her heart and the fear that trembled through her limbs eased a fraction.

"Did ya hear about what happened two days back? A rider dressed in black came riding up the road like the dogs of Sirius were bitin' at his heels."

Faye looked over to the chicken lady's booth, watching the woman flirt with the dairyman over a giant wheel of cheese. "Oh? Did anyone say—"

A trumpet blast cut her off.

Jane cupped a hand to her ear and asked, "What?" but Faye ignored her.

The noise in the market died down as a short man dressed in bright green-and-gold silk stepped up onto the back of a cart, then onto a crate. He unrolled a scroll and squinted at it with his beady eyes.

"Hear ye, hear ye!" he shouted.

The people crowded closer, murmuring. Faye shuffled along with them and stood on the toes of her right foot.

33

"On this day, the second of Thrimilchi, it has been officially announced that the Crown Princess Colette de la Rou of the kingdom of Revayr is dead."

Faye's heart stopped. She gasped and staggered back. But she had only just seen Colette last night. She couldn't be dead. Not dead. She was in the Underworld, with the rest of her sisters.

Right?

But no one here knew that. To them, she and her sisters were long missing. A faded memory. So why did they suddenly think Colette was dead?

Pathos. It had to be his doing. The panic rose. Clawed its way up her throat. He killed her because Faye had looked at Leo with unguarded affection.

He killed her.

The thought pulsed over and over in her mind.

Whispers, quick and fierce, spread through the crowd.

"Serves her right, half-blood mongrel."

"Her and her kind were a crime against nature."

"That's too bad. Colette was lovely for the eyes."

"It was those cursed Fae. They did it."

Faye couldn't breathe. Couldn't speak. Her sister wasn't dead. Colette was *not* dead. If she was, Faye would never be able to forgive herself.

"Love? You alright?" Jane's gentle hand pressed down on Faye's shoulder.

Blinking, Faye nodded and looked up at the herald. "I'm well. Don't worry about me." Her voice sounded distant to her own ears.

The herald continued speaking. His words jumbled together in her mind. She blinked hard to bring her vision back into focus. Focus. She needed to focus.

"Hereon this day, His Majesty King Richard ap Owen has announced that he will be holding a series of masquerade balls for His Royal Highness Prince Lionheart II. The balls will be held at the palace, starting on the twentieth day of Ærra Litha, and ending on Midsummer Night's Eve. At the last ball, the prince will choose a bride."

The women in the crowd all squealed and began to talk in earnest. All mention of Colette was forgotten in the wake of the news.

Faye stood numb, thoughts jumbled. She pressed her fingers to her temple. Colette wasn't dead. No. Of course not. It was impossible.

Fifteen days. That was how long she had before she would be able to return to the Underworld and prove that the herald's words were a lie.

Beside her, Jane grabbed Faye's arm and squeezed it tight.

"I can't wait to see which powdered princess he chooses!" she whispered.

The herald nodded to the trumpeter beside him. A single blast rang through the air. The noise died down as the crowd waited in anticipation.

"This year, the king has announced that every eligible maiden is permitted to attend with the intent of winning the heart of our beloved prince. This is an extension of goodwill from the king to show that he is of the people. Thank you."

The market was now in an uproar as the women rushed about, whispering to each other. Jane's hand was a noose around Faye's arm, growing tighter and tighter.

"Did ya hear that? Did ya hear that? We all get to go. Blimey!" And she rushed off to join a group of maids.

Faye turned, forcing her way through the crowd. Arms and torsos and legs all pushed back, wanting to trap her. Lowering her head, she shoved back harder. She needed to get out. She needed air.

As soon as she broke free, she collapsed on the cobblestones. The basket bounced from her arm and she slapped her shaking hands over her mouth to fight back a cry.

This was not the end. This couldn't be the end. Colette was alive. Colette was alive and safe. There was nothing to worry about. The panic in her chest eased as she gulped in deep breaths.

Eggs. She needed eggs. Rising, Faye brushed off her skirts and picked up the basket with shaking fingers. Fifteen days until she saw her sisters again. Then, she would know if what the herald had said was the truth.

As she staggered through the market, the whispers and excitement that buzzed around her grated on her nerves. They were all too quick to forget Colette and move on. Faye gripped the basket hard. So what if King Richard was throwing a ball for Leo? So what if it was a chance to meet him after being separated for three years? He had rejected her. Denied her. Who was to say he would actually care if she showed up?

"At least Pathos would never reject me," she whispered to herself.

The thought didn't bring any comfort.

There was no chance that she would be able to go. When the herald said every eligible maiden, he'd meant every maiden with fortune. With benefits. With full Human blood. And she had none of those. Besides, she didn't even own a ball gown. All she owned was the simple dress she wore now, and a few hand-me-downs from Delphine.

Turning to the chicken lady, Faye sniffed. It wasn't like she wanted to go anyway. Just the thought of attending a masquerade ball made her want to scream. Already she was forced to dance for the Midnight King. She certainly didn't want to dance for King Richard. He was just as horrid, passing the edict that kept her in hiding. No, she wouldn't go. Even if it meant not seeing Leo again.

The city walls loomed before her. Faye stared at the gray stone. She must have wandered too far. Cold dread filled her chest. She inched her gaze up until she saw them.

Wings. Huge, feathered, leathery, and dragonfly thin. All hanging in a row along the walls. They were the wings of every Titanian Faerie that King Richard had executed. Silence pressed in around her. A frigid breeze rustled the deep brown feathers hovering just inches from her face. A shudder ran across her skin. It was horrible. So, so horrible.

These Fae died just because of what they were. It was cruel. Heartless. Faye couldn't help but imagine her own mother's wings hanging on the wall. Tears pricked her eyes, but she pushed them back. What if Leo was just like his father now? What if he hated those of magic blood?

When Faye returned to the cottage, Delphine was waiting for her at the door. Her eyes were pinched. "Mama's in a lot of pain today."

Faye nodded. Whatever chronic illness Madame Leroux had, the doctors were unable to treat it. She had searched everywhere for a cure but found nothing. Only the ancient Faerie remedies Faye made could ease her pain.

Madame had admitted once that it was like having fire burning away at her limbs, constant and unending. It was hard to imagine what that even felt like. Some days it wasn't bad. But other days it grew worse. And Madame transformed from a gentle bird to a roaring lion.

"Faye!"

Faye cringed. Delphine grabbed the basket and jerked her head toward the hall. Faye sucked in a deep breath and suppressed the last of her fear. Her worry for Colette still clawed at her mind, but she couldn't let it overwhelm her.

Plastering on a smile, she pushed open the door to Madame Leroux's room. The interior was cloaked in darkness, the heavy green drapes pulled shut.

"Yes, Madame?" she asked, her voice a pitch higher than she liked.

She curled her hands and hid them in her skirts. If she could convince Madame to take her herbal concoction, then maybe her wrath would be soothed with the dulling of pain.

"Twenty minutes and eighteen seconds at the market. Do you care to explain just what stalled you?" Her silky voice held a note of irritation. She stared at Faye from the shadows of her monstrous bed, watch in hand, her green eyes glowing like a cat's.

"I ..." The announcement of Colette's death rang through her head and she couldn't find the words to continue. Hot tears stung her eyes and she widened them to make the tears dry. She would not cry. Not now. Not ever. "I was distracted. I'm sorry."

Madame snapped her pocket watch shut. "No matter. Just be sure to keep your head on next time. Hand me my walking stick. Silly Bonnie left it by the chair."

Faye tensed. Bonnie. Had she said anything? Had she told Madame about the stories?

Cautiously, she grabbed the walking stick by its polished silver panther head and placed it in Madame's hand. She then supported the woman's arm and helped her make her way out of the room.

"I have news," Faye said quietly, hoping to ease the tension between them. "That is why it took me so long to return."

Madame Leroux froze, her brows bent in a frown. She leaned back and gripped the head of her walking stick. "News of a good kind, I hope?"

"A messenger from the king came to the square." The floorboards creaked and Faye glanced to her left.

Bonnie peeked out of her room, eyes bright. Glancing back to Madame Leroux, Faye licked her lips.

"He had an announcement. The king is holding a series of masquerade balls." She fought back a shiver at the words. "He has also announced that every eligible maiden is invited."

Madame Leroux stiffened and closed her eyes. Faye's heart pounded in her chest. Was she still displeased?

"I—I don't want to go myself. I just thought, maybe, this news would be exciting for you and Delphine. Perhaps she could—"

"Silence!" Madame Leroux hissed, squeezing her eyes. She leaned heavily on her stick and pulled in a deep breath. Her full lips curved up in a smile and she chuckled as she set the pace again. "Forgive me. That is the best news you've ever given me. Thank you, dear Faye." She patted Faye's hand.

Delphine entered the hall just then, carrying a platter filled with steaming eggs and toast. "I've finished your breakfast, Mama." She stopped and frowned as Madame Leroux continued to laugh. "What's going on?"

Madame Leroux gave Delphine a soft smile. "My dear, I do appreciate your efforts to please me. You are the best child a disgraced countess could ever have. It would be almost a shame to lose you."

Faye frowned and opened her mouth to speak, but Delphine beat her to it. "Mama, I don't understand. What do you mean?"

"The king is hosting a ball for his prince, where he is to find himself a future wife." Madame Leroux's eyes shone bright and she straightened a bit. "You and Faye will try for Prince Lionheart's hand."

Chapter Five – Leo

Leo sat slumped on the plush window seat. Outside, servants bustled through the courtyard and soldiers trained in the fields beyond. Their shouts echoed up to Leo's window.

Jack had to be wrong. And yet, he couldn't refute the evidence he had seen in his father's room. Leo closed his eyes and wished he could wipe the horrifying image from his mind.

"A load of balderdash," he mumbled to himself.

It couldn't have been the work of Enchanters, like Jack said. The Enchanters were dead. Gone. The whole lot of them rotting to nothing underground.

If Colette was dead, then that meant her sisters could very well be dead as well. It meant that Desi, Adalie, Estelle, Genevieve … Faye. They were all gone. Brutally murdered by a monster who was supposed to be dead.

Leo's throat tightened as he gazed past the foggy glass and out toward the village beyond the castle walls. There were so many things he wanted to tell her. So many things he had left unsaid. He'd never get the chance to apologize. To tell her that he was wrong, running away like that. That he had no choice. He'd never get another chance to tell her that he was so, so sorry. That he loved her. That he was going to finally push past his ridiculous fears and confess that she had captured his heart and soul.

He snorted at his own thoughts. What a ruddy romantic.

Still, he couldn't help but remember Faye's gentle smile. The way she'd always seemed to be so genuinely interested in everything he had to say. How she would laugh at his jokes, even when they weren't funny.

Guilt gripped his stomach and he shoved himself off the window seat. Now, his father had officially announced the ball being held *in his honor*. Leo rolled his eyes as he flopped into his favorite stuffed blue chair situated before the fire.

The whole blooming event had nothing to do with Leo and everything to do with his father's machinations. He planned to name Leo the Crown Prince while establishing a betrothal for him before Leo became old. At this point, Leo knew his father was desperate to see him married before he turned twenty-five.

And all of this would end on not only Midsummer Night's Eve, but on his birthday as well. At least he'd be able to drown his sorrows in a thick slice of cake. His stomach rumbled at the thought.

Leo shifted position and rested his elbow on the armrest. A loud knock interrupted his thoughts.

"Who is it?" he called.

"Me, Your Highness."

Jack. Leo sighed.

"Alright then. Come in if you must."

Jack opened the door and strode across the blue-and-gold rug that dominated the stone floor. He leaned against the mantelpiece, right next to the mace Leo had won in a tournament last year. Raising a large, bushy brow, Jack eyed Leo.

"Are you alright, my lord?"

"Yes. I'm fine. I'm only sitting here, feeling miserable because …" He couldn't say it. He screwed up his face to keep from crying like a dolt.

Jack's expression shifted to something that seemed like an attempt at sympathy.

"I understand." He cleared his throat and looked away.

Leo dropped his head in his hands. He couldn't stop the images of Colette and Faye lying dead somewhere, brutally murdered. Killed by a monster made of darkness. The image sharpened in his mind, as if suddenly, Leo was standing right next to them. The sisters gripped each other's hands, their blank eyes locked on one another.

A man dressed in black knelt beside the bodies. A crown of iron spikes rested on his head. When he looked up, he wasn't a man, but a wolf.

With a gasp, Leo jerked upright. The image faded and he shoved to his feet. His whole body shook. It was so real. So clear in his mind. Not even his dreams held that much weight.

Turning away from Jack, Leo made his way across the room on wobbly legs and collapsed onto his bed. He leaned against the wooden post and gripped the dark blue drapes in his trembling fist.

"Your Highness?" Jack pushed away from the mantel and took a step closer. "Are you sure you're alright?"

"It's just …" Leo rubbed at his eyes. The image was still burned into his mind. "So much … so much to take in."

A heavy, pressing silence descended on the room. Leo kept his eyes locked on the floor. Inhale. Exhale. Inhale … Ropes of fear bound his chest, making it hard to breathe.

"I think I might know something that will cheer you up, Your Highness," Jack said, scratching his head.

Leo glanced up at his guard. "What? Please don't tell me a game of croquet."

"I know where the box was found."

"You … what?" Leo's heart throbbed in his ears. Excitement shivered down his spine. He jumped to his feet. "You know where?"

Jack nodded. "At the edge of the Northwind Forest, just across the moors. It was discovered by the village patrol."

The Northwind Forest. It was naught but two leagues away from the castle. Leo went there many times on his rides across the countryside. He looked out the window. The sun was making its way toward the horizon.

He could go there tomorrow. Look around. Come back before Father grew suspicious. Leo rubbed the back of his head as he thought. This was the only way he'd find the truth. He had to find an answer. Some clue as to who left the box and note.

Turning to Jack, he grinned. "How do you feel about going for a hack tomorrow?"

Chapter Six – Faye

"Wh-what?" Faye gasped.

This didn't make sense. Madame Leroux wanted *her* to go to the ball? She couldn't do that. Going would mean facing Leo. And after Pathos' actions last night, she wasn't sure if that was something she could ever do again.

"I can't possibly—" Faye started.

"Mama, I don't—" Delphine began.

Madame Leroux held up her hand. "My dear, the life of a queen is much better than the life of a seamstress. Why settle for rags when you could have riches?" She beamed. "Once our honor is restored, we'll no longer be forced to live in this hovel."

Delphine clamped her lips together and shook her head. "Mama, it's not that bad here. I love our home. What good will our honor do us if … if …" Her knuckles paled as the tray shook in her hands.

Bonnie came clattering into the hall. Her wide smile faded as she looked from one face to the other.

"Mama? Are we eating breakfast soon?" Bonnie asked in a small voice.

Delphine turned and marched back toward the kitchen, tray in hand. Faye wrapped her arms around her middle, unsure of what to say.

"Go on, Bonnie. You can have my breakfast." Madame steered Bonnie back toward the kitchen, leaving Madame and Faye alone.

Faye glanced out at the sitting room, at the cold fireplace. "Madame, I … I can't."

Madame Leroux pinned her with a hawkish glare. "You can and you will. You are beautiful, Faye, with a natural grace and charm. Any prince would want to marry you."

Faye shook her head hard. "I … I'm forgetful, a klutz. There is nothing desirable about me."

Sighing, Madame Leroux placed both hands on the snarling head of her walking stick. "Oh, Faye. Do you think I don't know who you are? Or, I should say, *what* you are."

Faye's heart froze. No. She couldn't know. There was no way she could have found out. Not unless … Bonnie. She must have said something. Fear curled around Faye's chest and she backed away.

"I don't know what you mean. I'm just a commoner." She reached up and touched her hair to make sure her ears weren't visible.

"A commoner Revayrian who just happened to end up in Eura?" Madame's gaze softened. She placed a gentle hand on Faye's arm. "Come. Let's talk where the others can't hear."

Numb, Faye followed her. Madame shut her bedroom door behind them and shuffled to her bed. Lowering herself into the plush green cushion by the window, she sighed. She swallowed and rippled her fingers over the head of her walking stick. Pulling her watch from her pocket, she flicked it open.

A sigh escaped her lips. "Well, it will be lunch soon, so there's no point of us eating now, is there?"

Faye perched on the edge of Madame Leroux's bed. The ticking of the large grandfather clock across from the bed filled the silence. Faye knotted her fingers together as she waited for Madame to speak.

Madame Leroux shrugged. "To be completely honest, I didn't know who you were at first. An orphan? A runaway? It didn't matter to me. I needed help and you were willing to work, so I didn't think much on the matter. But as the years passed, I began to study the way you moved, as if you're always on the verge of dancing, the distinct honey coloring of your hair. Then, there were those stories you told Bonnie. You ought to know by now, my little girl can't keep a secret."

Faye brought a hand up to her cheek. None of this made any sense. And yet, there was an ease to Madame's voice, a gentleness Faye hadn't seen before that kept her from running. If Madame had known her identity for this long, she could have turned her over to the king ages ago. But here Faye was, safe and sound.

"I planned to return you to your parents but tracking down Fae bloodlines is a tricky thing to do, especially here in Eura. And Eura makes it nearly impossible to contact anyone in Revayr." She leaned forward, dark skin glittering in the half-light. "Then I discovered your curse."

Faye's hand fluttered. She knew. Madame knew about the curse. For some reason, the thought brought a measure of relief. She opened her mouth, but Madame stopped her.

"One night, when I awoke, I saw you vanish into the fire. And then I knew. Few still believe in the story of the White Lady and the Midnight King, but you're looking at one of those believers. It's just terrible, knowing that monster has you on a leash."

The relief quickly turned to dread as Faye listened. If she knew about the curse, did she also know that Faye was one of the lost princesses? It didn't matter. Any citizen of Eura could earn five thousand pounds for turning in a Faerie. Madame could use the money for her daughters. She could give them a better life.

Faye's stomach churned and she steeled herself. She would rather know now than face the betrayal when Madame turned her in.

"Are ..." Faye licked her lips and wrapped her arms around herself. "Are you going to turn me in?"

"No, sweet child. For years many in Revayr pushed for a peace treaty between Magical and Human kind, myself among them. We all longed to protect both and believed we could live together in harmony. My husband and I were the very first to sign the petition. Eura is a cruel, dark place for any magical creature to live in. What puzzles me is why you haven't returned home on your own?"

Faye's throat constricted. "I can't go back," she whispered.

Leaning forward in her chair, Madame looked at Faye with her jaw set and eyes blazing. "If you destroyed those shoes that connect you to the Underworld ..."

"It's not that easy," Faye said, blinking away tears. "If I destroy my shoes, I'll ... I'll never see my sisters again. And I can't go home. Not without them."

"He has more of you captive? That beast! Then if you refuse to break your shoes, we have no other choice. We must break the curse completely."

"How?" Faye held her breath, afraid of the answer.

She couldn't dare to hope. It wasn't her place to hope for something she knew would never happen. Yet, she leaned forward to catch Madame's next words.

"By marrying a Human, my dear." Madame leaned back in her chair. "Only a binding vow and contract of equal weight can undo the curse of the Underworld. Whether you charm the prince, or any of the other young men at this ball, should you gain a proposal, you will be free."

Free. An impossible word. Could she really believe this? That one day, they would be able to return home? Faye shook her head. No. It was impossible. Unthinkable. They had been trapped for three long years, and Faye had tried thousands of different ways to break her family free. And now Madame had placed the solution so easily in Faye's lap. She wasn't even sure if she deserved it.

"You and Delphine should both go to the ball. That way you have a chance to be free and my daughter will have a chance at a better life, and I will fain the opportunity to build a better future for all magicfolk." Madame Leroux stood and shuffled across the room. "Come. I need you to make that potion." She patted Faye's shoulder as she passed and slipped through the door.

Standing, Faye followed. Her head spun with a thousand thoughts. Madame Leroux was a magic sympathizer. She wanted Faye to go to the ball and face Leo. A man who had left her waiting for a promise that never came. And the threat of Colette being dead could very well be true. It was too much. Too much to handle. Too much to think on.

Entering the kitchen, she picked up various jars of herbs and began to mix Madame's potion. Delphine and Bonnie were laughing as they twirled about the sitting room in an awkward waltz. Bonnie fell on her seat and released a wild giggle.

Delphine's smile slipped for just a moment. She gazed at her latest creation draped on the overstuffed chair. A blanket covered in an embroidered phoenix in brilliant reds and golds. Faye had told her more than once it was her best work yet. Delphine had more talent in her pinkie than most girls did in their entire bodies. She deserved a chance to become the seamstress of her dreams.

Faye turned her back on the scene. They were both prisoners caught up in a twisted game. Only, where Delphine had no choice, Faye had built her prison. And Pathos held the key.

Chapter Seven – Leo

"Remind me again, my lord, why we're sneaking behind your father's back just to look for clues," Jack called out from behind Leo as they rode across the open moors.

"You're the one who told me the location," Leo called back.

"Yes, but I didn't think it'd lead to this." Jack scowled. "I hate rain."

Most of the time when it rained in Eura, it was a thunderstorm. But today's rain was a light drizzle—a pleasant rarity. Leo tightened his grip on the reins as worry grew in his chest. With a rain like this, the chance was high that by the time they reached Northwind Forest all evidence would be gone. Still, they had left the city as early as possible, with the sun climbing the horizon beyond the distant trees.

And while the vision from yesterday was already fading from memory, he could still see Colette and Faye's lifeless bodies, lying side by side with a dark figure looming over them.

But he refused to let it dampen his spirits. The vision was just that. A part of his imagination stretching to fill in the gaps. He would no sooner put stock in it than he would in his father promising to let the Draconians cross the border in peace.

Leo's horse bounded across the open moors, nearly flying. Power churned in its muscles, and Leo leaned into its neck, mane whipping his face. Adrenaline surged through his body and he let out a wild whoop. Neither drizzle nor downpour nor thunderstorm could crush him. He would be happy today, and he would find an answer.

As they neared the forest, Leo pulled his horse into a trot. Jack thundered past, then slowed his horse to a walk and circled back.

"The only other thing the patrol found was boot prints. Though, I don't think those will help, my lord, as the rain's most likely washed them away by now."

Leo's horse snorted and shook its head, and Leo grinned. "I agree with Ghost. It should still be somewhat dry in the forest since it's just a drizzle."

They reached the forest's borders, crooked trees bent over by centuries of harsh winds. Leo patted his horse's shoulder, then gripped its white mane as he dismounted. His feet sank into the loamy earth with a wet splash. Jack followed, and soon they were ducking under the moss-laden branches of Northwind Forest.

Leo's boots crunched dead leaves as they picked their way forward. A carpet of heather grew in between the trees, interspersed with moss and giant, feathery ferns. Above, squirrels scrabbled across branches and birds flitted from tree to tree, calling out warnings.

"Where exactly did they find the box?" Leo asked as he searched the ground for any sign of disturbance.

Jack pointed ahead and to the left, toward a small clearing. Here, the ground was disturbed by at least a dozen hoofprints churned up in the mud. Leo frowned.

"Well, they made a right mess of things, didn't they?"

He left his horse next to a poplar tree and stepped into the clearing. Tracking was hard enough without snow in the wood. The patrolmen just had to ruin any further chance of discovery.

But there was … something. Leo cocked his head as random heavy drops of rain splashed on him. It was a trail, like a heavy object had been dragged away, deeper into the wood.

"This way. Come on, Jack."

Leo jogged across the clearing and pushed through the ferns to follow the trail. It swept back and forth, almost like the edge of a cloak. But who would wear a cloak heavy enough to leave a trail?

"I don't think this is a good idea, my lord," Jack said as he followed behind, leading both horses. "What will your father say if he finds you out here?"

Leo rolled his eyes. "Don't be such an old maid, Jack. When we return, I'll tell him we went for a jaunt over the moors." The trail ended and Leo paused. He squinted. "We went and saw some sheep ... chased a cow or two ... and went ... home."

There was something behind one of the trees. If it hadn't moved, Leo wouldn't have noticed it. He could have sworn he'd seen a wolf. Leo whipped out his hand to Jack. His leaf-crunching steps ceased.

Reaching for his belt, Leo grabbed the hilt of his sword. It would be almost completely useless against a wolf, but a lone wolf wouldn't be foolish enough to attack two Humans and two horses. Leo waited, muscles tense.

A dark green cloak flashed, and a person bolted into the wood. Leo straightened, surprise rippling through him. An image flashed into his mind—the man with the wolf head, crouching over the bodies of Faye and Colette.

"Hey!" Leo shouted.

He burst into a run. The cloaked man skittered from tree to tree, hiding among the low branches of the trees. Ducking, Leo watched the man's pattern. He veered to the right, running at an angle—drawing closer and closer to the right side of the forest. If Leo moved fast, he'd be able to cut him off in a matter of minutes.

Jumping over a log, Leo brushed past a bramble patch and slipped in between two trees. The man was right next to him now. With a yell, he slammed into the man and they both fell to the ground.

Leo drew his sword and pressed the tip against the man's back.

"Reveal yourself, sir!" he shouted.

The man lifted a shaking hand as he turned over. He pulled down his hood, revealing a youthful face covered in freckles and framed by matted brown hair. The boy stared up at Leo with wide, terrified eyes.

A beggar boy. Jack was right. This was all just a waste of time.

"Am ... am I in trouble, Your Highness, sir?" the boy whimpered.

"What were you doing running in the forest?" Leo barked, irritation mounting.

"N-nothing, sir, Your Highness, sir!" The boy picked up a sack that lay next to him. "I found this, back there in the clearing. I thought it might have some food or something in it."

Leo snatched away the sack. He sheathed his sword and jerked his head toward the moors. "Go on. Get out of here."

The boy shot to his feet and bolted away. Leo watched him run as Jack approached with the horses.

"Find anything?"

"No." Leo tossed the bag to the ground. "Nothing but this and a beggar boy. Whatever *this* is."

Jack came closer. His horse rubbed its forehead on his shoulder as he examined the bag.

"What's in it?"

Leo shrugged and frowned. "I don't know. But whatever it is, that beggar boy must not have wanted it that bad to leave it behind."

Crouching down, Leo grabbed the top of the bag and unwound the rope holding it shut. After throwing the rope aside, Leo lifted the bag and dumped its contents on the forest floor. Something colorful fluttered down to rest among the ferns. Leo dropped the bag and picked up the cloth.

All the blood drained from his face. The forest tilted. In the distance, he heard Jack let out a curse.

It was a dress. A beautiful white dress, with frills and lace. And splashed all over it was blood. The bodice was ripped, as if a knife had stabbed it multiple times, and the crimson stain spread out like a rose.

Leo's hands shook. It wasn't just any dress. He remembered, on the night that he left, how beautiful Faye looked beneath the trellis covered in fresh-blooming roses, her white gown blending her with the moonlight.

Faye's dress.

This had to be a lie. Leo's heart pounded and his limbs shook as he searched the forest floor for a note, a scrap of paper, anything.

"My lord?" Jack left the horses behind and approached Leo slowly. "My lord, what is it?"

"Do you see anything? A note, or a card, something with words." Each word flew from his mouth, hard and desperate.

Jack bent and picked up the rope. A small scrap of paper fluttered from a section of it, tied on with string. Leo lunged forward and snatched the paper from the rope. With shaking hands, he smoothed it out on his knee.

With this, we announce that another princess is dead because you refused to surrender to us the one with the White Lady's blood. More will follow until none are left.

The words burned themselves into Leo's mind. She was dead. Irrevocably, unequivocally, dead.

It was getting harder to breathe. Leo stumbled back, the dress slipping from his hand. He collapsed into a mess of ferns.

Jack bent to pick up the dress.

"Don't touch that!" Leo shouted. He scrubbed at the mess on his cheeks and gathered the dress into his arms.

"Your Highness …"

"She's dead! Don't you see?" Leo's words rasped against his throat. "She's gone because …"

He choked, unable to say more. *She's gone because I failed.*

It was a lie. It had to be. Because if Faye was dead, then Leo would never get the chance to say he was sorry. How he never meant to break her heart. To tell her he loved her. To propose. To promise to her the rest of his life and the best of his years.

Now, none of that mattered. His words would never reach her. She was gone.

Chapter Eight – Faye

One by one the days inched by until they all blurred together. Faye watched the moon wane every night, both dreading and hoping for it to disappear. Her feet slowly healed as Delphine and Bonnie prepped for the upcoming masquerade. Faye could only pretend, and hope, that her fear was hidden.

Delphine set to work, sewing her own ball gown, determined to finish it in time to show off her mastery of the skill. It was her own defiance, proving to her mother that she could care for herself.

Faye too threw herself into her work, but only to keep the wild thoughts at bay. If she remained too idle, the whispers would come creeping back and threaten to consume her whole. Never before had she longed to return to the Underworld as much as now. And the thought scared her.

When the full moon finally rose, Faye rushed to the hearth, her legs lighter than feathers. Without resisting, she dashed into the embrace of the magical cords, snatching her mask before it fully formed, the twisting, metallic butterfly wing biting into her palm. She squeezed her fist around it, breathing in the pain. Absorbing the strength.

Poneros gripped her hand with stiff fingers as he helped her into the boat. A nervous energy spilled from his tense shoulders and stiff limbs. It sent a shiver of worry into Faye's own limbs, twining around her lungs and squeezing tight.

Faye glanced at her sisters as they settled into their own boats that drifted across the lake and counted the occupants. Colette was still missing. Faye clutched her skirts in her fist, picking at the embroidery.

"Poneros …"

The word had just slipped from her tongue.

He looked down at her, his rat mask hiding his expression. Shrinking back, Faye wrapped her arms around herself. She waited, heart pounding, to see what he would do. With silent precision, Poneros slid the pole into the lake and pushed. Across from Faye, Helaine kept her expression carefully blank, even though her fingers twitched.

They glided across the lake in silence, the heavy air muffling all noise. Faye peeked up at Poneros. He was looking out over at the other boats.

She's dead, she's dead, she's dead. The thought spun through Faye's mind. Colette was dead. She had to be. Phagos had killed her as punishment and dumped her body in the upper world. Faye bit her lip to keep from screaming. From crying. There was nothing she could do. Absolutely nothing.

I'm so, so sorry, Colette. Please forgive me.

Colette was dead because of her. She was dead and Faye could have, *should* have prevented it. How, she didn't know. But she knew in her bones that it was her debt to pay.

Would Desi be next? Fear gripped Faye and she looked over at her sisters. What would happen if they were all killed, one by one? Panic seized her and she gripped the edges of the boat as it scraped against the sand. Poneros jumped into the shallows of the lake. As he pulled the boat ashore, Faye leaned forward.

"Please, Helaine," she whispered, "tell me what's going on. Is Colette dead?"

Helaine shrank back. "I don't know. I haven't heard anything."

She scrambled from the boat before Faye could say anything else. Poneros followed, then took Estelle's arm.

Adalie looked back, her blue eyes dark in the flickering lights of the forest. The fingers of her left hand rippled in a wave. Faye's heart quickened as she waved back. Longing overtook her and she imagined herself wrapping Adalie in a tight hug and never letting go.

Phagos tracked Faye's movements as they walked. Animosity poured from him in sickening waves. Slowing her steps, Faye fell back, out of the crazed gaze of his bull mask.

It was hard, wrapping her mind around the fact that Phagos and Pathos were brothers. As Phagos jerked on Adalie's arm, a small, selfish part of Faye was glad that Pathos had chosen her instead.

It was a foolish thought. Guilt stabbed Faye in the chest with a white-hot iron, deep and burning. *She* deserved the abuse, not Adalie. Adalie had done nothing wrong.

The trees shifted from diamond to a deep purple, glowing with veins of amethyst light. Where the diamond trees were smooth as cut glass, and transparent, these trees were rough and gnarled, their branches twisted and patches of their trunks scorched black, as if burned.

The castle came into view as the trees thinned and the ground fell away into a sharp slope that led down into a chasm filled with a rushing river of black water. A bridge of stone and twisted metal stretched across the chasm, leading to the outer castle wall. The drawbridge lowered for them and two shadowy guards stood waiting. Arches lined the bridge intermediately, each decorated with a pair of gargoyles, their mouths curled in hungry snarls.

As they crossed, Faye placed her hands protectively on Belle and Margaux's shoulders. Old, tattered banners waved from bent poles. They snapped in a cold wind that blew from the direction of the castle. Of all the things here in this shadowy Underworld, the banners were the most colorful, holding onto faded tones of blue and white.

Her shoes clicked against stone as the gargoyles tracked their movements with shining red eyes. Faye kept her gaze ahead. As long as she showed no fear, they wouldn't attack. She hoped.

Quickly, they crossed the bridge and paused in the castle courtyard. Belle clutched Faye's leg, and Faye placed a protective hand on her head.

Phagos positioned himself next to Faye, Adalie on his other side. His posture was casual. Mocking. Power oozed from his stance. As if he knew they wished to speak and was lording it over them.

Faye curled her fingers into a fist. It was now or never. Stepping back, she slipped from the line.

Phagos' hand slammed down on her shoulder. "What do you think you're doing?" he growled.

"Please, I—"

Phagos grabbed Faye's wrist and leaned in close, so close that Faye could see his round black eyes.

"You were just trying to speak to Adalie. You know it is forbidden." He lifted his hand as if to strike her.

"Phagos." Pathos didn't yell. His voice was smooth and cold.

Pathos stood on the steps leading into the castle. Without the darkness surrounding him or the spiked crown, he looked like an ordinary man in his tailored suitcoat with its gold-tree flower tucked neatly in the lapel. But, with a flick of his fingers, darkness swirled across his shoulders like a cloak. He turned his wolf mask toward Phagos and cocked his head.

Slowly, Pathos descended the steps and crossed the courtyard until he stood before Phagos. Reaching out, he placed a hand on his brother's shoulder.

No one moved. Faye held her breath as Phagos' grip tightened.

"Dear brother," Pathos said as he shifted his hand to touch Phagos' neck. "*No one* touches Faye."

Phagos released an angry snort. He whipped toward Faye, wrenching out of his brother's grasp. Leaning in close, he spoke in a low growl. "If you keep running off, little lady, I am going to add another scar to Adalie's beautiful face."

Hot breath smelling of rot blasted Faye's face. Phagos' deep black eyes bore into hers and she nodded. He released her wrist, shoving her back.

Pathos caught Faye as she fell. She struggled from his arms and straightened. Lifting her chin high, she snapped open her own fan, even as she trembled inside. She *needed* to speak to Adalie, no matter what threats he poured out. "I'm not afraid of you, Phagos."

He laughed and, gripping Adalie's hand, walked away.

Pathos straightened his jacket as he watched Phagos. He looked Faye in the eye, a warning in his voice. "You should be."

∞

The moment Faye saw Colette on the dais, it was as if a heavy weight lifted from her chest. Tears of relief filled her eyes, but she kept them in check. She didn't know how Pathos would react to her crying. Especially after what happened in the courtyard. He had protected her. And yet Faye found her fear of him deepening.

All throughout the night, she kept her eyes on Colette, drinking in the sight of her alive and unharmed. As they danced, Pathos whispered in her ear that he would grant her a chance to speak to Adalie. Faye nodded, accepting his offer as her heartbeat pounded in her ears.

With the last notes of the dance, Faye curtsied as Pathos bowed. He moved closer and leaned down to whisper in her ear.

"By the drinks table. Ten minutes is all I can give you. Anything more and it will upset the balance of magic."

Faye nodded. She peered up at the dais through her eyelashes once more. Once again, Colette's pale face was smooth as marble. Her half mask with the large phoenix wing fanning out from the right looked overly bright. Worry gnawed at Faye again. Something about all of this wasn't right.

Pathos made his way across the room, his steps sending ripples across the floor. Harsh whispers floated through the air the moment he met with Phagos. Together, they climbed the dais steps. Faye kept them in sight as she made her way over to Adalie.

"Come with me," she whispered.

Adalie touched the yellow moth wing on her mask as she dipped her head toward the brothers. "But what about the Midnight King?"

"Just come on."

They made their way over to the table, where several of the shadow-like courtiers backed away. It was as if there were a barrier between them, one they could never cross. Adalie's breathing quickened and she kept her head cocked toward the dais. Faye picked up one of the crystal cups. The surface was slick in her sweaty palm.

"I need you to tell me something."

"Yes?"

"Why is Colette here, in the castle?" Faye picked up the ladle from a bowl of deep red liquid. She shuddered at its uncanny similarity to blood.

"She married Nosos."

The ladle slipped from Faye's fingers as she gasped. It clattered against the bowl, quick and sharp. Up on the dais, Pathos looked back. He held up his hand, displaying five fingers.

Faye rubbed her forehead, a headache starting to build. Why would Colette ever do such a thing? While Pathos had made his intentions clear several times, the thought of marriage had never crossed her mind.

"Why?"

"It was a deal she made with the Midnight King. Don't you already know this?"

Faye shied away. "No. Pathos—I mean, the Midnight King won't tell me anything."

Adalie knew nothing about Faye's freedoms. None of her sisters did. It was something she would never be able to tell them. If she did, she would lose their trust and with it, their love. And just the thought of it sent panic shooting through her limbs.

Pathos had told her that she was special, that she could walk above ground because she was different than the others. But Faye hated it. Every waking moment under the sun was just another reminder that they were stuck while she, the one who had brought this upon them, was able to walk free. Faye should be the one imprisoned in the cliffs. She should be the one trapped in darkness. Not them.

But she couldn't let Adalie know. If she found out, she would hate Faye forever. And Faye couldn't bear the thought of losing her sisters completely.

"I may have found a way to break the curse," Faye whispered.

"How?"

"No time, I can't tell you everything. Just pass it on to the others. They need to hear this." She dropped the cup onto the table and took Adalie's hands in her own. Her sister's skin was warm and soft and *alive*. "But I promise you, I *will* get us all out of here."

Adalie's chin quivered and she nodded, a fierce light shining in her eye. She squeezed Faye's hands in a strong grip, and Faye squeezed back.

Behind Adalie, Pathos descended from the dais. Faye released her sister's hands and scrambled back. Adalie gave Faye one last nod before turning and making her way toward Phagos.

Pathos held out his hand to Faye and she took it in her own. As they made their way to the dance floor, Pathos remained silent. Curiosity burned through Faye, but she bit her tongue. The music swelled, a slow, gentle piece. Pathos and Faye took their places in line across from each other. As the dance began and they circled one another, Pathos spoke.

"Phagos will never touch you again. You have my word." He said the words with a fierce sort of pride.

"Thank you," Faye whispered, knowing he would want to hear the words. But they burned like acid on her tongue.

"I'm afraid Nosos has done something terrible. With your mother."

Faye's heart skipped a beat and she wobbled, missing a step. "What?"

"She has been placed in the valley of the shadow beasts."

His words drained Faye of any elation she had from talking to Adalie. She had only heard of the shadow beasts from Phagos's mad rantings. Estelle, Faye's younger sister by a year, had been thrown among the shadow beasts three months back as punishment for Genevieve missing three steps. Estelle returned a different girl. Once so vibrant and defiant in her dances—twirling her forest green skirts and stamping her glass slippers as she danced with Poneros—she now moved as if she were nothing but a shell.

From the way Estelle's shoulders hung crooked to how her neck seemed too thin for her head, it was as if the shadow beasts had stolen her very spirit. Faye could only imagine what they would do to Mama.

The thought made her sick. It was another secret Faye kept from her sisters. How their mother was trapped too. And while Faye hadn't seen her at all, sometimes Pathos would whisper to Faye about her mother's condition. Of how Pathos kept her in the castle dungeon, along with the courtiers from Revayr that had been swallowed by the Underworld as well.

"Is she alive? How long has she been there? Please."
Faye's throat tightened. "Will you help her?"

Pathos turned his face away, the wolf mask catching the
muted light. "I will do what I can. You have my word as the
Midnight King."

Faye clenched her jaw and pointed her toes, placing her
foot delicately on the floor and sending out a deep gold
ripple. She spun and curtsied. And she prayed to anyone who
would listen that Madame's plan would work.

She would go to Leo's masquerade balls and she would
dance. She would find a husband. And she would not fail.
Because failure was not an option.

Chapter Nine – Leo

Leo marched into his father's study and slapped a stack of papers on the desk.

"Father, explain this."

Sunlight, bright and splendid, shone down on the wretched papers from two large windows. Leo would have enjoyed it, if it weren't for this atrocity he had found printed in ink.

Father peered at the papers through his spectacles. He raised one eyebrow. "These are the lists I spoke to you about. Of those attending?"

"Yes, but you haven't invited anyone from Titania, and I can assure you, the Faerie Queane can be a handful when not invited. Don't you remember what happened to your grandmother? She was cursed by the queane to sleep for one thousand years."

The thought of his father spurning the Fae Queane was not only appalling, but downright frightening. If the queane grew angry and decided to curse the whole blasted country, Leo would have no one to blame but his father. Then again, with his current actions, Father was making a right mess of things already.

Father sighed and leaned back in his chair. He rubbed his eyes as the grandfather clock chimed seven. "Son, these are all the people I am inviting, and no one else. It would be a foolish thing to do, inviting the enemy into our very home."

"But Faerie Law dictates that when the queane is invited to a celebration in peace, she cannot bring harm to the kingdom. She may not like the idea of coming here, but she'll be obligated by law to leave us alone, at least until it ends." Leo crossed his arms, daring Father to contradict him.

"No." Father shook his head. "Those with magic blood are dangerous and need to be put in their place. Just look at what happened with Revayr. King Raoul let magic run wild in his kingdom and even married a *Faerie*." He spat the word like it was the most disgusting thing he had ever tasted. "Now his wife and half-breed daughters are gone, and I blame no one but the Fae."

Leo flinched. He reached for the crumpled letter in his pocket, the bloodstained note he'd found in Northwind Forest.

"What about King Raoul?" Leo paced in front of the desk. "Raoul is Human, and a very kind man. He's not on your list. If you want to prove that the treaty between Eura and Revayr still exists, you need to invite him."

Father glared over his spectacles at Leo. "*King Raoul* is the main offender. Why would I invite him to the masquerade?"

"Because he's *Human*, Father!" Leo couldn't believe the man sitting in front of him. Was he really that hypocritical? "Please, if you won't invite him for yourself, do it for me. King Raoul was like a second father to me. I owe him for his kindness. Please, Father."

Silence cloaked the room. The grandfather clock ticked on, unperturbed. Father tapped the butt of his fountain pen against the worn wood desk.

Leo waited. He wasn't inclined to make his father angry, but this was one point he couldn't back down on. The only way he could continue to search for the princesses was to talk to their father, and since Leo couldn't travel beyond Eura's borders, he had to bring Raoul here.

Finally, Father spoke, his voice low. "This isn't about that de la Rou girl, is it?"

Leo's gut twisted. Her name sounded almost like mockery on his lips. But even as the pain surfaced, Leo steeled himself. Faye was gone. That he could not change. But he could honor her memory.

It was no use fighting with his father on this. Leo took in a steadying breath. For now, he would acquiesce. For now, he would do what his father demanded. But he would not stop searching for a way to end this murderer so that the monster could never hurt another soul again. And to do that, he needed to find the descendant of the White Lady.

Leo bowed his head. "Forgive my impudence, Father. This is not about *Princess* Faye de la Rou. I spoke only hoping to keep the peace." He bit off the rest of his thoughts, not wanting to anger his father more.

Father nodded and bent back to his paper. "Apology accepted. Now go on. I have business to attend to."

Leo picked up the list and scanned the names. So many pompous and snobbish men and women. He paused at a particular name. Brianna MacNamara. She was a nice girl, a perfect duke's daughter with a heart of gold. She and Leo had been childhood friends, as her father would make constant trips to the castle. But as they grew older, they had grown apart, Brianna absorbed in preparing to take over her father's estate, and Leo learning how to rule the kingdom. As much as Leo had enjoyed Brianna's company, he couldn't imagine marrying her.

He glanced at his father, at the broad set of his shoulders and the chiseled jaw and steel-colored eyes. The battle-scarred hand that gripped his pen. Irritation bent his brows and his mouth was locked in a straight line. Leo dropped the paper back onto the table and folded his hands behind his back.

"But Father, what if …" He frowned. "What if I don't love her?"

Father laughed. Leo's cheeks flamed as irritation mounted.

Father leaned his elbows onto his desk. "You will learn to love, my boy. In time. But ruling a kingdom with a wise partner is more important. You'll learn to live with each other if you remember to put—"

"Duty before self." Leo mumbled the words, tired of hearing them.

"Exactly so."

Leo crumpled the list in his hand and dropped his gaze to the wrinkled paper. What good was a loveless marriage? Neither he nor his future wife would ever be truly content with one another.

But Father wanted Leo to marry, and marry soon, for his crowning ceremony would take place on the night of the last ball, which also happened to be Leo's twentieth birthday. He would become the crown prince and Father would keep him home. Then Leo wouldn't be able to search for the princesses, or the White Lady's descendant any longer. And if he couldn't rescue at least one princess, then there would be no hope for peace.

Leo turned toward the door, then paused. He looked back at his father, busy with whatever it was that had captured his attention. Should he say anything and risk his father's anger? Leo shrugged. Why not?

"What if the princesses were still alive and one happened to come to the ball?" He came back to Father's desk and rested the heels of his palms on the wood. "Desideria, perhaps. Or maybe Adalie or Estelle. Would they be considered potential brides?"

Father was already shaking his head as Leo spoke. "No. No!" He rose from his desk, pushing back his chair with a loud screech.

Leo backpedaled.

Father's face was crimson, and his eyes flashed. "Lionheart ap Owen, you promised you would drop this. It has been three years, three years since those half-breed daughters disappeared, and I say, good riddance! No son of mine will *ever* marry a Faerie, even a half-blood."

Each word struck Leo like a harsh blow. He hardened his jaw and kept his eyes locked on Father's gold-and-red collar.

Anger, sharp and hot, crackled through Leo's veins. Leo tightened his grip around the paper, crumpling it in his fist.

Beneath their feet, the ground rumbled. Leo's anger surged with the quake. Father's pen rolled across the desk and fell to the floor. The ink bottle shook and the windows rattled in their frames. The noise pounded against his skull in time with his racing heart.

Leo staggered. Father fell back in his chair. Gripping the edge of the desk, Leo braced himself. But as soon as the quake started, it stopped. He looked up at Father, shocked. Eura never had quakes. Ever. It was something that only happened in other countries. But Leo couldn't deny what he had felt.

Father's face was white as he stared at Leo, jaw hanging like a drowning fish. Leaning forward, Father took off his spectacles with a shaking hand and threw them onto the desk. He cleared his throat, once. Twice.

"Please, son. Stop looking. I know you and the girls had some sort of special bond but it's over. It's time to move on. As long as magic exists in this world, we must fight against it. Fight until we have the upper hand and the Fae are put in their place, just like the Enchanters. Underground."

Leo's anger had been drained away, replaced with a heavy sort of weariness. He shook his head. It wasn't worth it angering his father any more.

Bowing stiffly, he said, "Forgive me, Father. I misspoke. I shall not bother you again."

Straightening, Leo marched stiff-legged from the room. His father was impossible. Incorrigible. A man too set in tradition.

Jack pushed away from the wall next to the door.

"I take it your conversation with His Majesty didn't go as planned?"

Leo let out a humorless laugh. "Not exactly."

He balled up the guest list, stormed up to the nearest window, and chucked it out as hard as he could. He watched it sail away and thrust his hands deep into his trouser pockets.

Jack came to Leo's side and raised his heavy brows. "That was the list," he said, but not as a question.

"Yes. It was the list." Leo planted his hands on the windowsill and stared out at the distant mountains. "Father wants me to give up looking."

Leo wouldn't give up on them. Not now, not ever. Not until he knew that each girl was undoubtedly, irreversibly dead. No longer would he mourn for them, doing nothing like he had for so long.

Once, there was a time when he thought like his father did. A time when he too had looked down on the Fae, thinking them an inferior species and in need of control. Labeling them as wild, undisciplined, and dangerous.

But when he arrived in Revayr, his views were shaken. Fae walked the streets side by side with Humans. A woman with black-and-orange striped hair. A man with yellow eyes. A girl whose toes never touched the ground. There was even one Faerie he could recall, a little girl named Wyn who could shift into the form of a black-and-white bear. Her kindness and willingness to help a poor sot like him proved to him that Fae were just like Humans. The only thing that set them apart was magic.

Then there were the princesses themselves, and their mother. Queen Nimue had instantly made him feel at home among so many foreigners. Being Eurish herself, she had taken him under her wing, and her soft, gentle demeanor helped him grow accustomed to life in Revayr.

Time spent with the sage queen was bittersweet, for she reminded him of his own mother, who had died when he was very young. The thought brought back an age-old ache in his chest. He couldn't even remember his own mother's face.

"I don't think you should give up on them." Jack's voice was quiet. "I think what you're doing is right."

It was comforting, knowing that Leo had at least one ally. He slapped a hand on Jack's wide shoulder.

"Thank you, friend." Leo turned back to the courtyard below. "If only I knew where to start."

Jack shifted on his feet, his leather armor creaking. "What we found the other day ... it had me thinking. I know someone who might have more information on this descendant of the White Lady."

"Brilliant! We'll go ask your friend tomorrow. How far away are they? I might just ask Father later to allow me to go on a hunting trip." Leo began walking at a brisk pace as he spoke.

If this informant of Jack's knew anything, perhaps they could point Leo to this Enchanter with White Lady blood flowing in their veins. And the sooner they found them, the sooner Leo could free Faye's sisters. If any still lived.

His guard remained silent.

Leo looked back. "Jack?"

Jack was still beside the king's study door, unmoving, eyes trained on the floor. "This ... informant ... isn't fond of royals. No offense, Your Highness."

Leo's enthusiasm faded, but he gave Jack a firm nod. "Then go. And hurry back as quick as you can. I don't like waiting."

Relief loosened Jack's shoulders and he bowed. "Thank you, Your Highness."

Turning, the guard marched quickly down the hall.

Leo sagged against the window. The cold stone bit into his skin and made him shiver. Pulling the crumpled note from his pocket, he stared at the dark brown stains, the sharp, slanted writing. Tears blurred his vision and for a moment, he let them escape. Faye's face came to mind, a blurry image from distant memories. Pain gripped his heart so hard he feared it might burst. Leo covered his eyes with a hand.

Jack was right. As long as Leo had breath in his lungs, he would search. He would look, and keep looking until he freed Faye's sisters, or until he found their remains and brought them home. He would not stop until the kidnapper was brought to justice. He would fight for them, with every ounce of strength. And maybe, just maybe, he could begin to make up for the mountain of mistakes of his past.

Chapter Ten – Faye

Faye's dresses arrived three days before the first ball was to be held. Faye's stomach churned as Delphine circled the gowns with a critical eye.

"Well, they are beautiful." She fingered the beads that graced the top with a sort of reluctance. "It would be a shame to ruin them."

Faye fingered the fabric. One was a brilliant gold, the next deep silver, and the last a shimmering white. They were made from the smoothest silk that slipped through her fingers like water. She recoiled and scrubbed her palms against the rough cotton of her working dress. They were too much like the enchanted ball gown. Even the tiny crystals sewn into the bodices were too familiar. Uncanny.

Faye shook her head. No, this dress had been made by hand, crafted from fabric woven on a loom and then cut and sewn and patched together by real, living Human hands. Not pulled together by some magic glamour.

Madame bustled into the sitting room, carrying a long, oblong box. "I need you to look your best, so if there is anything that is not to your liking, be sure to tell me." She grinned as she held out the box to Delphine. "Here are your masks. One for each dress. I tried to get them to match your designs as closely as possible, Delphine."

Delphine opened the box and squealed. "Oh, Mama! They are stunning!"

She pulled one out and held it to the light. Faye stared. She had to admit, the mask *was* stunning. It was a colombina mask made of stiff paper-mâché and painted a deep, sapphire blue. Tiny blue crystals rimmed the eye holds, giving it a subtle shimmer. The nose was a long black beak curved slightly and a plume of emerald green peacock feathers formed a crown along the top. In the front, two golden feathers accentuated the colors, complimenting the delicate swirl of green on each cheek.

Holding it up to her face, Delphine turned to Faye, a wide grin stretching her mouth. "What do you think?"

Faye pushed away the images of the monsters waiting for her in the Underworld. She wouldn't let them keep her from enjoying this moment. She smiled. "I don't know. Do you think many men will fall for a beak like that?"

Delphine held the mask by its black silk strings to her face and struck a pose, her hand to her cheek.

"If a man can't appreciate a girl with a beak, then I think they're utterly hopeless." She grinned and twirled in a circle. "And when all the men flock to me and beg for my hand in marriage, you'll be sorry, Faye."

Laughing, Faye picked up another of Delphine's masks—a green moretta mask painted with brown branches and spring-green leaves—and covered her own face.

"I don't know, I think being a forest maid would be much more attractive."

Delphine sniffed and pointed her nose in the air in mock offense. "Well then, I don't think you quite know the definition of beauty, dear Faye."

"I fear you're quite right, dear Delphine." Faye giggled as she placed her hand on her forehead and struck a languid pose. "Poor me, such a drab and boring creature."

Delphine burst into a fit of laughter.

"Let's see yours!" she said as she carefully put her masks away and turned toward Faye, an eager light in her eye.

They crowded together at the table, Bonnie at Faye's right elbow and Delphine on her left side. Grinning, she flipped back the lid. All feeling left her limbs as she stared, stunned.

Butterflies. Each one perfectly crafted in silver, gold, and diamond, the shape of their wings too familiar. Faye slammed the box shut, her heart beating at an odd pace. She closed her eyes as her limbs trembled. All the laughter stilled.

"Faye?"

No. Faye's stomach turned, and the room spun. She couldn't do this. Those masks would *never* touch her skin.

"Faye, what's wrong? Don't you like them?" Delphine's voice held a hint of reproach.

Trembling, Faye turned to Madame Leroux, who leaned on her walking stick, shock in her eyes. Suspicion, sharp and heavy, filled Faye's chest. She immediately shoved it down. Madame couldn't be involved. Could she?

"Where did you get these?" she asked in a low voice.

"From a mask maker. Where else?"

Faye's blood ran cold.

"What did he look like?" She almost didn't dare ask. "Was he … wearing a mask?"

"Why, yes." Madame Leroux frowned. "It was quite odd. A silver mask in the form of a snarling wolf."

The room spun and Faye clutched the table. He knew. He *knew*! And yet he said nothing. She dug her nails in the wood and took in deep breaths, willing herself not to scream.

Pathos had been there that day when Leo rode by. She hadn't just imagined it. He'd been *right there*, inches away, standing in the sunlight.

The daytime was the only time she ever felt safe from him. Separated from the night and all the horrors that walked within it. But now, she wasn't even free of that. The sacred line between night and day, between peace and fear, shattered, all because Pathos couldn't stay where he belonged.

Maybe it was a warning. A warning that she would never be free. Once the thought wormed its way into her mind, she couldn't escape it. And all because of three stupid butterfly masks.

Holding back a shudder, she wrapped her arms around herself and left the kitchen.

"Faye, wait!" Bonnie rushed after her, but Faye slipped out the door before Bonnie could follow.

She rushed down the pebble-lined path, past the sunflowers, and into the tiny garden with its stone-wall fence and climbing vines. Leaning against the cool stones, closed her eyes and turned her face up to the sun.

"We can do this," she whispered.

It was rude of her to walk out on Madame Leroux like that and refuse to go to the ball. So what if Pathos had sold Madame the masks? So what if that meant he could follow her to here, to Eura? If going to the ball meant there was hope for her and her sisters, then she would go, masks or not.

A chill ran down her spine and she searched the garden as a creeping sensation filled her bones. He could be anywhere, watching her, waiting. If Pathos had found some way up, she would never be safe again.

Shadows flickered beneath the trees, and Faye's heart leapt into her throat. She searched for any sign of a wolf, frozen to the spot. But all that she could see were sunspots and the waving grass. Quickly, she rushed back inside.

For the rest of the day, Faye kept thoughts of Pathos firmly locked behind iron doors by throwing herself into her work. She cleaned the kitchen, scrubbing the floors and the table, dusting the furniture and polishing the silver. Anything to keep the cold at a distance.

She paused amidst washing the laundry and scrubbed at her skin. Terror gripped her in its tight embrace. She couldn't get the feeling of someone watching her to go away. It prickled down her neck and across her spine. Dug deep into her shoulders and spread into her fingers.

Voices drifted into the kitchen while Faye sat on the floor. Delphine and Madame, talking just above a whisper. Faye paused to listen, her heart pounding in her ears.

"There's something going on here, Mama. Something I don't understand."

"I believe there is some form of history between Faye and that mask maker. She's told me next to nothing of her past, so anything could have happened before I found her."

"I just wish she would talk to us and stop being so secretive. Then maybe we could help."

Faye couldn't stop the tears that filled her eyes. She scrubbed at her cheeks with the back of her hand. She didn't need their help or their sympathy. There was nothing either of them could do for her. They were wasting their worries on a girl worth less than the ragged dress she held strangled in her fists.

⊗

Faye lay awake long after Madame, Delphine, and Bonnie had fallen asleep. Staring into the fireplace, her pulse pounded in her ears. Pathos had come above ground. He had come on a night when the moon wasn't full. But he and his brothers were supposed to be trapped underground. They couldn't escape. It was impossible. Unthinkable.

And yet he had. He *had* to have come and sold the masks to Madame Leroux. It was the only explanation. No one else knew of the butterfly mask.

Faye needed answers. And she needed them now.

Pushing up from the couch, she threw her blanket aside and dropped to her knees on the worn rug. Scrabbling at the brick that hid the slippers, she snagged the edge with her nails and pulled. She removed the slippers in her shaking fist. The glass was cold against her skin as she slipped them on.

Magic, sharp and frigid, crawled up her legs and into her chest. She sucked in a gasp. The air in the fireplace shimmered. Faye reached out a trembling hand and touched the back wall. It swung open on silent hinges as the clock chimed ten.

Faye tensed all her muscles as her heart fluttered against her ribcage. The magic burned along her skin, revolting against her choice to enter before her time. She was crazy. An absolute goosecap. She couldn't go to the Underworld. Not now. Not before her time.

I need answers. I need to know why. She repeated the thoughts over and over as she crouched on the hearth, joints locked, unwilling to let her go.

A tug of magic snagged at her chest and Faye rubbed at the spot. Pathos. He knew she was coming.

Taking in a deep breath, she plunged into the darkness.

This time, her nightgown didn't shift into the brilliant gold dress. The gold-trees shimmered in a light of their own making, blossom-heavy branches bowing down to meet her. Each step felt like a mile. Faye's slippers clanked against the steps as loud as the ring of the city bell.

Gold light shifted to silver, and the trees faded into the tunnel walls. There, at the end, stood a silhouette. Faye's steps faltered and she gripped her skirts. She should run back up the stairs. She should turn and flee and never come back to this place.

"Faye." Pathos's voice was deep and musical. A soft call that beckoned her onward.

Her feet moved of their own accord, carrying her closer and closer to Pathos. He held out his hand and she found herself reaching. There was no reason to fear him. He had never hurt her, not once. Pathos cared for her. He protected her. At least, that was what she told herself as fear clogged her throat.

"My lady," he said, bowing. "Why have you come?"

Faye paused just out of arm's reach. Letting her arm fall, she folded her hands over her chest. She felt naked without her mask, dressed in only her nightgown.

"I ... I want to know ..." Faye struggled to find the words, but her mind drew a blank.

Pathos nodded, the wolf mask looking monstrous in the twilight. "I knew you'd come. One day."

"What's happened with Colette?" She forced the question past her lips. "Why is she married to Nosos?"

"She made a deal with me. Marry Nosos and she can go above ground. Just like you."

"But I'm not married to you, Pathos."

He remained silent at that. His gloved fingers curled and uncurled.

"What about the others? Do they have to marry your brothers?"

"Only if they want to. I promised I would never force them. Phagos can't hurt Adalie in that way." His tone was filled with sympathy and Faye imagined his face softening with the words, how the hard lines of his brow would smooth, and his lips would quirk in a smile. Only, she had never seen his face before.

"Did you come above ground today? Did you sell Madame Leroux the masks?"

Pathos took a step closer. "What masks?"

"The butterfly masks." She spat the words as if they were poison. "Did you sell her the butterfly masks?"

"No. You know I can't leave, Faye. But whoever did must have known how beautiful you look in them."

He was lying. She could hear it in his voice. But she could ask the same question over and over and get only the same answer. She needed a new tactic.

Faye brought a trembling hand to her cheek. "Do you know about the masquerades? And don't lie to me, Pathos. I want the truth."

Silence fell between them. Heavy, impenetrable silence. Pathos took a step back, black boots scuffing on the diamond-strewn path.

"Yes. I know about the masquerade balls being held in *Prince Lionheart's* honor." He spoke as if Leo's name was venom. "You can't go, Faye."

"I must."

"You can't. The Midnight King will get angry and something horrible will happen. Think of your sisters. Do you want them to suffer?" His voice was rough. Angry.

Faye shuddered at the way he spoke of himself. Always, there was a separation between Pathos and the Midnight King. They were one and the same, and yet even Pathos knew he was different when he wore the crown.

"If I don't go ..." Faye bit her lip.

She couldn't tell him about breaking the curse. He would only fight all the harder to keep her here. She straightened, standing as tall as she could. She had only one choice. Only one thing he could not back down on.

"Pathos, I want to make a deal."

Chapter Eleven – Leo

The whispers were everywhere. Princess Colette de la Rou had been seen in the streets of Westshire. Every servant Leo passed—Colette's name was on their lips.

Even out in the training yard, the soldiers muttered together. A particularly tall fellow with a full mustache murmured, "It's her ghost, I tell you. Got herself murdered and now she's haunting the moors."

Leo itched to jump on his horse and ride out to Westshire that very moment, but if Father got wind of his leaving, he would send the whole brigade after Leo to drag him home. Instead, he listened to the gossip and paced the halls, waiting for Jack to return, hopefully with some worthwhile news. Wherever it was that he'd gone, it was in the direction of Westshire so he might have learned something.

As Leo made his way back inside, he tried to block out the whispers. It had to be a cruel joke started by those in Westshire, to gain visitors. If anything, they had just seen a banshee or a werewolf. Nothing more.

The darkness of the stairway enveloped him as he placed his foot on the first step. Images flashed through his mind, faster than he could make sense of them. His chest constricted and he stumbled, knees slamming into the steps.

Faye stood right before him—eyes filled with tears. Dressed in a bridal gown, her lips were a pale blue. Skinny fingers clung to his hands as they danced together in the dark.

"Leo," she whispered. "Leo, don't you know me?"

Butterflies peeled from her skin and danced around them in hues of silver, gold, and white. They swirled around Leo's head and then flew away, taking with them the warmth in Leo's veins.

Bit by bit, Faye's skin bled of color until she was a ghost. They continued to dance, until the darkness swallowed them both.

Leo pulled in a gasp like a drowning man, his head tilted back. The darkness dissipated and natural sunlight filled the stairwell once more. Leo collapsed on the steps and fought for breath. The vision … it seemed so real. He could still feel her frozen breath on his neck, her ice-cold fingers on his shoulder and hand.

Staring at his fingers, he shook his head. That was it. He was going bonkers. Absolutely cracked. What he needed was to sleep more. Sleep more and worry less.

A derisive laugh edged its way up his throat. That was nearly impossible. He wouldn't be able to stop worrying and stressing and wishing and searching until Faye's sisters were found, safe and sound.

Pushing up onto shaky legs, Leo straightened his jacket, smoothed his hair, and brushed off his trousers. Walking like the prince he was supposed to be, he continued up the steps. Shoved the vision from his mind. It meant nothing. It would never mean anything.

And yet, he couldn't shake the fact that he had seen the vision of Colette and Faye dead before he found the dress and note.

"It's utter balderdash," he muttered to himself. "That's all it is. Infernal balderdash."

There were more important things to do than ponder visions that could mean absolutely nothing. After all, Father had finally granted him access to the archives, but only if he agreed to considering one of the preferred candidates. He'd told Father he would pursue Brianna McNamara just to get him off his tail. At least, a life with a girl he knew would be better than a life with a stranger.

Hopefully, the archives would show him something, anything that involved the lineage of the Enchanters, so he could find if there was, in fact, a descendant of the White Lady. And if not, he would just have to wait until Jack returned.

The library was bigger than he remembered. The last time he had stepped foot in here was more than six years ago, long before he had traveled to Revayr. Rows upon rows of dark bookshelves marched in even lines across the floor and lined every wall.

Leo moved toward the back of the library where the castle archives hid. The door was locked and bound with a heavy chain, but luckily, Leo had the key.

With a rattling clang, Leo unlocked the chains. They slipped through his fingers and he tried to catch them. One chain slammed into the floor with a loud clash of metal on wood, while the other swung free. Leo froze and looked back. A librarian appeared from between the shelves and scowled at him over the rim of her wire-framed spectacles.

"Sorry," Leo whispered.

The librarian shook her head and retreated among the books. Taking in a breath, Leo turned back to the door of iron mesh and slid it open. Surprisingly, it was silent on its hinges. Leo slipped inside, leaving the door ajar.

Ten bookshelves filled the cramped space, along with an overcrowded desk. Piles of paper and bookbinding material were everywhere. Stepping lightly, Leo peered around for the archivist.

"Hello? Anyone in here?" His voice was muffled against the rows of ancient books.

Only silence answered him. Shrugging, he continued farther into the room. If he knew Father, the lineage of the Enchanters wouldn't be easily accessible. However, Father would be a fool to throw them away, so Leo guessed that the book would have to be somewhere in the back corner, alone and forgotten.

Leo reached for the nearest pile of books and held his breath as dust exploded into the air. Setting them down on an old, rickety chair, Leo waved the dust away as his eyes watered and a cough crept up his throat.

The first few books held the lineages of old Highland families, back when Eura and Draconia had been the same country. A few of the names were crossed out, while others had a giant red X next to them. From what Leo could remember, the crossed-out names meant the child died at an early age or was ostracized from the family, and the red X meant that the family was a traitor to the crown.

Most of the other books were the same. Half of them were ancient families that no longer existed, and the other half were Draconian families Leo had no idea if they still existed. With a sigh, he pulled down the last stack. These held names that were completely unfamiliar to Leo. He tried to read some of them, but they were too long and complicated. When he reached the third book, he paused, his heart kicking up a notch.

Right there on the page, written in swirling black ink, were the words, *Lineage of the Lords and Ladies of Everland*. And right beneath that was the name of the very first White Lady. *Artemis*. An odd name, but it had a pretty ring to it.

Leo traced his finger down the page, his heart pounding loud in his ears. The names only stretched down for nine generations. The last name on the list was --. Leo frowned as he checked the date scrawled next to her name. *1100-1202*. According to this, she was the current White Lady when Everland fell. He squinted at the page. There was another name beneath hers, but it was scratched out. Leo tilted the book toward the only window in the room.

"Cassiopeia," he whispered.

He looked up and repeated the name to himself. Something about it seemed familiar. He wasn't sure what, but it just rolled off his tongue as if he'd been saying it his whole life.

He snapped his fingers. Of course. Many ladies of the court were named Cassie, and Father had told Leo that his great-great-great grandmother was named Cassie. An unusual name, but not uncommon.

Still, the name rattled around his mind like a tune he couldn't place.

Sighing, he shoved the books back onto the shelf. That didn't help him any. This Cassiopeia didn't live very long at least, for Enchanter. More than likely, she had died in childhood. Which meant that either there were names missing from the lineage, or she had been the last of her line.

Disappointment curled inside Leo's stomach and he shoved his hands into his trouser pockets in a very unprincely manner. This whole thing was a waste of time. All this translated to the fact that these murderers were obsessed with finding someone who did not exist.

What in all the Five Kingdoms would they even want with the White Lady's descendant anyway?

Chapter Twelve – Faye

"Those are dangerous words, Faye de la Rou." Pathos took a step closer.

Faye slid one foot back. "You *will* let me go to the masquerade. You won't interfere."

"And what do I get out of this? Deals go both ways." Pathos moved yet another step closer, sending his wolf mask into shadow.

"You …" Faye searched her mind for something, anything he would agree on. "I'll dance an extra night every new moon."

Pathos shook his head. He reached up and touched the base of his mask, as if he were about to take it off. Instead, he lowered his hand and cocked his head to the side.

"That won't do. I have a better proposition. You will go to the masquerade balls. You will dance with your precious Leo and everyone will be enamored with the mysterious girl in the butterfly mask. You'll be the talk of the city. Everyone will want to know who you are." His voice was low. Dangerous.

Faye swallowed and backed away. This wasn't what she wanted. But with every word he spoke, she felt something inside her tighten, inch by agonizing inch.

"You'll have three days to make the prince fall in love with you. He *must* say those words, or you'll lose. And when he says those words, you will bring him here to me."

Shock rippled through Faye. He wanted Leo? Why?

"However, you will *never* be able to speak of the curse. Nor will you be able to say your name. And at the stroke of midnight, you *will* come to the Underworld as you normally would, or else the deal is off. If you break this in any way at all, you will live in the Underworld forever, just like your sisters. You will never see the sun again."

Pathos' words rung in the air like a death knell. Faye couldn't breathe. Couldn't move. Couldn't speak.

"And if I win." Faye ground out the words. Forced them into existence. "If I win and make Leo fall in love with me, then my sisters, my mother, and the courtiers all go free. We all leave this place for good."

Something flashed in Pathos' eyes. "If you win, then you and your loved ones go free. Agreed?"

There was no way she could agree with this.

But if she didn't, she would never have this chance again.

Faye gritted her teeth. "Swear to it."

"I swear."

With those words, pain blossomed in her chest. Faye cried out and clutched at her breastbone as searing pain carved its way across her bones. She fell to her knees as she sucked in ragged gasps.

Pathos came to her and placed a gentle hand on her shoulder. The burning eased, leaving her with a cold ache. He placed a finger under her chin and tilted her face up. She gasped and her hands flew to her face. Gently, he grasped her wrists and pulled her hands away.

"I've seen you without your mask before."

His words carried the weight of a thousand memories. Of the time before the curse. Of midnight dances in the rose garden. Quiet conversations of hopes and dreams. Sharing stories of magical lands under the stars. Giving her time when her sisters were too busy for her.

He was the first to call her beautiful. The first to see her as she truly was. He drew her in, capturing her heart and mind. He had promised her a future of bliss. And she had believed his pleasant lies.

Faye lowered her hands and let him look at her, let him see the girl she had tried so hard not to become, the girl she

90

tried so hard to escape. Pathos knelt before her and took her hands in his. When he spoke, his voice was gentle.

"How beautiful you look. You remind me of my mother."

Curiosity filled Faye. "Your mother?"

"Yes." He turned his face away. "She was trapped with us, lost in an eternal sleep. There's nothing I can do to help her."

Even though she wished she could keep her heart of stone, pity drilled its way inside. She reached out, hesitant.

"I'm sorry."

Pathos moved closer and gripped her shoulders.

"Why do you go back to them, my lady? Why do you return to the land of Humans when you know it's all just a lie? There's nothing for you there."

Faye's throat tightened and she closed her eyes, each of his words a dagger twisting in her heart.

"The Humans will never accept you. No matter how well you dance, how fine your speech, you will always be a half-blood to them. A mongrel. They all hate you and your kind. If you showed them who you truly are, they would kill you." He choked on his words.

"That's not true." Faye could do nothing more but whisper the words. "Madame Leroux—"

"Is a liar." Pathos leaned forward until his forehead touched hers. The grooves of his metal mask dug into her skin. "She only pretends to like you and fight for your cause because of what you can offer. A place back in the king's court. She was a countess, respected and well loved. But since her husband's death, she has been cast aside and she wants her power back.

"Up there, you're an outcast. A nobody. No one will ever appreciate who you really are."

A tear slipped down Faye's cheek. He was right. She had to hide her true nature every time she stepped out on the streets. She had to be careful with what she said so no one would suspect who she really was. It was so, so tiring, keeping up the charade every single day. She wanted only to be accepted. To be loved.

"Only I can understand how you feel. Only I know what it's like to live a lie. Even if Leo chases after you at the ball, he will only be chasing after the image of you. If he found out who you really are, he would reject you, just like he did last time. And if that happens, Madame will cast you aside. You'll no longer be of any use to her. Then what, Faye? What will you have?"

Agony, deep and sharp, dug into every inch of Faye's body and she fought back a sob. "No one."

Pathos cupped her face in his hands. "That's right. You will have no one. You'd be all alone on the streets once more, lost and abandoned. All because no one can accept your blood."

His tone turned feverish and his words rushed from his mouth like a river. "If you would only stay with me, marry me, Faye. Then I could turn you into an Undead, and you would be free. Free of everything. Free of the upper world, free of your fears. You would be free to embrace who you really are."

Who she really was. But what exactly was she? She wasn't Human, pure and perfect. And she wasn't Fae, wild and magical. She was stuck somewhere in between, never able to fit in either world.

But she couldn't be an Undead. She couldn't be like him. She never wanted to lose her connection to the upper world. To lose sight of the sun. Standing, she pulled away.

"I can't. I can't be with you." She turned and raced back up the tunnel toward the stairs.

"Everything that has happened so far has been your fault." His words froze her in place. "You know that, right?"

Faye gripped her nightgown in her shaking fists. She would never let herself forget.

"You chose this. You chose to lead your sisters to the ball that night." He shuffled closer. "You signed the agreement with the Midnight King the moment you put on those slippers. You are the cause of their pain. Not me. *You.* But despite this, I want you. I want you to stay with me forever. No one else will ever want you. Remember what they called you? A monstrosity. A disgusting half-breed. Half-magic. Half-human."

"No!" She whirled around and looked Pathos in the eye. "No! I will never be with you, Pathos. I could never marry you!" She screamed the words. Using as much force as her lungs allowed, shrieking until every word vibrated in her chest.

Her words echoed in the tunnel, bouncing off the walls and back into her head. They were harsh. Cruel. Pathos hunched his shoulders as if stung. He marched toward her until he was an arm's length away.

"What would your sisters think, if they learned about our deal? About how you get to run free in the sunshine while they shiver alone in the darkness? Do you think they would forgive you?"

Faye pushed the question past her lips. "Would you tell them?"

Panic cinched her lungs closed and she struggled for air. He wouldn't tell them. He couldn't. Her sisters would never forgive her. Never.

Pathos sighed. He bowed his head and a lock of his black hair fell before his mask. But he didn't answer. Faye watched him for several agonizing heartbeats, waiting. Waiting for his reply. But it never came. Instead, he took two steps back. Allowing her to run.

Faye inched her way backwards until her heels bumped the bottom step with a quiet clink.

"Just remember, my lady, that if you marry a Human, nothing will stop my brothers from slaughtering your family, starting with your dear mother." Cold permeated his voice.

Turning, Faye fled up the stairs.

It wasn't until she reached the top of the steps that she slowed and collapsed. The open fireplace was just an arm's length away, but Faye suddenly felt too tired to crawl through once more. Leaning against the wall, her hand pressed against something cold. She lifted her palm. There, shining in the dim light, was the tiny comb Pathos had given her. Faye picked it up with shaking fingers.

A beautiful thing made of twisting branches of gold and tiny white pearls; it was the first gift Pathos ever gave her. And the thing that caused this whole mess. Faye squeezed the comb in her fist, feeling the teeth prick her skin.

At least there was one thing she could trust about Pathos. He *always* kept his word.

Chapter Thirteen – Faye

The carriage bumped and rattled down the streets, carrying Faye, Delphine, and Madame Leroux to the castle. Outside, night had fallen, and a slash of late evening sunlight shone on the streets, casting the city into sharp relief.

Faye gripped the sleek wood of the door, keeping her hands well away from her silver skirts. At first, she had told herself to wear the gold one and get it out of the way, but the more she had looked at it, the more she was unwilling to touch it. Pathos may force her to wear gold every night, but if there was one thing she could control now, it was the color of her dress. Still, the feeling of the fabric against her made her stomach turn.

Men and women dressed in flamboyant costumes paraded down the street. Their masks a grotesque display of wealth and the darkest of imaginations, each one blurred by the carriage's motion. One man turned toward the carriage as it passed—his mask too close to a snarling wolf.

Madame looked the perfect picture of a predator, perched in her side of the carriage. Dressed in black silk, her hair was styled in braids that draped across her shoulder. A clay mask shaped like a panther's head hid her face, and her green eyes glowed like a a cat's eyes. She pulled out her watch with clawed fingers.

"The ball will start in eighteen minutes. At this current speed we should arrive two minutes early." She snapped the watch shut and dropped it in her handbag.

Beside her, Delphine fidgeted with her moretta mask, her full lips pinched into a frown. She glanced at Faye and gave her a weak smile. Faye tried to smile back. She couldn't blame Delphine for her reluctance. They were both trapped in this cage of a carriage, heading toward a future neither wanted.

95

"I wonder what styles of dresses we'll see? I heard that there's a new style among the nobles of the northern Highlands that's been influenced by the Draconians." She smoothed her hair with a gloved hand.

Faye held a hand to her stomach and tried to block out Delphine's words. Her voice grated against Faye's ears. Everything inside her ached. Her heart pattered harder than it ever had—so hard she felt faint. It was too stuffy in the carriage. She needed air.

I can't do this. She gasped for air as she dug her nails into the door. *I can't do this!*

Air. That was what she needed. Faye shoved the carriage window open and stuck her head out. Closing her eyes, she breathed it in. The scent of woodsmoke floated on the breeze. It reminded Faye of fire. Fire and fireplaces. Fireplaces that opened to a winding staircase. A staircase to a twilit world and a man in a wolf mask.

Faye flinched back inside the carriage and slammed the window shut. Air refused to enter her lungs no matter how hard she tried. Madame reached across and brushed a strand of hair from Faye's face.

"Leave the window shut, dear. You don't want to ruin your hair."

As they came closer and closer to the castle, Faye's grip on the door tightened. It wasn't the prospect of dancing with strangers that frightened her so much as the prospect of dancing. And at midnight ... what was she to do? What would happen to her? Would she have to run all the way home? That would make her late. And if she was late, would he count it as a loss? Would she immediately lose her freedom, right then and there?

In preparation, Faye wore her glass slippers. She kept them hidden beneath her skirts in hopes that Madame and Delphine wouldn't notice and ask questions. Magic buzzed through her limbs, tugging with tiny claws as the night deepened, adding to the anxiety that shook her to her core.

And Leo. Three years of distance between them. Three years of not knowing whether he had forgotten her.

Faye knew for certain that on that night in the garden he made his decision. One that could not be changed. But now she had to face him again. To dance with him, laugh with him. To make him love her. Only, would it even be real if she couldn't give it in return? She gripped her shaking fingers as shame washed over her. All it would be is deception for the chance of saving her sisters. Could she really break his heart just to see her family free?

Broken hearts can be mended, she told herself. *Dead sisters can't be brought back to life.* She would never get another chance like this.

As the carriage rolled to a stop, Madame leaned forward, both hands on her walking stick.

"This is our chance, girls." Passion filled Madame's voice. "This is our chance to change the wrongs of the world. We must present ourselves honorably tonight, and you two must gain favor with the prince. If we can climb the social ladder to its head, then we can reverse the laws that keep the magicfolk oppressed."

Delphine nodded, but dropped her gaze to the carriage floor. "I won't let you down, Mama."

Madame smiled and turned to Faye. "I know you'll try your hardest."

Faye took in deep, shuddering breaths and picked up her mask. The metal wing burned into her palm. Her stomach churned and nausea overtook her.

"Smile wide and smile proud." Madame straightened. "Let them know we mean business."

Faye put on a wooden smile and waited as Madame Leroux exited the carriage, then Delphine. When she made to leave, her feet wouldn't leave the carriage floor. Terror gripped her throat. Around her, the world dipped and swayed. She couldn't do this. She should just return home and accept her fate.

But she couldn't do that either. If she gave up on her family, then she could never face another sunrise knowing she could have tried harder. She pushed away her fear, replacing it with anger. For three years, she'd lived with a broken heart. It was time Leo did the same.

"Come along, miss," the driver said, impatient.

Faye tied her mask in place, took his hand, and exited the carriage. Her heart skipped a beat as she looked up at the castle.

The walls were made entirely of grey stone. Not as impressive as her own castle's white marble, but still enchanting. Green ivy climbed alongside the doors, ending in an arc above with tiny yellow flowers peeking out. Faye could just imagine how it must look on the inside.

Dazzling dresses of pink, red, green, and yellow surrounded her. Winking jewels and black suits and white gloves. Polished hair and wide smiles. Masks of varying colors, shapes, and materials. So, so many masks. They crowded in around her, leering down at her, transforming into the dark and twisted masks of the Midnight King and his brothers.

Her lungs squeezed. There were too many of them. Too many. They all stared at her, waiting to devour her whole. To drag her down into the deep, deep darkness where she would be trapped, trapped in the presence of the monstrous king.

"Faye, come on!" Delphine appeared before Faye, her dark skin burning a beautiful umber in evening light.

She gripped Faye's arm and dragged her through the sea of masks, up the polished steps and into the castle, Faye stumbling behind.

Madame waited for them in the castle foyer. Above, chandeliers spilled yellow light, splashing across the black-

and-white marble of the floor. Frescoes of past kings and their numerous victories were painted onto every surface of the walls. Suits of armor stood sentry at every corner of the room. Or were they soldiers? They stood so still, backs straight, polished pikes glinting in the light.

Everything about the castle was both familiar and foreign. All the people. All the fluted buttresses, the grand staircases carpeted in red, the gold enamel on the walls and ceiling. It almost felt like she was home. And yet it wasn't her home.

On her left loomed a painting of what looked to be King Richard running a Faerie through the heart with his sword, his foot planted on her stomach. The Faerie's wings lay crumpled beneath her and her eyes were wide with shock.

The image burned itself into Faye's mind. The Faerie looked so helpless. Faye's stomach twisted and she feared she would be sick.

Faye reached up and made sure her ears were covered. She had no doubt now that Leo sided with his father. How could he think any differently, growing up with King Richard as his father? A small voice whispered that Leo deserved to be dragged into the dark. And yet … And yet, could she really commit the same evil as before?

"Come, it's time for us to make our entrance." Madame Leroux moved toward the double doors leading to the ballroom with a sort of vicious grace—the crowd parting before her as if she were a shark cutting through the sea waves.

Faye followed, with Delphine at her side. She held her head high and stepped with purpose, even as her mind screamed for her to turn, to run back. But tonight, Faye wouldn't let her fear control her. She had to do this. For Adalie. For Colette. For Mama.

Only, when she reached the double doors, her courage withered. Madame and Delphine continued on, leaving Faye behind. Everyone in the ballroom looked so happy. Not a single one of them aware that the girl in the butterfly mask was here to steal their prince. None of them knew that he would be the next to disappear. Faye's skin crawled with the thought of becoming the villain all over again.

She could retreat, find an alcove and hide. Wait until all the guests were inside. No one would see her leave. In fact, she could leave right now.

No. Faye shook her head. This was the moment she had been waiting for. The moment she needed, for her sisters. This was the moment she could see Pathos lose. Then he would have to help them escape and go free.

Heart pounding, Faye tightened the strings on her butterfly mask, until the leather cut into her skin. She stepped toward the doors. Put one foot in front of the other. Smoothed a hand over the silky fabric of her silver ball gown. And made her way through, into the light of the chandeliers.

Faye's breath hitched in her throat as she hovered at the edge of the ballroom.

There he was.

Prince Lionheart stood in the middle of the ballroom, holding Delphine's hand. His red hair burned like fire, complementing the scarlet of his jacket. The bright yellow lion gatto mask couldn't hide the boyish grin she had come to love so many years ago. There was a light about him, a certain kind of happiness that drew Faye closer.

Faye placed a hand to her chest as it hit her. This was real. This was all real. It was no dream, no trick. He was here. He was *right here*. Standing before her, a look of surprise and awe on his face.

Leo began to move toward her. Faye panicked. Should she walk to meet him? Should she just stay still? The room grew stifling and Faye's hands began to sweat within her silk gloves. He was coming closer. She needed to move.

Soft clinks accompanied her movements, step by shaky step. The masked crowd watched her, murmuring behind lace fans and goblets of wine. Among them all, Leo stared, enraptured, as if she had stepped out from a folktale.

Pathos's words rang through her head. *Everyone will be enamored with the mysterious girl in the butterfly mask.* Faye fought back a shudder. None of them would even look her way if they knew who she was. If they knew what she was here to do. Instead, they'd be demanding to see her neck inside a noose.

Faye met Leo in the middle of the dance floor—her heart quickening as she found herself lost in Leo's beautiful, silvery eyes.

"My lady," Leo murmured. Faye's throat tightened and her legs wobbled. "Would you care to dance with me?"

She shouldn't. And yet, he held out his hand, a small smile on his lips. And yet, her heart yearned to hear his gentle laugh, to feel his callused palms take her hands, to hear her name on his lips.

She swallowed back the tears forming and spoke in a whisper, trying not to choke on the words. "I would be delighted, my prince."

He took her hand gently in his and swept her onto the dance floor.

The dance was a sweeping waltz, simple yet beautiful. It brought back too many memories as Leo led her across the floor, one hand gripping hers, the other on her waist. Memories she fought hard to keep at bay.

The last time she had danced with him, he had stepped on her toes. The memory brought a smile to her lips. She almost laughed at the absurdity of it all. Here she was, with the last man in all the five kingdoms she had ever wanted to meet again, and she was *smiling*. Smiling like a fool.

Leo's eyes held a dreamy look, and his ears turned a brilliant shade of red. Faye's heart fluttered in her chest. Even after all this time, she still found it endearing.

What should she say? What *could* she say? She longed to spill everything right here, right now. To scream her name so loud the entire room would be able to hear her. She wanted to slap Leo so hard his head spun. Perfect, adorable, frustrating, ridiculous Leo.

Still, the only reason he danced with her now was because he was enamored with the girl he thought her to be. Normal. Human. Not Faye, the half-breed.

"My name is Leo," he blurted in a loud voice. His freckled cheeks turned a darker shade of red as he gave her that lopsided grin. "And who might you be, mysterious lady?"

Faye's heart skipped a beat. "I—" Her throat caught, and no noise came from her mouth. Of course. She almost forgot she couldn't speak her name.

Leo cocked his head. "My lady? Are you well?"

Putting on her best smile, Faye let out an airy laugh that sounded more like a cry. "Oh, yes, I am perfectly well. I am just … amazed to be here, dancing with the prince."

The brilliant smile returned and he twirled her about. "Ah, so you are from Revayr. Your accent is quite strong. I hope you will not leave me in suspense, mademoiselle. Will you tell me your name? Or will you make me guess?"

Faye stared at the shiny brass buttons on his coat, her skin suddenly cold. The way he looked at her, as if she were some creature of magnificence … it was wrong. Pathos had done this to her, *making* her charm the crowd. It wasn't real. None of it. She was bait. And Leo couldn't even see the trap right before him.

"I am no one, Your Majesty." She took in a shuddering breath. "No one."

"No one? That's hardly the truth. A girl as beautiful as you surely has a name. Let me see, does your name start with an A?"

Shaking her head, Faye scanned the room for a way to escape. The ceiling seemed to be pushing down, pressing her into the floor.

It was useless. There was no reason for her to stay. The dancers swirled around her, their laughter filling the air. Faye stumbled in Leo's arms and searched the crowd for Madame Leroux. She had to tell her she was ill and needed to leave, immediately.

A grey mask caught her eye and Faye gasped.

Pathos was here, watching her. Standing just on the edge of the crowd. Leo took her through a spin and Faye tried to keep her gaze on Pathos. But when they came back around, he was gone.

"My lady? Are you alright? It's like you haven't heard a word I said." They had stopped dancing, and Leo's eyes were pinched with concern.

Faye backed away. "I'm sorry, my prince. I … I'm just so nervous. I got lost in my worries."

Leo remained silent at that, and they finished the waltz. Faye kept an eye out for Pathos, but she couldn't see him anywhere. She fought off a shiver and turned her gaze back to Leo's deep-grey eyes. It was just her imagination. Pathos wouldn't dare come here.

Yes, he would.

Of course, he would. Pathos had come to see her fail. If only she could say her name. If only she could speak just one single word. If only she could make Leo understand.

Tears pricked her eyes as her tongue remained silent. *I am Faye de la Rou!* she wanted to scream. *Leo, don't you know me? Don't you know me?*

"Don't you know me?" she whispered.

"What was that?" Leo asked as he led her across the floor in a lively dance.

Faye hitched on a smile and shook her head. "Nothing, my prince."

Nothing at all.

The dance ended and Faye curtsied low to Leo. He lingered, as if wanting to ask her to dance again. But Faye turned her back on him and searched the crowd for someone, anyone else.

Music spilled down from the musician's balcony as Faye danced with a gentleman in a green coat. Faye only half listened as he talked throughout the entire minuet. The same infatuation glowed in his eyes. His smile was too wide. His enthusiasm too much. Faye kept her eyes firmly locked on the wrinkles in his white shirt.

Dance after dance, noble after noble, Faye's skin crawled. What was Pathos trying to prove? If anything, it seemed like he wanted her to win. But that wasn't how Pathos worked. If she won, he would never see her again.

Faye searched the crowd for Madame Leroux once more. She stood next to another matron, and they spoke in low tones. Heart constricting, Faye pushed through the crowds of masked faces. There were so many of them, staring at her with deadened eyes behind those black masks. When she reached her guardian's side, she was shaking.

"Madame Leroux," she breathed, curtsying. "Please, I need to speak with you."

Madame Leroux turned from the woman with whom she was conversing and cocked her head. When she saw Faye's face, she moved a step closer. "My dear, what on earth is wrong?"

Faye gripped her wrist and dragged her away from the noise and the dancers, into a quiet corner near the doors.

"Faye, what happened? You should be dancing, smiling, having a good time. Not crying." She reached out and brushed the tear from Faye's cheek with the backs of her fingers.

"I can't speak of it." She bit her lip as another tear fell. "I can't say anything about the curse, or I lose. And if I lose, they'll be stuck forever, and all of this is my fault!" Her words grew more frantic as she spoke, panic coursing through her veins.

Madame grabbed Faye's shoulders. "Slow down, dear! What do you mean you'll lose?"

Faye reached up to tear the mask off, but a face in the crowd stopped her. A man dressed in blue and white. Something about him was familiar. The broadness of his shoulders. The tilt of his jaw beneath a close-cropped beard. A mask decorated in blue and white hid half his face, and his hair was more grey than brown, but there was no mistaking him.

Could it really be?

"Faye, answer me! What is going on?"

Madame's voice snapped Faye back into the present. She stared at the windows. It was pitch dark. The moon, round and full, looked down at her, framed by heavy velvet curtains.

"What time is it?" she blurted.

Madame Leroux frowned and pulled out her pocket watch. She looked at the golden face. "Almost midnight. Why?"

Her heart skipped a beat and a cold chill clutched her spine. Faye clutched her stomach and leaned over, letting out a moan. "No, no, no, no!"

Tearing out of Madame's grip, Faye gathered her skirts and bolted for the door. Several voices called after her, but she didn't slow. The sharp scent of magic burned inside her nose as the clock ticked closer to midnight. If she could make it out of the ballroom, perhaps she could find a fireplace, or a doorway, anything. Just as long as it was away from people. Memories of the last time she had been in a ballroom flashed before her eyes, making her stumble.

The floor shaking. A wide fissure snaking across the ballroom, cracking the wood. The world tilting as a black hole opened. Screams. So many screams as one by one, men and women slid inside, followed by her sisters. Her fingers scraping wood as she clawed for a handhold. And then Pathos's voice in her ear, telling her that everything would be alright.

A hand landed on her arm and Faye spun to see Leo.

"Are you well, my lady?" he said softly.

Faye gasped as a ripple of magic gripped her spine. She staggered, falling into Leo's arms. In the distance, she heard a clock chime. *Midnight.*

Pushing away from Leo, she curtsied, her legs wobbling, heat roaring through her cheeks. "I—I have to go. Thank you, Your Majesty—" Another wave of magic tugged at her, making her stumble. She turned and fled.

"Wait! Mademoiselle!" Leo's voice pulled at her, begging for her to come back.

But Faye raced out of the ballroom, away from the masked faces, away from the dancing, and into the empty hallway.

The clock chimed again, and her heart jumped. Faye dragged in a shallow breath as her feet turned, carrying her down a narrow corridor.

A nearby maid squeaked when she looked up. She flattened herself against the wall even as she called, "My lady! You cannot be here!"

Faye ignored her and raced through the twisting servant's halls until a kitchen came into sight. She burst in, frightening the cooks. She paused next to the fireplace long enough to shout, "Get out!"

The servants scrambled to obey, leaving her alone. The magic pull was so strong that Faye let out a cry as pain seized her muscles. She fell to her knees, shoved her arm through the flames and pushed the fireplace's back wall. It creaked open and she plunged through the flames and into the Underworld.

Chapter Fourteen – Faye

Faye gasped for breath as she stumbled on shaky legs through the tunnel, her once silver dress now a deep gold, the colors twisted by the magic of the Underworld. Tears slipped from her eyelids and ran like hot coals down her cheeks.

If only this were a dream. If only this were a nightmare. If only she hadn't taken Pathos's hand that night. If only … if only. Biting her fist, she slumped to the ground, her back pressed against the wall. Her mind screamed where her voice could not, wishing for the walls of the Underworld to crash down around her. To leave her buried beneath the rubble, forgotten by the world.

The way Leo had looked at her. It almost felt real. But it was all a lie. Whatever Pathos had done to her had enchanted him. It was not real love. It would never be real.

Stone crunched underfoot and a shadow blocked out the pale light. Faye sucked in a breath and looked up. Pathos knelt by her side, his silver wolf mask catching the light. He was silent, watching her.

It was unusual for him to be here. He always waited in the castle, on his throne, as the Midnight King. But here he was, at her side, gaze fixed. Faye could almost imagine him delving into her thoughts, extracting each one and reading them like a book.

"I know it's hard, but it must be done. Still, if you aren't up to the task, there is always another option."

Faye pressed her hands over her ears and squeezed her eyes shut.

"If you would just marry me, Faye, I could help you. I could release your mother. She would be free to return home."

His words circled her mind, over and over, tempting her. She could agree to his words. She could marry him, and her mother would be free. She could marry him, and she would never have to see Leo again. Never have to experience that same heartache over and over, knowing that he would never accept her. She could lose herself in the darkness.

But settling for marriage meant Adalie would be trapped in the arms of a monster. Colette would never be free of Nosos. They would all remain prisoners. And Faye couldn't do that. Not knowing that she had been the one to bring their fate upon them.

Struggling on aching feet, Faye stood. The glass slippers dug into her skin. She leaned against the wall. A moment. That was all she needed.

"Come, Faye. We must be going."

Faye didn't move. Didn't want to.

Strong arms wrapped around Faye, lifting her off the ground. Faye gasped and opened her eyes. Pathos was carrying her from the tunnel and toward the boats. Already, her sisters had climbed into theirs and were floating across the still surface. A sixth boat bobbed among the subtle black ripples.

Lowering her into the boat, Pathos climbed in on the other side and pushed it from the shore.

"He'll never love you." Pathos's voice was quiet. Almost pitying. "He can't love you. No one can. Not really. Who could ever love a traitor?"

Who could ever love a traitor?

Pathos's words echoed through her mind. Pain pierced her heart at his words, but she bit the inside of her cheek. He was right. He was always right.

But she couldn't stop trying. Not yet. Not while there was still a chance.

They remained silent for the rest of the trip across the lake. Faye stared at Pathos's thin shoulders, hunched beneath his suit coat and cape. The ears of his mask were just visible above his slicked-back hair. His very presence left Faye cold inside. But, more often than not, so did the truth. There was nothing warm about the truth.

The boat scraped against the opposite shore. Pathos jumped into the water and scooped her into his arms once more. Faye laid her head on his shoulder as he walked into the forest. His skin was freezing. No heartbeat thrummed against her ears. A shudder gripped Faye's spine. It was like being carried by a corpse.

"You're lucky you found a fireplace when you did. Otherwise, you could have pulled down the entirety of King Richard's court with you. This is why you can't be loved. You're a danger, Faye. A risk. You can break kingdoms and destroy countries, all because of a simple curse you created."

"I know," Faye whispered. She struggled with her thoughts. But no matter how hard, she couldn't get them in order. She licked her lips. "If you'd only let me speak, let me tell him who I am, I could bring him to you. I could." An odd sort of desperation filled her voice.

"And what do you think the prince would do when he learns of your identity? Love you? Willingly follow you? No, I put that curse on your tongue to protect you. If you even let it slip that your name is Faye de la Rou, they would turn on you. Burn you at the stake. Call you a monster. And Leo would be there, laughing with them as they plunged your soul into the afterlife."

Faye closed her eyes as the words rushed over her. Leo could never love her, the *real* her. Not after what she'd done. Not if he knew.

"Faye, my jewel, I only want to keep you safe. The world is a horrible place, and Humans will stop at nothing to purge it of all that is beautiful and good. But, if you insist on breaking the contract for your sisters, one of equal blood and royalty must be traded. You have until the final ball to bring Leo to me. Do you understand?"

Faye nodded and turned her face away.

∞

Her movements were wooden as she danced that night. She placed each step in perfect time with Pathos'. As the floor shifted color and the symbols glowed beneath their feet, with each flash she saw Leo, smiling down at her, his eyes sparkling with laughter. Light touching everything he looked upon. He was too good. Too perfect.

Between the tears that stung Faye's eyes, she could see Adalie dancing on bloodied feet, her glass slippers stained crimson. Her hands were bandaged and Phagos laughed each time Adalie missed a step.

"Is this for letting us speak?" Faye choked.

Pathos turned his face away. "The Midnight King placed the punishment on Adalie instead of you. He wanted to protect you."

It should have been me.

Faye ducked her head. Shame washed over her in waves. She should have been the one punished. Not Adalie. She should have been the one to bleed.

∞

By the time Pathos and the others rowed them across the black lake, Faye could barely keep her eyes open. The moment she reached the cave, she tore her shoes off, feeling the cool stone beneath her aching feet. More blisters had formed, and Faye had to fight back tears. They were less than what she deserved.

She rushed up the stairs, through the crystal, gold, and silver forests, her mind racing. Where would this tunnel let out? At home? Or at Leo's castle? What would Madame Leroux say when she arrived home without them with her ball gown covered in soot?

She pushed the door open and peered out. Then cursed. She was still in the castle kitchen. How to sneak out?

Carefully, she stepped into the fireplace and out into the kitchen. The room was empty. Her heartbeat roared in her ears, making it hard to listen for approaching footsteps. Sneaking through, she darted down the hall, peering into rooms until she found a washroom. Rows of line were strung up along the ceiling, with a variety of clothing hanging to dry.

Faye snagged a skirt and blouse with trembling fingers and tugged them on. They were a little baggy on her small frame—the skirt trailing the floor—but they were better than running around the castle in the ball gown. She wrapped her slippers up in her dress and shoved the blasted things into a laundry bag.

After that, she found linen strips in a cupboard and wrapped her feet. If she were going to cross the city streets with blistered feet, she may as well make it as comfortable as possible.

She met only one other servant on her trip out of the castle. The slim young woman blinked at her with bleary eyes, stopping in the middle of the hall.

"So, the party is over now, I expect," the maid said in a sleepy voice.

Faye nodded. "Yes." She shuffled backwards, heat filling her cheeks as she scrambled for something to say. She held up the laundry bag. "Um … one of the ladies … no, lords … left his, um, jacket."

She winced. The maid would see right through her lie.

Instead, the maid just nodded and yawned. "One of the Revayrian servants, are you? Can't believe that King Richard didn't make a bigger fuss over King Raoul showing up out of the blue without even an invitation to the ball. But oh well. It's not my business what the kings do." She blinked sleepily, then yawned again. Her gaze flicked down to Faye's feet. "Hurt yourself, love?"

Shock rippled through Faye. Had she heard the maid right? Was her father really *here*, at the castle? Last night … it had to have been him. Faye swayed. He had been so close, and she didn't even know it.

The maid's brow furrowed with concern.

"A cup!" Faye said quickly. "One of the cups broke and I stepped on it. Cut right through my nice shoes, too." She let out a weak laugh.

Shaking her head, the maid sighed. "I knew something like that would happen one of these days when the cooks started lacing the punch." Nodding, the maid looked up. "Well, you go on and deliver whatever it was you said you had. Be careful and mind your manners. Nobles are always cantankerous in the morning, even without the lack of sleep."

Faye nodded and gave her a wobbly curtsy. "Thank you, miss."

The maid smiled. "And make sure you have Angelina look at your feet whenever you come back. Infections can be nasty."

Nodding to herself, the maid shuffled down the hall with another yawn. Faye darted in the opposite direction, heart pounding. *Thank the heavens!* It was a good thing the maid hadn't asked any more questions. Faye wasn't sure what else she could have said. Her head still spun with the thought of her father being here, *here* in King Richard's castle.

The urge to search the palace for him filled her. But what would she do if she found him? He might force her to stay here, keeping her from bringing her mother and sisters back home. She couldn't do that. Even though the thought tore her up, she needed to leave the castle—and her castle—behind.

Voices rose as she neared the servant's entrance to the courtyard. Two men were speaking in low tones, their argument heated. One of the men had a thick Revayrian accent. Faye stilled. Did someone from her country come to Eura for the ball? Excitement tingled down her spine. She knew most of the names of the gentry and nobility. At least, she had. There was no way of knowing how many of them were still alive.

"I don't understand, Prince Lionheart," the Revayrian man said, desperation lacing his voice. "Why won't you believe me when I say I saw one of my daughters here?"

Faye's heart jumped in her throat. He was talking to Leo! She had to get out of the castle, and quick.

"I am sorry, Your Highness, but it just doesn't seem possible."

They rounded the corner, and Faye ducked her gaze. She rushed past Leo and the man, glancing up once to take in the Revayrian's features. He had brown hair streaked with gray, and a short, trimmed beard. Something about his voice was familiar. It called to her, daring her to remember. Faye continued on and blocked out their conversation.

When she reached the servant's entrance to the courtyard, Faye hopped onto the back of a cart heading out to market. The driver hummed as he swayed on the bench, the draft horses trotting with lively steps. Faye leaned against the sacks piled in the back of the cart and closed her eyes. If she could rest, just for a moment …

A hand touched Faye's shoulder. "Wake up, miss. We've reached the lord's homes."

Faye sat up and blinked hard. Where was she? She looked around with bleary eyes and pristine manors looked down at her from both sides of the street. She groaned and rubbed her pounding head.

"Come along, miss. I've got to keep going." The cart driver looked at her with a kind smile crinkling the corners of his eyes.

Faye eased her way out of the cart and onto her aching feet. She cursed under her breath as her legs threatened to buckle.

"Thank you for the ride, monsieur."

The man's smile stretched wider and he tipped his straw hat at her. "Any time, mademoiselle."

As the cart rumbled away, Faye limped the rest of the way to Madame Leroux's cottage. When the house came into view, she trotted awkwardly up to the gate and slipped inside. The morning was bright and cloudless, the sun just over the horizon, and Faye guessed it had to be at least seven. Which would give her time to start breakfast and rub some salve on her feet. With any luck, the Leroux family would still be asleep.

She had just finished wrapping clean linen around her feet when Madame Leroux appeared in the kitchen. Judging by Madame's expression, she was not happy. Faye scrambled to her feet.

"Madame Leroux, please—"

"Where have you been? I was worried you'd never show up!" she croaked, eyes bleary as she shuffled along, her walking stick thumping against the worn floorboards.

"I ..." Faye searched the room for Madame's daughters, but neither were in sight. Most likely still in bed. "I came back in the kitchens of the castle."

"Were you seen? Where is your dress? Did anyone stop you?" Madame gripped Faye's shoulder, concern wrinkling her brow. "If anyone saw you skulking around, they might think you a spy and our whole mission would be forfeit."

"No, no one saw me." Faye shrank from the intensity in Madame's gaze.

Madame's growls smoothed and she nodded, catlike gaze fixed on the mantel. "Go on. Get some rest. You'll need your strength for tonight."

"No, I'm alright. I just need—"

"Faye." Madame gave her a gentle push toward the sitting room. "Rest."

Madame Leroux turned away, leaving Faye alone in the kitchen. Falling into a chair next to the table, Faye crossed her arms on the table and buried her face into the crook of her elbow.

Even though she was tired, she felt restless. The constant energy crawling through her skin always came after spending the night in the Underworld. She longed to run out into the sunshine and soak it into her skin until every fractured piece of her glowed. Until the darkness and fear of the Underworld could never touch her again. But at the same time, she longed to crawl beneath her blanket and drift into a world where emotions didn't exist until either the sun consumed the earth, or she died.

Chapter Fifteen – Leo

Someone was pounding on Leo's door. Leo groaned and buried deeper beneath his silk sheets. It was much too early to rise, and he had a splitting headache.

The pounding came again. "Sire, it's me. Jack."

Leo pushed himself upright and turned to the door with blurry eyes. "A moment, please!" he called.

Hopefully, Jack would have some good news. He had been gone long enough.

Rolling over, Leo managed to sit up. Sunlight speared through the heavy drapes over his window and into his eyes. He squinted. Why did the rotten sun have to be right there? It was just what he needed, making his headache worse.

Images from last night swam in his mind. The girl in the butterfly mask, looking dangerously like a Faerie straight from the Blackwood. And King Raoul. The man insisted that the girl was his daughter. And not just his daughter; he had the audacity to call her Faye de la Rou. Leo's chest tightened.

And it was the oddest thing. Leo had been more tired that night than he'd ever been at any ball before. One minute, he was full of energy, and the next, he felt like he was about to fall on his face from lack of sleep. The feeling still persisted, clinging to the edges of his limbs.

Rising from bed, Leo threw on shirt and trousers and stumbled toward the door. He tripped over the edge of the rug, landing in a plush chair near the fire. Leo debated standing up but decided not to risk standing again. At least this was as good a place as any to talk to his guard.

"Come in!"

The door opened and Jack stepped inside. His hair was disheveled, and mud spattered his cloak.

"What did you do, ride through every mudhole in Eura?"

Jack bowed. "Forgive my appearance, Your Highness. I've just returned from my errand."

Leo slapped the armrest. Any news was good news.

"Go on then. What have you learned?"

"First, I thought you'd like to know that not one, not two, but eight villagers who live in Westshire claimed to have seen the ghost of Princess Colette."

"Oh? What did they say?"

"The same thing. They saw a young woman dressed in red wandering across the moors. Some even claimed to see her carrying a lantern at night, searching for something."

Leo folded his arms as he thought this over. There was a good possibility that these people were making up tales. But there could also be the slim chance that Colette could, in fact, be alive. Still, after seeing the bloodied dress that belonged to Faye, Leo wasn't so sure of that.

"Go on. What else?"

Jack's black brows lowered. "Well, I don't know how helpful it is, but I've been to the Blackwood."

"The Blackwood? Are you joking?" All of Leo's previous enthusiasm was quickly replaced with incredulousness. Of all the harebrained things Jack could have done ... "There are werewolves, pixies, banshees!"

Jack held up a large hand. "I know, Your Highness. I didn't go far. My sources led me to a wise woman who lives on the border. A strange lady. She wears tinted glasses and was carrying an umbrella around in her house."

Odd. "And? What did she tell you?"

"Something strange. It seems there was once a feud that went on between the Midnight King and the White Lady long before the war began. The White Lady had at first joined him in his search for immortality, but after her daughter got involved—"

"So, the White Lady *did* have a daughter?" Excitement buzzed through Leo's veins, remembering the name he found in the library. Cassiopeia.

If she had a daughter, then that meant the daughter could very well have survived beyond childhood after all. Then, all Leo would have to do was find her and ask for her help in saving Faye's remaining sisters. They could use her as bait—with her permission, of course—and lure the kidnapper in before killing him.

"Yes, but it pains me to say, her daughter died in the fight. It was her death that turned the tide of the war and the White Lady defeated the Midnight King. As a result, she cursed the Midnight King and his sons."

Leo's heart sank. There went his plan. If she was dead, then who was to say that there was a descendant still alive? He flopped back into his chair and glared at the empty fireplace.

"Strange," Jack muttered.

Leo frowned. "What?"

"Oh, nothing, Your Highness." Jack shifted and dropped his gaze to the red-and-gold rug. "Just, it seems odd of the wise woman to mention the day the White Lady's daughter died. The eighteenth of Winterfylleth."

His words brought a shiver to Leo's skin. That was the same day as his mother's death seventeen years ago. Leo had only been three years old then, so he didn't have any memories of his mother. But Father would never speak of what happened. It was almost as if she had just vanished.

Leo pushed himself to his feet and clapped a hand on Jack's shoulder. "It's not much, but you did good work. Thank you."

And, with that, he wandered out the open door, into the halls of the castle, keeping his gaze locked on his boots.

This whole plan was going to rot. Every new breakthrough just turned into a dead end. If they didn't act soon, who knew when the murderer would strike again and—

Leo ran a hand down his face. He couldn't even think of it. With the White Lady's daughter dead, what chance did they have of catching this kidnapper before they killed them all?

He gripped the crumpled note in his pocket. If there was one thing he excelled at, it was hunting. Ever since he was twelve, he had hunted wolves and even brought down deer with a single arrow. He would hunt this murderer down. He would make sure the kidnapper never preyed on an innocent life again.

Chapter Sixteen — Faye

Heavy mist pressed against Faye's skin as she slammed her shovel into the ground. Chunks of peat crumbled down the side of the hole and landed in a pile. Below, Jane stacked the pieces as Lyr, Jane's brother, hefted the peat into the back of a wagon. Just beyond, more servants worked, stacking the wagons to the brim.

Faye drove her shovel into the soil with a ferocity that made her muscles ache. But listening to the hiss of metal biting earth and the soft thumps of dirt was more pleasant than the whispers that floated across the moors. Whispers of the girl in the butterfly mask. Everyone spoke of her with excitement, all eager to know just who this mysterious princess was.

With a grunt, Faye slammed her shovel into the ground again.

"You want me to take over, love?" Lyr called from beside the wagon.

Faye wiped strands of damp hair away from her face. "No, I've got this."

Lyr squinted up at the sky, freckled nose wrinkled, then nodded. "Looks like fog's comin' in thick, so we'll have to hurry if we want to get back."

"Alright. You think I've got enough?" Faye asked as she leaned against the shovel to rest.

Nodding, Lyr scratched his strawlike hair. "That should do it. We have enough for both your Madame Leroux and our Mrs."

"Oh, good." Faye squinted at the horizon.

The wind blew, sending the fog rolling toward the distant forest. Behind her, the city looked like a ghost town, the servants trundling toward it like spectral beings returning home.

A lone rider passed the servants. Faye stumbled back as a particularly strong gust of wind snagged her hair and whipped it into her face.

"I wonder who that is," she said as she watched the rider canter across the moors.

Something tugged at Faye, drawing her toward the rider. They seemed familiar. Before Faye knew it, her feet drew her across the moor.

The wind swirled around her, dragging the mist behind it. Jane's voice rose with the wind, but the words were muffled. Turning, Faye searched the mist for Jane and Lyr. But all she saw were wild tufts of grass and heather springing up from the loamy ground.

A snort announced the arrival of the lone rider. Faye scrambled back, away from the road. As the rider came into view, Faye sucked in a gasp.

It was Leo.

His horse looked like a ghost in the mist with its brilliant white coat, and he its spectral rider. Shoulders slumped and head bowed, Leo rode at a sedate walk, the reins limp between his pale fingers. He passed by without looking up once. With a swish of its tail, his horse carried him under the boughs of the Northwind Forest.

Faye brought a hand to her forehead. When did she walk this far? How did she get here without even knowing? Her head spun. She needed to get back, before Jane and Lyr went looking for her. With this mist, they could easily get lost. And, if she left now, she would still have time to stack some peat in the garden to dry before sundown.

Still, curiosity pulled her feet onward. With careful steps, she inched her way under the boughs of the Northwind Forest. The fog thinned as she approached the trees, and Faye could just see Leo ahead, dismounting. His horse's grey tail swished as Leo stroked its neck. Soft murmurs filled the air and Faye strained to listen.

She inched closer, careful to step on roots and lumps of dirt, avoiding the leaves as best she could. Pausing behind an ancient oak tree, Faye pressed herself against it and listened.

"… hard, Ghost. Just everything, all of this, is too hard. I want to find them, I want to find—" Leo paused, his back to Faye. When he spoke next, his voice shook. "I want Faye to be alive. I want that note, that bloody dress, all of it to be a lie."

Faye clamped a hand over her mouth, shock rippling through her. He thought … she was dead? What note? What dress? Her heart picked up its tempo.

"And then Father, well, you know what he's like."

Leo's horse snorted and shook its mane.

Laughing, Leo patted his horse's shoulder. "You and me both, Ghost. He's a ridiculous, goosecapped old fop!"

With a whinny, Leo's horse threw its head up, as if laughing. Leo turned to the side and Faye could just see the grin on his lips.

"Oh, you think that's funny, don't you? You want me to say it again?" Leo cupped his hands around his mouth and shouted, "King Richard is a ridiculous, goose-capped old fop, and I don't care who hears it!"

When he lowered his arms, his eyes grew watery and he collapsed onto a mossy log. He dropped his head in his hands and soft sobs filled the forest, his shoulders shaking.

Tears stung Faye's eyes. Why did he believe her to be dead? And did he really care that much? Her heart ached as she watched him. She should say something. Call out to him. Let him know that she was alive, and she was here, and if he wanted her to, she'd never, ever go away.

But what would Pathos say? Faye shrank back. He would be angry if he found out that she wanted to talk to Leo.

Then we don't tell him, her mind whispered. *We keep this to ourself.*

She could do this. Pathos didn't have to know. It was just one small moment. That was all she wanted. Just a single moment.

Trembling, Faye stepped out from behind the tree. She gathered her courage and took in a deep breath to call out. But when she tried, nothing came. Her heart sank, and a longing cut through her, so deep it hurt. Of course. The curse. Still, she stayed where she was. If he looked up, if he turned around, he would see her. If he just looked up, if he just called out her name—

A hand pressed against Faye's mouth and an arm snaked around her waist. Before she could scream, she was jerked backwards, and darkness clouded her vision.

Magic scraped against her skin, dug into her bones. Faye struggled in her captor's arms, fear gripping her tight.

With a final tug, the darkness faded, and Faye found herself on the moors. In the distance, she could hear Jane and Lyr calling her name, but the fog hid them from sight. She stumbled forward, bent as she fought for balance.

"What were you doing?" her captor yelled.

Ice filled Faye's veins and her head suddenly grew light. She turned to see Pathos, wrapped in a heavy cloak, the hood pulled up. A sharp wind blew, tugging at its edges, and for a moment, it looked like the cloak had turned to smoke.

"Answer me, Faye de la Rou," Pathos growled behind his wolf mask. "You almost broke the contract. What do you have to say for yourself?"

Faye struggled to find words. "I ... I didn't—"

"Your actions won't go unpunished." He whirled and began to march away.

"No!" Panic gripped Faye by the throat and she rushed after him. "No, Pathos, please, I'm sorry, I really am, please don't hurt my sisters, please—"

"Enough!" He whirled, bringing his arm up.

Faye ran into him and fell back. She hit the soft ground, elbows sinking into the dirt.

"No amount of pleading can save you this time, my lady. You've gone too far. For this, your sisters will spend the rest of the moon's cycle with the shadow beasts."

No. Faye scrambled to her feet. No, she couldn't let him do this. She couldn't let her sisters get taken by the shadow beasts. Poor Belle and Margaux, they would lose any innocence they had left. Kamille, Linette, Genevieve—

"No!" she screamed.

Lunging, Faye scrabbled for any part of Pathos, any part of him she could grab hold of. Anything. Anything but the shadow beasts. Anything—

She scraped the edge of his mask. With a vicious tug, she yanked it off.

It was harder remove than she thought it would be. Almost like peeling off a second skin.

Pathos let out a roar as the mask fell away. He scrambled back, covering his face with his hands.

Clutching the mask in her hand, Faye stormed after him. Her entire body trembled with the anger that coursed through her veins.

"You want this back?" she shouted, her voice too loud in her own ears. "You want this back? Promise me you won't send my sisters to the shadow beasts. Promise you won't hurt them!"

Pathos snarled. It was a deep, wolfish sound, one that Faye never thought she'd hear. It shook her to her very bones. When he lifted his face from his hands, Faye bit back a scream as she saw him for the first time.

His skin was pallid, lips blue. His flesh was sunken and hanging off his face like another mask that didn't quite fit. Crooked and sharp, his teeth were like jagged pieces of glass.

Two black spheres were pressed into the sockets of his skull. He snarled at her as he hunched, arms tucked close.

It was almost pitiful. She stared at him—mask forgotten. Beneath the hideous veneer, she could see the kindness in him. And she could see how, if he were living, he could have been ... well, not handsome. But not ugly. There was a sadness about him. A depth to his soul that pulled Faye closer to the monster cowering on the moors.

Every threat, every deal she had planned in her heart died on her lips. Faye reached out to Pathos and he let out another vicious snarl.

"Now you see!" he shouted. "Now you see that I am a hideous monster, a freak, just like you!"

Faye flinched back and tucked her arms in close.

Pathos rose to his feet and stood over her. The light slashed against his high cheekbones, carving hollows into his face.

"You think Leo would agree to come with you if he saw you? He mourns a dead friend, not a lover. He mourns an opportunity. Nothing he says is real. Do you hear me? None of it is real.

"I wish only to make you happy, Faye de la Rou, only to help you, and you make selfish demands, thinking only of yourself! Will you not let me have this one small favor? Everything I do is for you and you're too blinded by your greed to see it. Curse you!"

He towered over her, anger twisting his face and burning in his black eyes. Faye turned away. He was right. He only ever did things for her, always sacrificed his time and favor with his brothers for her. She was being selfish. She would always be selfish.

"You must agree to new terms. A single dance with the Midnight King at Leo's ball. That is all I ask. One dance. Do this, and your mother will be free from the shadow beasts. You have my word."

His words drew her back to him. Lifting her face, she met his eyes.

Pathos seemed to deflate, and he stepped back, shoulders slumped. "You know, this hurts me much more than it hurts you. I don't want to do this, any of this. But you've forced my hand." He was quiet now. Gentle, like always.

Faye's heart ached. He was willing to make a trade like this ... for her sisters, her mother? He was willing to help Mama if only she agreed to let him have a dance at the masquerade?

Faye bit the inside of her cheek to keep from screaming. The Midnight King side of Pathos would not make this easy on her. He would force her to dance with him, to make her seem untouchable. To make it impossible for her to win.

Could she even win?

"I can get her out of the pit. I can pull her away from the shadow beasts. Faye, your mother would be safe, if only you say yes."

Tears stung Faye's eyes.

She couldn't allow this to happen. But how could she call herself a devoted daughter, a devoted sister, if she sacrificed her mother and sisters for another night at a royal ball?

Faye would never forgive herself if she caused her mother's pain. It would be selfish of her to withhold this opportunity. She would just be proving Pathos right.

"I agree," she whispered. "One dance in exchange for Mama's safety."

Hesitantly, Pathos reached out. Faye remained rooted to the spot. Tucking a strand of hair behind her ear, his fingers brushed the point of her ear.

"We are both outcasts, you and I." Pain filled Pathos's gaze. "Creatures of darkness. We don't belong in this world of light."

The truth of his words sucked Faye's breath away. She was an outcast, unwanted. If Leo, or any of the nobles of

Eura, knew what she really was, they would be disgusted. They would cast her out before she had a chance to explain. Suddenly, the light of the sun seemed too bright, Jane and Lyr's voices too loud. None of this was for her. She deserved none of it.

Faye blinked hard. Shaking, she held out the mask. Pathos took it, but instead of putting it back on, he held it with limp fingers. Faye dropped her gaze to the ground.

"I'll see you tonight, then."

Taking her hand in his, he brushed his lips against her cheek. They stung like frostbite. She shuddered and closed her eyes.

"Until we meet again, my lady."

When she opened her eyes, he was gone.

∞

Jane and Lyr fussed over Faye the entire ride back into the city. Jane expressed how worried she was, and Lyr nodded in agreement. Faye let them talk. Let them worry. Let them fuss. She couldn't stop hearing Pathos's voice in her head.

One dance. One dance.

Faye couldn't stop trembling. She scrubbed at her cheek, still feeling Pathos' parting kiss, like a leech that wouldn't let go. The feeling in her limbs slowly faded, replaced with a bitter cold.

"Are you sure you're alright?" Jane asked, placing a gentle hand on Faye's back as they rattled into the city.

"I'm fine." She gave her a stiff smile. "Everything's fine."

Wrapping her arms around herself, she kept her head ducked low until they reached Madame's house. Lyr helped her stack a portion of the peat next to the door before driving off with Jane, both telling Faye to be careful.

Faye entered the house and locked the door behind her.

Everything was quiet. Madame, she guessed, was sleeping, while Delphine and Bonnie were out running errands. Leaving her alone.

Crouching next to the fireplace, she dug out the brick that hid her glass slippers. When she lifted one up to the light, she gasped.

The glass had turned an ashen grey.

Chapter Seventeen – Faye

Faye smoothed out the skirts of her white dress for the hundredth time as the carriage rattled down the street. Her own fears wrapped around her like a thousand snakes, sinking their fangs into her skin and squeezing the air from her lungs.

Pathos would be there tonight. Would he arrive before her? Or after? Should she search for him? Faye shuddered at the thought. She squeezed her eyes shut but Pathos' twisted face painted itself onto the backs of her eyelids.

"Do you remember that handsome duke who was dressed in green last night?" Delphine asked as she looked out the carriage window. Beside her, Madame dozed, head resting on her daughter's shoulder.

Faye swallowed. "No. Who was he again?"

"Lord Henry, son of Count Henry the Fourth of Faewalk. He was a nice gentleman." Delphine looked at Faye askance. "I'm surprised you don't remember him. You danced with him twice last night."

Gripping her skirts, she fought off the growing chill. "Oh? I hardly noticed."

"Why did you run out last night? Where did you go? Mama said that you grew ill and went home early but when we arrived, you weren't there."

"Your mother didn't lie. I grew sick. I had to leave." Faye's muscles stiffened. Why did she care so much?

"You only ran out to catch everyone's attention. All they can talk about is the girl in the butterfly mask. No one will remember anyone else." Delphine's dark eyes flashed.

"What are you trying to do here, Faye? I want only to make Mama proud and help her fight against the lies that have kept us destitute for so long. But it looks like the only thing you want is for everyone to think about you."

"No, I don't!" Faye's voice filled the carriage. The anger and fear that had been brewing inside her all day bubbled to the surface. "I don't want to be recognized or famous! I don't want to turn heads and become the talk of the city. I only want …" She choked and gripped her throat. Her deal with Pathos had cut her off.

Fighting back tears, Faye whispered in a shaky voice, "I just want to see my family again."

Delphine's eyes widened at her outburst. She looked down at her skirts and Faye buried her face in her hands.

All Faye wanted at that moment was to go home. A sharp pang filled her chest at the thought. It had been so long. So, so long that it was nearly impossible to remember what exactly her room had looked like. Or what color of roses and geraniums had been planted in the garden. Or what the servants looked like.

Her lady's maid had been a petite girl only a few years younger than herself named Christine. She had been a close friend and confidante. If Faye ever returned, would Christine even still be there?

It hurt too much to think on it. Faye rubbed her cheek with her hand and took in a shaky breath.

Twisting her fingers together, Faye spoke. "I apologize for my words. They were harsh and cruel, and you have every right to be angry." Tears burned in Faye's eyes, but she pushed them back. "I don't ask for your forgiveness because I know you have no reason to forgive me."

I don't deserve forgiveness. Not for anything.

Shaking her head, Delphine sighed. She looked down at Madame, a look of exhaustion crossing her face.

"Lord Henry is the only man I've ever met who seemed to actually care about my dreams. He promised someday he would give me my very own shop, right here in Brighthaven. I'm just afraid that if Mama knew … she might never let me talk to him again."

Faye sighed. "I know how you feel."

More than Delphine would ever know. As silence descended on the carriage, Faye curled her hands into fists, cinching her fingers tighter and tighter until her nails dug into her palms and pain shot up her arms.

∞

As Faye, Madame, and Delphine entered the ballroom, the occupants buzzed with not just wonder, but pure excitement. Faye searched the masks as they passed by until her eyes landed on Leo, who looked resplendent in a gold-and-white suit. This time, he wore a gold mask that covered the right side of his face, leaving the left side bare. While the sight of the mask made her shudder, seeing half of Leo's face, she could almost pretend that he wasn't wearing one at all.

That invisible tether around her heart tugged and guilt wrapped her in its heavy embrace. Only hours earlier, she had witnessed a side of him she'd never seen before. A side she never knew existed.

But she also learned he thought her dead. A hollowness crept into her chest and nestled where her heart was supposed to be.

Leo separated from the crowd and made his way toward her. Faye ducked her head and pretended not to notice, keeping close to Madame. Heart thudding in her chest, she locked her gaze on a short, bald man with a loud laugh. Out of the corner of her eye, she saw Leo keeping time with her steps. Faye hurried her pace, her cheeks flaming.

133

Leo lengthened his strides. Finally, he squeezed past three men dressed in black and halted before her.

He gave her an elaborate bow, an odd smile on his lips. As if his heart and his head had two different emotions in mind.

"My lady," he said, eyes sparkling. "Would you care to dance?"

No. Faye straightened her shoulders. "Yes."

Taking her hand, Leo led her through the dance, and she followed along as best she could, tripping over the glass slippers. The dance was kind of a fast-paced waltz, and Leo lifted her into the air more than once, setting her lightly on her toes. She winced each time her feet touched the floor.

Leo searched her gaze, grey eyes filled with worry. "You seem upset. What's wrong?"

Faye looked away. "I just don't care much for dancing tonight."

"Is there anything in particular that's making you upset?"

Shrugging, Faye kept her gaze firmly on Leo's embroidered jacket. She couldn't allow herself even one glimpse of his face. For if she did, she knew her heart would surrender. Even if her voice could not.

"It's alright. You can tell me. I don't mind."

"I really don't think it appropriate for a lowly maiden to tell the prince her woes."

"Well, a prince is supposed to serve his people, is he not?" Leo's eyes sparkled. "And if that means lending a listening ear, then so be it."

Faye couldn't help smiling back. Warmth filled her insides from the joy that spread across Leo's face. She ducked her head. No. She couldn't allow herself to fall in love with him again. Not Leo.

But wasn't this exactly what she wanted? For Leo to see her, to notice her, and maybe … perhaps … to love her?

"Where did you go last night? Why did you leave?"

Faye shook her head. "I can't."

"You can't tell me?"

Faye nodded.

Leo sighed and looked away, exposing only the unmasked side of his face. Her heart skipped a beat. When he looked back down at her, she forced her gaze to their feet, following the complicated steps.

"Why not?"

"I just can't. The words won't come."

"Are you under a spell?"

"Yes."

Faye gasped. The word had just slipped out. Something fluttered in her stomach and she tightened her grip on her skirt. Leo's grey eyes grew sharper.

"Do you know the daughters of King Raoul de la Rou?"

"Yes!"

Faye grinned wide as elation filled her. She no longer felt the pain in her feet or cared if she missed a step. There were loopholes to Pathos's deal. If she answered the right questions, if Leo figured out who she was …

Leo leaned in, gaze intense. "Are they safe? Are they alright?"

Shaking her head, Faye searched for the right words. "No … they are …" She tried to say *trapped* but her tongue refused to form the word. "Lost? No. H-hidden."

Frustration built inside Faye's chest. Neither were the right words. Her sisters were trapped. Locked up in the Underworld while she was given the freedom to roam and do as she pleased. Her reward for being their traitor.

"Please, what else can you tell me? Is there anything I can do to help you?"

Leo's gaze was so intense, so filled with concern that Faye choked. She pulled away, her heart thumping wildly in her chest.

"Why?" she choked out.

Leo had no idea who she was. So why did he want to help her? Was he really so enchanted by the magic Pathos had placed on her? The thought made her throat close. What if he thought she was someone else? What if … he never loved her back?

Leo ran a hand through his hair, tousling the thick red locks. "I once had a friend who disappeared three years ago. I loved this friend very, very much."

Faye trembled—his words far too sweet for her ears. Was he speaking of her? That he loved *her*? Truly?

"But now … now that friend is dead." He turned his gaze to her, sorrow clouding out his boyish joy. "I don't ever want to sit by and let something like that happen again. And that is why I want to help you."

She squeezed his hand, ever so lightly. If he thought she was dead, then this friend he loved—could it really be her? Or was he speaking of someone else? He had to be. It was too kind, too beautiful for her to dare hope for.

He stepped closer—his movements hesitant. "Tell me … are you one of the princesses? One of the daughters of King Raoul?"

Yes! she wanted to shout. Faye fought to keep her welling emotions at bay. *Yes, Leo, yes, I am here, alive! I need your help! I need you to save me.* But instead, she firmed her chin and kept the grief in check. It wouldn't do to cry. She had cried enough.

So, she looked him in the eye, begging him to understand that her next word was a lie. "No."

Leo deflated. But there was no way Faye could tell him the truth. Even if Pathos had not cursed her tongue, she wouldn't force him to come with her into the dark. He was too good for this world. No, she would find another way. A way that didn't involve betraying the last person in all of Eura who still believed in her.

Leo sighed. He looked over her shoulder, his eyes shining in the candlelight. Then he turned those beautiful, storm-glass eyes toward Faye. The muscles in his jaw bunched.

He leaned close and whispered, "Tell me where they are."

Faye closed her eyes. "I can't."

"Excuse me," a voice rumbled behind her. "I thought you had saved the next dance for me, darling. But I see you've found yourself a new companion."

Leo stiffened and placed a protective hand on Faye's back. Faye's head spun and she wobbled, turning to face Pathos behind her. Dressed in the same suit and wolf mask, Pathos adjusted a gold-tree blossom tucked in his lapel. His eyes shone with fire and his hands were curled into fists. He gave her a small bow but didn't take his gaze off Leo.

"My lady, if you wouldn't mind."

At that moment, Faye realized the music had ended. She and Leo had been dancing to silence. She took two long steps back until she stood next to Pathos, her cheeks hot.

Leo stepped forward, his eyes like steel and his fists clenched, as if he were a lion ready to tear into a jackal. "Pardon me, good sir. I don't think I know you."

Pathos gave Leo a flourishing bow. "Of course, you don't. It is a masquerade, after all."

Taking Faye's hand, he spun her away from Leo, his movements as smooth as those of a cat, leading them into the next dance. He held her as if she were made of porcelain. His touch remained gentle. Kind. And yet, ever cold. Ever distant. Not warm and genuine like Leo. She could no longer see the prince amidst the flaring skirts and multitudes of masks. Always, so many masks.

"What did you tell him?"

Faye dropped her gaze to Pathos's chest and remained silent. There was nothing she could say that Pathos wouldn't perceive as breaking their deal. Nothing she could say to save herself or her sisters. She let Pathos lead her across the floor in a slow reel, her skirts flaring about her aching legs, his hands keeping her from falling to the floor.

Dancing with him here was torture. Seeing him that morning, it had shaken her. But now, with Pathos holding her in his arms, her world began to crumble. It just went to prove that nothing in her life could last forever. Nothing whole or pure or even beautiful. He was right. She was darkness. She didn't belong here. She would never belong here.

The night stretched on too long. Panic clawed at her insides, tearing her apart piece by piece. Faye couldn't bear seeing everyone's masks. Seeing *his* mask.

Dance after dance, Pathos dragged her across the floor, never tiring. Her legs trembled and her feet felt like lead. Her movements became choppy and stilted. And yet she continued to dance. Finally, at the end of a song, Pathos paused. He held her with strong, steadying hands.

"You are tired."

Faye nodded, struggling to breathe. Not just from the dancing but also from being here. This place that had once held hope now just felt like a tomb.

Pathos wrapped an arm around her waist and helped her to one of the chairs that lined the room. She dropped into the seat. Giving her a small bow, he turned and walked away toward the tables of punch.

Faye watched him go, mouth dry. He was leaving her defenseless in a sea of men that slowly crowded closer and closer, each one begging for a dance. Their eyes glazed over with looks of helpless adoration, their smiles too wide, their voices too loud. She politely declined each offer, her heartbeat ratcheting with each new gentleman that came her way.

"My lady." Leo appeared at her side, brows bent with concern. "Are you alright?"

Nodding, Faye gave him a small smile, relief flooding her veins as the crowd inched away. "I just need to rest a moment."

She searched the crowd for Pathos. He was standing impatiently behind a group of women circling the punch table. Faye would have laughed if he hadn't been the beast of her nightmares. Still, despite sharing only one dance, she felt it would be better if she never danced with Leo again. Better if he never saw her again. Even if that meant willingly walking into the jaws of the wolf.

"Do you think you could have one last dance with me?" Leo asked, holding out his hand. When she hesitated, he looked back at Pathos and his jaw clenched. "Just for a moment."

Leo stood there, waiting. Hope in his eyes. His hand extended. Her lungs constricted. It felt like he was offering her the world. Endless sunshine and days of laughter. Freedom to do as she pleased, freedom to leave the Underworld behind and never look back. All of it rested in the palm of his hand. All she had to do was reach out and take it.

She bit her lip. If she danced with him, Pathos would watch their every step, waiting for her to lure him away. After all, she was just the bait, the shiny bauble designed to bring Leo to his doom. To keep him safe, she had to stay as far away from him as possible. Her sisters never deserved their fate. And neither did Leo. Even though it felt like sinking into a river and letting the water fill her lungs, Faye leaned back in her chair and shook her head.

As much as she hated Pathos, she would rather be dancing with him instead of sitting next to Leo like she was a broken doll he wanted to fix. To choose Pathos would mean, at least, her sisters would be safe. Because all of Pathos' attention would be on her. As long as he was here, the Midnight King wouldn't take him over. He would be here, her Pathos. Her Pathos.

The hope in Leo's eyes died. He took one step back. Two. Three.

The magic tugged at Faye's spine. She sighed. Finally. Standing, she slipped past Leo and curtsied.

"I am sorry, my prince, but I must leave now." She gathered her skirts and ran before he could stop her.

"No, wait! Come back!" Leo's footsteps clacked on the polished wood behind her.

Pathos came toward her, cutting through the crowd like a shark. Leo caught up to her and grabbed her sleeve.

"Wait, please, just tell me—"

Pathos reached Faye's side and yanked her from Leo's grasp. Faye stumbled. Pathos spun her behind him, as if to shield her from Leo. He took a menacing step toward Leo.

"Stay away," he growled.

Leo stepped closer until he stood toe to toe with Pathos. He looked Pathos in the eye and straightened his jacket.

"It does not behoove you to speak to the prince of Eura that way." Though he remained calm, a threat laced his words.

The magic yanked at Faye again and she tugged on Pathos' arm.

"Leave us alone," she growled at Leo, ignoring the hurt in his eyes.

Turning, Pathos gripped her hand in his and they bolted from the room.

As they ran, Faye glanced back once. Leo stood with his arms dangling at his sides, one foot forward as if he were about to run after them. He reached out one hand—his face twisted with hurt.

Faye's heart squeezed inside her chest and she smothered her sorrow that rose like a wave.

Chapter Eighteen – Leo

Desperation clung to Leo. There was something so familiar about the girl. He could almost believe that she was Faye, even though he knew she was gone. Even though everyone else knew she was gone. But his heart screamed the opposite.

She looked back once, and he caught a glimpse of her dark, dark eyes. He had recognized those eyes as they danced, remembering a time not too long ago when he had seen them bathed in silvery moonlight. There was no mistaking it. This girl, this Faerie, *had* to be Faye. And here he was standing like a fool, watching as some man in a wolf mask dragged her away.

It was strange. Leo felt he'd seen this man somewhere before. But it didn't make sense. Throughout his searches, it wasn't a man he saw, but a wolf. Just a regular gray wolf. Why would some man follow him?

Something jostled loose in his memories; the man with the wolf head from his visions. But they were just that. Visions. Delusions created by an overworked mind. This man and his visions couldn't be connected.

Fatigue weighed down his limbs and Leo's mind grew fuzzy. He should chase after them. Demand that this man unhand her. But it had looked like the girl had *wanted* to go with him. And he couldn't cause a scene if she willingly chose this man over him. Still, he needed answers. And he wasn't about to let the girl who might be Faye get away.

Shaking away the sleep that threatened to overtake him, Leo pushed through the crowds, dancing past powdered nobles and dressed-up commoners. When he finally escaped the last of the crowd, the girl and the man were gone. Leo rushed to the doors, his boots slamming against the wood floor. Once he left the ballroom, he slid to a stop, wobbling a little.

The hall was empty. Leo held his breath. An odd sound caught his ear. Almost like glass tapping on wood. But at a steady pace. Then Leo remembered. *Shoes.* Her dance slippers were made of glass.

Putting on a burst of speed, Leo ran down the hall. He rounded the corner in time to see the girl dart into a room, her brilliant white skirt flaring out behind her.

"My lady!" he called out.

The young woman came back out into the hall, panic written on her face.

"Monsieur!" she gasped. "Please, don't follow me!"

Leo approached with slow steps. "My lady, please, tell me why you have to run away. Tell me how I can help you."

Glancing into the room, the girl became like stone. The man came to the doorway and bent to whisper something in her ear. Then, the girl shuddered. Her butterfly mask gleamed in the moonlight that poured through the windows. Her voice was tight when she spoke.

"I cannot. Please, Monsieur, if I do not go—" She whirled and rushed away, the man following like a dark shadow.

Leo watched her go. He itched to get her away from the man, but what she had said made his blood run cold.

If I do not go—

What? What had she meant to say that she couldn't finish? Leo stared at the empty hall where she had once stood. Questions circled his mind, too many to count. There was something going on here, something that certainly involved magic. Leo could almost feel it in the air, rubbing his skin raw.

There was no denying it. This young woman was enchanted. And she knew something about the missing princesses.

Maybe she is *Faye.*

No. He needed to stop making that assumption. No matter how similar her eyes looked, or how familiar her touch felt, there was no evidence. For now, he had to do what his father always told him. *Rely on the facts. The facts never lie. To trust in your gut is to trust a fleeting fancy.*

The facts. First, the young woman was enchanted, and the man in the wolf mask had to be involved. Second, this girl was his first and only lead on finding the princesses. And the third fact—she was gone. He couldn't let her go, not with the risk of another princess being killed.

Whoever this wolf man was, Leo wanted to give him a swift knock in the jaw. Teach him some manners. Just who was he? His mask was strange and his clothing ancient. As if he had stepped from another era. A living relic of ages past. And heavy magic leached from the man's skin.

Whoever he was, he was powerful. Very powerful. And he needed to be stopped before that poor girl got hurt. The urge to command his guards to capture this brute and have him hanged filled Leo, but he stopped himself from calling out. No, this wolf man could not be stopped by mere Human soldiers. And it would be foolish to risk putting the girl's life in danger.

The bloodied dress and Colette's finger filled Leo's mind and he fought off a shudder. For now, he would leave them be, for the sake of Faye's sisters. There was one night left for the ball. Hopefully, the girl would return. And he could find a way to break her enchantment. And if he could do that, then maybe, just maybe, he could finally get the answers he so desperately needed.

Leo turned back to the ballroom. Light splashed from the door and the laughter that echoed inside promised smiles and high spirits. As Leo reached the double doors, he found Jack waiting for him, his hand resting on his sword.

"Is there trouble, Your Highness?"

Leo waved a hand. "Nothing to worry about." He thought a moment, then asked, "What do you know about enchantments?"

∽

A loud thump startled Leo awake. He looked up to see Jack standing next to his bed.

"Jack, what in the blazes—?"

"Good morning, Your Highness." Jack had a particularly vicious grin on his face. "After your vague question, I did some digging and I've found some books I thought you might enjoy perusing."

Rubbing his head, Leo rolled over and glanced at his nightstand. A stack of old, dusty books rested on the carved table. Each one was at least a hand's width thick with yellowed pages.

"Read fast, Your Highness, because technically these books aren't supposed to leave the library. Or be read. Or exist." Jack cleared his throat.

Leo raised an eyebrow. "Are you saying these books are banned?"

"Indeed, Your Highness."

Leo grinned. "Excellent." Just what he needed.

Picking up the first book, Leo flipped through the thick vellum pages. Each one was gilded in gold trimming, with illustrations painted throughout. There were several entries on the subject of enchantments, mainly about transforming someone into a frog or a swan. There was even an enchantment that described a person turning into a pig.

He shook his head and skipped those pages. Obviously, the mysterious girl was not transforming into a creature of some sort at the stroke of midnight. Otherwise he would have been chasing after a goose or some such creature. He paused. Or would he have been chasing a butterfly?

You're getting sidetracked, he chided himself.

The next book was a tome of spells. Leo fanned the pages. Most of the spells involved elements like moving rocks or bringing down rain. Nothing that involved curses.

Sighing, Leo picked up the third book. The writing scrawled across the cover wasn't even in a language Leo could read.

"Nothing yet?" Jack asked as he flipped through the spell book.

"Nothing." Leo picked up the fourth book.

After what felt like a million pages, he finally came upon an entry on dark magic. One passage spoke of a Necromancer who had raised an army of the dead, and only by killing him could the enchantments end. Leo shuddered. He was glad that this Necromancer was gone.

When he neared the end, he found only one passage involving the stroke of midnight. His pulse quickened as he scanned the page. It spoke of a serving girl who was enchanted by a Faerie to become a beautiful princess as a trap to lure away a prince. However, it was easy for the prince to see through the curse, and the spell wore off at the stroke of midnight.

Leo shook his head in disgust and slammed the book shut. The mystery girl had been terrified for her life. Whatever was going on was much more complicated than that.

Leo bit the inside of his cheek to keep from cursing and flopped backwards onto his bed in a very unprincely manner.

Utter balderdash, he thought. All these books were a great waste of time. Leo flipped to the last story and paused. He squinted. Something about it seemed familiar.

The Midnight King is an entity that has been around for as long as the written word has existed. His real name has been lost amongst history, but what is known is that he came from a tribe of enchanters, said to have come from the fabled island of Everland. He was known for his dangerous experiments and his discovery of the gift of immortality—but this came at a great cost. For every year he wanted to live, he had to rip out the soul of an innocent victim. This left the world in turmoil as more and more innocents were executed in this horrific way.

He took on the title of Midnight King in defiance of the White Lady, who was averse to his ways. Their war lasted more than an age.

When at last the great White Lady, the leader of the Humans, caught the Midnight King, she locked him away in the Underworld where he could no longer hurt others. But what she didn't count on was his sons, Undead creatures able to stalk through the world at night.

Many men and women began to go missing. It was rumored that he was using them in his twisted experiments as a way of escape. But as long as he ruled the Underworld, there would be no saving them.

Over the recent years, however, word of the Midnight King has been scarce. The last that was heard was an incident that happened between him and the now-disgraced Pandalian Faerie, Aurore. The Midnight King had demanded that the Faerie give up her daughters in marriage to his monstrous brothers. She refused him, and as a result, her husband and eldest child, a son, were killed.

One other incident was one year ago, when the king of Revayr accused the Midnight King of kidnapping his daughters. However, it is believed that they were taken by their Faerie mother into Faerie Land.

He bolted upright and thrust the book under Jack's nose. "Look at this!"

Jack leaned backwards while frowning at the page. His eyes darted as he read. Then his eyebrows rose. "That's the account of the fight between the Midnight King and the White Lady."

"Yes, but look!" Leo stabbed the page at the part that spoke of King Raoul.

Jack blinked. "Well, now, that's interesting."

"Interesting indeed." Leo scrambled off his bed and snatched up a red silk robe draped across the end of his bed. Shoving his arms into the sleeves, he grabbed the book from Jack's hands and bolted for the door.

"Your Highness!" Jack called. "You're not dressed properly!"

"No time!"

Leo rushed through the halls, grateful that the castle was still asleep. It would be severely vexatious if any of the servants saw their prince dashing about like a madman clothed in nothing but a robe and nightclothes. Especially embarrassing if his father caught him.

After making his way up three flights of stairs, he hurried down one long hall and threw open a set of heavy oak doors that led into the library.

Leo ran between the shelves, pausing as he scanned the spines. It had to be in the library somewhere. Leo grabbed hold of a rolling ladder and pushed it across the floor until it collided with a bookshelf that sat against the wall. Climbing up the rungs, he reached up and snagged the corner of a thick red tome. It fell from the shelf and Leo scrambled to catch it. His fingers slipped across the leather cover. With a loud thud, it hit the floor.

Sucking in a breath, Leo waited for several heartbeats for the librarian to appear and chide him for the disturbance. He didn't know if she would awake at this hour, but he wouldn't be surprised.

When he didn't hear the clicking of shoes, he let out a breath and made his way back down the ladder. With clumsy hands, he picked up the heavy tome and opened it to the last few pages.

It happened so suddenly. One moment, I was sitting on my throne, laughing with joy as my daughters danced with guests on the ballroom floor, and the next, the floor had crumbled beneath their feet. My daughters, my wife, all my guests and friends … all gone. Then the floor had reappeared as if nothing had happened. As if none of them had ever existed.

But I remember. I remember before this happened, my daughter, Faye, had come into the ballroom with a boy I didn't recognize. He had been wearing an odd mask that covered his entire face. What exactly it looked like, I can't recall. But I remember that boy.

Leo's heart beat hard against his ribs. *This* was what he had been looking for. He remembered reading it years ago and dismissing it as the grieving king's mad fancies. But, after seeing the mysterious girl and the masked man, he couldn't brush it off anymore. King Raoul really had been telling the truth the whole time, and no one believed him.

The Midnight King was real. Very, *very* real. The thought sent a chill through Leo's bones. And that girl, the daughter of King Raoul and Queen Nimue of Revayr, was trapped in his clutches.

Leo snapped the book shut. That meant that the man in the wolf mask had to be the Midnight King, or at least one of his sons. All this time, it hadn't been bandits or murderers or fanatics. All this time, it had been the most powerful Enchanter in existence.

There was only one thing to do. He would follow this man in the wolf mask to the Underworld. Even if it meant facing his father's disapproval for the rest of his life. He could take the shame. But he couldn't live knowing that he had turned a blind eye on the fate of an entire family—not when he could have done something to help.

Chapter Nineteen – Faye

Silence wrapped around Faye like a heavy cloak. She shivered in the corner of the Underworld ballroom alone. Guilt, sharp as broken glass, filled her heart, scraping with every steady beat. The moment they entered, Pathos had left Faye standing here while her sisters lined up on the dance floor. But Faye couldn't make herself follow them. Not yet.

Colette sat alone near the ballroom floor, back hunched and head bowed. It was as if she was wilting before Faye's very eyes.

Faye sucked in a deep breath. Enough was enough. It was time. Either Faye confessed to her the truth of what happened three years ago or spend the rest of her life hiding behind a lie. She needed to tell them how sorry she was. Even if it meant they rejected her forever. Because once they were free from the Underworld, there wouldn't be another chance.

Faye shivered and wrapped her arms around herself. Soon she would be left alone, for good.

Faye knelt at Colette's feet. Cold crept inside her chest. She took in a shuddering breath. If she didn't speak now, she never would.

"It's my fault," Faye whispered.

"What?" Colette leaned forward.

"It's my fault. I was the one who cursed us all."

Colette's hands fluttered, the bandage on her right hand restricting the movement of her remaining fingers. Her mouth fell open in shock.

Faye looked back. Nosos had spied them and was coming their way. She turned and spoke as fast as she could. "I did

149

it. Pathos, he came to me and promised me a magic world of dance. He showed me the Underworld. He gave me the glass slippers. Told me that if I put them on, I'd be able to come and go whenever I pleased. I went into the ballroom that night to bring you all with me. But when midnight came, the floor crumbled beneath our feet and we fell." Faye's throat constricted. "We all fell, and it was my fault and I'm sorry, Colette, I'm so, so sorry."

Nosos grabbed her arm. "What are you doing? The king won't like this."

Faye wrestled against his grasp. She needed to finish. "I knew what would happen!"

Colette struggled to her feet. Nosos gripped Faye's other arm.

"I knew when I walked into that ballroom, the spell would take us all. But I didn't care. I was too angry at Leo to care. I was selfish."

"Faye!" Nosos' voice shook. "Be silent!"

He dragged Faye backwards, away from Colette. Colette took a wobbly step. Then another. She lifted a hand as if to stop Nosos.

"No!" Faye screamed. She scrabbled at his hand as he dragged her toward the dais, desperation clogging her throat.

Nosos threw her down at the bottom of the steps. Faye's elbow hit the marble, sending a shock of pain up her arm. She struggled to push herself upright.

"Brother, this girl needs to be punished. She was talking with her sister."

Faye looked up, tears blurring her vision. Pathos would punish Nosos. He would hurt him for hurting Faye like this. Only, it wasn't Pathos who sat on the throne. The iron crown rested on his head. It was the Midnight King.

He turned toward Nosos. "I will not tolerate you treating Faye that way."

The Midnight King rose from his throne.

Faye's throat constricted, even as her heart forgot to beat. She slid back across the marble, trembling, as the Midnight King floated down the steps toward them. He reached out to Nosos and gripped his brother's throat.

Nosos choked, scrabbling at the Midnight King's hand. But Pathos was unmovable. His fingers squeezed tighter, tighter, until bone cracked. Faye winced. Nosos's head hung at an odd angle. The Midnight King dropped him.

All was still for several breathless heartbeats. Then Nosos' leg twitched. His neck straightened, snapped into place. Nosos gasped and lay on the floor, chest heaving. The Midnight King knelt beside his brother.

"Hurt her again, and you will go to the shadow beasts." The room shook with his voice, deep and resonant.

The Midnight King paused before her, silent. Faye ducked her head. She bit her lip hard until she tasted blood. He knelt and placed a shadowy hand under her chin.

"Look at me." A chill filled his words.

Faye lifted her gaze to the silver wolf mask. He tilted his head to the side. He didn't speak a word, yet his voice resounded in Faye's head. Shouting, screaming, whispering. Telling her that she was worthless. That she was horrid. A monster.

All warmth fled her body as she slapped her hands over her ears. She bent over and whimpered as the voices bombarded her, scraping against her skin, clawing at her, clinging to her soul. Until her own voice was drowned out by the voice of the shadowy king.

"You know you aren't allowed to speak with your sisters." His voice was a hiss and a boom at the same time, like waves of the ocean, pounding against her. "You have disobeyed my one and only rule."

"Yes," Faye whispered.

"But I cannot have you breaking my one and only rule. Am I not generous? Am I not kind to allow you freedoms?"

"Yes." The darkness was crawling into her skin.

"Then why do you show contempt toward me by breaking the rule I have so carefully created to keep you and your sisters safe?"

Silence replaced the voices. A deep, crushing silence. Faye held her breath and waited.

The Midnight King rose and made his way back to his throne. Faye stared after him, unsure of what to do. The absence of his presence was both a relief and a stab in the chest. She hated when he was like this. And yet she wanted Pathos more than ever, to hold her and protect her from the dark. She shivered and wrapped her arms around herself.

Slowly, awkwardly, Faye climbed to her feet. She straightened her skirt and dropped her arms to her sides. She fought to keep herself standing upright.

Poised. Perfect.

The Midnight King lifted a hand and the music began again.

"Dance," he commanded.

Faye's feet began to move. Her glass slippers tapped on the floor in an elegant dance. Her arms followed, rising and lowering according to the steps. Faye held back a scream. She was dancing, but not of her own volition.

And the Midnight King pulled the strings.

Faye's sisters clustered around the edge of the dance floor. Belle and Margaux began to cry. Adalie reached out as if she wanted to grab Faye and pull her away. Colette fell to her knees and her skin paled, as if she no longer had the strength to stand.

Faye gritted her teeth and threw herself into the dance. Determination gripped her bones. The floor lit up beneath her feet, brighter than ever before. The symbols flashed in rapid succession. Over and over they appeared, each one drawn by her movements.

The ground shook. Faye wobbled but never stumbled. She would find a way for her sisters to escape. She would break their slippers herself and release them all. Even if she had to die to do it.

∞

When Faye came home that night, through the fireplace of Madame Leroux instead of the castle kitchens, she did not cry. She struggled to her feet, her ball gown covered in soot and ashes. The glass slippers rubbed against her raw skin. Exhaustion pulled at her every limb. Still, she did not cry.

By the time she had struggled out of the ball gown and into her night dress, her eyes were hot, and her thoughts spun. The Midnight King's voice echoed through her head.

Dance. Dance. Dance.

Slipping off the glass slippers, she stared at them, the delicate carvings, the columns of spun glass the only thing supporting the heel. They were a deep charcoal color now, darkness swirling inside the glass. Beautiful. Breakable. Yet cursed to forever remain this way.

With a muffled cry, Faye aimed to throw them at the fireplace. If she broke them, this would all be over. If she broke them, she would be free.

If she broke them, she would never see her sisters again.

I will not cry, she said fiercely to herself. *I will* not.

Burying the shoes in the fireplace ash, Faye stumbled to the sofa and collapsed, not bothering with the blanket. It wasn't until dawn peeked through the window that she fell asleep.

∞

Faye woke minutes before the others arose. She dressed quickly and hurried out to the garden before Delphine or Bonnie tried to speak to her. One by one, she pulled at the weeds poking up between rows of cabbage, digging her fingers into the cool soil. The sun warmed the back of her neck and hair, but it couldn't reach down to fill the empty spaces in her hollow chest.

She had danced until her feet bled. Danced even after she begged for rest. Danced until the sun rose and she collapsed. Pathos had to carry her out to the black lake. Faye could still feel his stiff arms around her and hear the lack of heartbeat in his chest.

Though her feet still ached, and blood was dried on her toes, she had shoved her feet into her shoes and marched out into the gardens. Pain was better than feeling the panic that threatened to swallow her whole.

Spots danced in her vision and Faye rested her hands in the dirt.

Dance. Dance. Dance.

Her limbs trembled. Faye wiped at the sweat beading on her brow. It was too hot outside.

"Faye!" Madame Leroux's voice floated through the open kitchen window. "Could you come here a moment, dear?"

Rising on wobbly legs, Faye clenched her jaw. She blinked hard as darkness consumed her vision for a moment. Hunger gnawed at her stomach, but she pushed past it. She could eat later when her nerves had settled.

Madame was sitting at the kitchen table when Faye entered the room. She held her pocket watch in one hand and a cup in the other. Snapping her watch shut, she dropped it into her pocket.

"I was thinking of getting Bonnie some dance shoes. She's old enough to start lessons. I'd like for you to come to the market with me. Delphine's already left for the seamstress shop."

The thought of dancing shoes made Faye's stomach curl, but she nodded. "Of course. Is there anything else you need?"

"No, that's all. I think Bonnie's around here somewhere." Madame shuffled toward the kitchen entrance. "Bonnie! *Ma petite* are you dressed? We're going to the market."

Faye wrapped her arms around herself and shuddered. A restless feeling took hold of her bones even as sleep tugged at her eyes. She paced in circles around the kitchen as she waited for the others. Her shoes rubbed against the abrasions on her feet. Faye closed her eyes and concentrated on the pain. As long as she felt it, she could push past the numbness that hungered to eat her alive.

∞

Madame Leroux, Bonnie, and Faye stepped through the market as the clouds overhead growled warnings of a coming storm. They had just come from the shoemaker's shop and were planning to head to the bakery when the skies grew darker and flashed with white-and-purple lightning.

Madame sniffed the air, her green eyes glowing in the gloom. "We had best hurry home. This storm is coming sooner than we think."

Around them, shops closed, and people scurried home. Faye couldn't blame them. When it stormed in Eura, it never just rained. Winds would come and tear through the streets like rogue ghosts, howling and sweeping unsuspecting travelers off their feet. The gusts would rip at shingles and thatch—anything they could tear loose.

Madame pulled out her pocket watch and nodded. "If we leave now, we'll make it home at least ten minutes before the storm arrives." She took Bonnie's hand. "Come along."

Faye moved to follow, but something caught her eye. There was a pattern in the cobblestones of the street. It looked almost familiar. Faye placed her foot on the first stone a lighter grey than the others. A buzz ran through her leg.

One more step. One more brick. There was magic here.

A single raindrop touched Faye's cheek. She opened her eyes and blinked. The city market was empty. Madame and Bonnie long gone. No carriages rattled by. No hawkers shouted. It was as if the inhabitants had all vanished into smoke.

More rain fell, slow at first, then harder. Faye's hair and dress were soon soaked. Still, she couldn't find it in herself to leave. Lightning flashed against the cobblestones before her, bright yellow, and she laughed.

Faye clamped a hand over her mouth. Had she just laughed? A wild, unfathomable joy tingled across her limbs and she threw out her arms as if to embrace the sky and rain. Or was it madness? If it was, Faye embraced it all the harder.

She couldn't explain it. And maybe, she didn't want to. But here, in the midst of the storm, with lightning crashing all around, she felt suddenly, and inexplicably, free. Lightning could touch her here. No one could force her to do or say anything. She was unshackled, a bird that had finally grown its wings. Another laugh rang out into the silence. Then, she started to move.

Slowly at first. She swayed in place, sodden dress slapping against her legs. She slid one foot out, then the next. Following the pattern of the stones. Letting the magic cling to her skin, her hair, her fingertips. Before she knew it, she was dancing.

It wasn't something she had learned in Revayr. Nor was it something Pathos had taught her in the shadowy halls of the Underworld. This dance had no name, no form to it, no rules. She twirled and splashed through the forming puddles, leaping into the air with toes pointed. She bent back, her hair dragging the ground, before twisting and sliding her toes through the pooling water.

She moved in time with the wind as it pushed the rain in different directions. She leaped with the lightning. She swayed between the drops, fingers passing through without breaking the delicate orbs of water.

And she laughed. *This* was freedom. *This* was dance. This was something she would never be able to do in the Underworld, something she would never do again after today.

This was her final dance, her last moment of freedom, her goodbye to the world she hated to leave behind.

Beneath her feet, the cobblestones began to glow. A deep, burning blue. Every stone her feet touched, the glow grew brighter, until new, brilliant patterns had formed on the stones. Patterns of summoning. Of calling and darkness and midnight.

Faye slowed her dance until she stood still, letting the rain drip from her eyelashes. From amidst the swirling patterns a form took shape. Darkness coalesced, hardening until Pathos stood before her, dressed in his black suit with a gold-tree bloom in his lapel, metal wolf mask in place.

He hovered within the blue light, unmoving. Faye held her breath as she stared at the looming figure. She hadn't realized she could do such a thing. But at the same time, it had felt natural, as if she had called upon a skill she had learned as a child.

"When did you learn summoning magic, my lady?" Pathos asked between rolls of thunder.

Faye laughed. "I don't know! I just did it!" She twirled beneath the clouds and splashed into a wide, shallow puddle.

"Why have you called me?"

Stepping up to Pathos, she looked him in the eye. "I want to change the deal."

"Why?" Surprise filled his voice. "Don't you want to save your family?"

"Yes." Faye wrapped her arms around herself to suppress a shiver. "But I refuse to give Leo in exchange. I'll become an Undead. I'll give you my magic. But in exchange, you must let my family go. My life for theirs."

Pathos stood still. The rain made tiny pinging sounds as it bounced off the metal of his mask. He reached out a gloved hand. Faye placed hers in his.

"You understand why the Midnight King did what he did, don't you?" His voice held a certain insecurity, a note of what sounded too much like fear.

Faye nodded. "I understand."

"Just know it won't ever happen again."

Again, she nodded, unable to speak.

Pathos gripped her hand tight.

"Then I accept your terms. Your magic, your life for theirs."

Chapter Twenty – Leo

It was only befitting that the rain fell on the same day as the last ball, threatening to cancel it entirely. Still, the rain couldn't dampen his spirits. After all, tonight was his birthday, and he intended to enjoy it. It was also his last chance to speak to the girl in the butterfly mask. If all went well tonight, he would finally learn the truth of just what happened three years ago.

Thunder shook the castle, rattling Leo's windows. Jack cursed under his breath and moved closer to the fire.

"Oh, come on, Jack, it's not all bad." Leo watched as a spear of yellow lightning hit the ground. "Thunderstorms are fascinating affairs."

"And what happens when the lightning strikes the window?" Jack muttered. He crossed his muscled arms and leaned against the fireplace. "You get an eyeful of broken glass."

Leo shook his head and leaned against the cold windowpane. Below in the courtyard, a figure was wandering through the rain. Leo squinted. It looked like …

"What in the blazes is King Raoul doing?" he muttered.

Turning, Leo raced from his rooms and down the spiral steps until he reached the ground floor. He hurried toward the small side door that led out to the courtyard. When it came into view, he slowed and paused. Cool air blasted into the hall through the open door. Lightning flashed, silhouetting the figure outside.

Leo stood in the doorway.

"Your Majesty?" Leo shouted over the sound of thunder.

Raoul staggered, then turned. He had his head tilted, as if he were listening.

"I can hear them," he shouted back, the rain muffling his words. "They're calling to me!"

A chill ran down Leo's spine. He clutched the doorframe. "Who?"

Raoul looked at Leo, his dark eyes wide and wild. He ran both hands down his face. "My girls. My girls are calling to me."

The king had finally gone mad. Utterly, hopelessly mad. Leo's heart sank at the thought. For three years Raoul had been ignored and ridiculed. And now, when he believed that he'd seen one of his missing daughters at the ball, he finally caved.

With a sigh, Leo shrugged off his jacket. Mad or not, the king would catch his death of cold if he stayed out in the rain much longer.

Taking in a breath, Leo plunged into the rain. The freezing drops slammed into his back with surprising force. A shiver snaked across his skin and he shielded his face with his arm. Wrapping an arm around Raoul's shoulders, he steered the king toward the door.

"No," he gasped. "No, I must find them! I must find them before it's too late!"

Leo's stomach clenched and he shouted over the wind. "We'll find them, don't worry! But we must get out of this rain!"

Raoul struggled in Leo's grip, but Leo wouldn't let go. He gripped the king's soaked shirt and dragged him toward the door. As they neared, something about the ground seemed to shift. Leo stumbled and Raoul fell to his knees. Leo's hands slapped against the wet stones, sending up a splash of water.

Beneath his fingers, the stones warmed. His vision dimmed. Something inside him shrank, leaving behind an empty, gaping hole. All the energy in his limbs weakened, and Leo collapsed against the ground. A chant rose, a thousand whispers that filled Leo's mind.

Dance. Dance. Dance.

A shiver spread through Leo's arms and up into his back. He jerked away from the ground, but the tingling sensation remained. To his horror, his hands began to *glow*.

"Your Highness!"

Leo looked up to see Jack dashing out into the rain, a cloak thrown over his uniform. Splashing through the puddles, he came to King Raoul's side. Together, Leo and Jack helped Raoul to his feet, Leo careful to keep his hands out of Jack's line of sight.

"Are you alright, my lord?" Jack shouted to Leo over the pounding rain.

"Yes," Leo said hurriedly. "Take him inside. I'll be right behind you."

Jack nodded and helped Raoul back across the courtyard. Leo followed at a slower pace. He pulled one hand from behind his back, almost too afraid to look. His skin was back to its normal pale coloring. No glow. No shimmer of light.

Leo released a breath and examined his hands. Had he just imagined it? Or had he really been glowing?

Shaking his head, Leo jogged to catch up with Jack and Raoul. It was just a trick of the light. A flash of lightning in the corner of his eye. Nothing more.

When they entered the castle door, two servants stood waiting with blankets. They wrapped the wool blankets around Leo and Raoul while Jack shook water from his hair.

"What is going on here? Leo, why are you soaked?" Father's voice snapped over the now-muted thunder.

"Nothing, Father." Leo's voice shook. He cleared his throat and gripped the blanket tighter around his shoulders. "Jack, make sure His Majesty is properly seen after."

Jack bowed to Father, then led the Revayrian king down the hall. Father watched them leave.

"That mad king went out into the storm." It wasn't a question. Father's lip curled. "I should have known Raoul would crack."

"Father, try to be kind," Leo snapped.

Father's eyebrows rose and his cheeks reddened. "Kind? Why should I be kind to a man who would dare to marry a ... a ... *Faerie*!" He spat the word as if it tasted vile.

Leo rubbed his forehead. "Why are you so against the Fae and magic? Every time I ask, you never give me a full answer and I'm tired of it. It's ridiculous!"

"I don't have to explain my reasons to you." Father threw his hands in the air. "What was he doing out in the rain anyway? Catching fish?"

Leo's stomach churned at his patronizing tone. "He heard something. That's all."

"That man is going mad, and you're too blind to see it, Lionheart."

"Too blind? Too *blind*?" Leo couldn't believe this. "If anyone is blind, it's you, Father! All this time, King Raoul was telling the truth about what happened three years ago, and you would be sorry to not pay attention to what's happening here."

"What's happ—"

"Yes, what's happening. The Midnight King is very much alive and real, and he has kidnapped the princesses, as well as the queen of Revayr. Wouldn't you be heartbroken if something like that happened to me and I was the one—"

"Enough!" Father curled his hands into fists and marched closer to Leo until they stood eye to eye. "I don't want to hear anymore of this nonsense. I've tried to keep you away from their influence, but it seems all you want is to throw your lot in with *them*."

Leo glared back into his father's pale green eyes.

"You have a choice to make, Lionheart. Either you put this ridiculousness behind you and become the prince you are meant to be, or you can throw your lot in with them and bring shame upon us all."

Father's words hit Leo in the chest. Leo staggered back a step. Curled his hands into fists. Father wanted him to give up. To pretend that what happened three years ago never did. To act like Faye and Colette never even existed. Pain twisted his heart. He wanted Leo to hate magic, to hate the Fae. Why was his father this way? Why?

Leo clenched his jaw. There was no point in yelling at Father. He would never see reason. Would never look beyond his own prejudices to help someone in need. All because they had different blood. Like a good prince, he bowed his head and backed away.

"Forgive me, Father. I shouldn't have yelled like that. I let my emotions get the best of me. I never meant to say things that are untrue." The words were bitter on his tongue.

"You are forgiven, Leo." Father gripped Leo's shoulder, his fingers like a vice. "And as tonight is your crowning ceremony, you'd better clear your head of all this nonsense and folktales. Eura needs a king with a stable head on his shoulders, unlike other rulers who have proven themselves too unfit for the crown they bear."

With those words, Father turned and walked down the hall, shoulders stiff. Leo stood alone, shivering as a cold wind blew through the still-open door. He kicked it shut with the heel of his boot. The resounding boom did nothing to ease his anger as it slammed shut and swung back open.

Tonight, he would be named heir. Tonight, he would have to choose between saving the last of King Raoul's daughters, or finally become the prince Father always wanted him to be.

Leo's becoming tightened at the thought and his heart ached, as if it were being ripped apart. How could he possibly choose between them? How could he make that decision in good conscience?

He couldn't. Logic told him to forget these tales, and yet his heart whispered to keep going, keep looking. The only thing he could think to do was nothing. To sit back and watch as he let all the answers slip through his fingers and disappear. To let go of that girl. Of that naïve hope.

Leo pulled the crumpled note from his pocket. The rain snagged at the ink, making the words blur together and drip down the page like tears. A gust of wind blew past and tugged the paper from his numb fingers. He watched it fly across the courtyard, then turned and marched back into the castle. There was nothing he could do. Nothing that could undo what was already done.

Chapter Twenty-One – Faye

The rest of the day wore on longer than ever before. Faye found herself checking the clock above the mantel as often as Madame Leroux pulled out her pocket watch. Pathos' words rang in her head, over and over.

Your life for theirs. Your life for theirs. At least Pathos had agreed to give her time to say goodbye. Still, the thought didn't bring as much comfort as Faye hoped it would.

When Madame had called out for the girls to get ready, she almost cried in relief.

But now that she was standing in the ballroom of Prince Lionheart ap Owen for what would be the last time, she couldn't understand how she felt. Pathos was bound to appear at any moment and take her away before she could even say goodbye.

She clutched at her throat. Would it be better to stay away from Leo? Or was it really alright for her to speak to him one last time, before she left the upper world forever?

Faye watched as Leo paced the ballroom, a golden cape thrown about his shoulders. Just an hour ago he had been crowned prince. Faye and the others hadn't arrived soon enough to witness it.

The tables were filled with all sorts of delicacies as well as a variety of drinks. A cake almost as tall as she was set on the center table along the left wall. More than once, Faye had watched Leo drift over to the table and take a piece.

Music filled the room, light and exuberant. Faye paced in her corner, unable to join the others on the dance floor. She brushed her hands over her skirts. Over and over. The detestable, horrible, disgusting gold fabric ran like rippling water under her sweaty palms.

She bit her lip and searched the crowd for Madame Leroux. How much time had passed? An hour? Two? Or had it only been several minutes? Faye pressed her cold hands to her cheeks.

"Mademoiselle." Leo's soft voice sounded behind Faye and she jumped.

It took more effort than she cared to admit to turn around.

Leo stood before her, an extravagant lion mask covering the upper half of his face. He bowed low to her and held out his hand. When he straightened, there was a weight to his gaze, a certain kind of sadness. Faye would almost call it longing.

"May I have this dance?"

Faye choked on her reply. She couldn't do this. She couldn't involve Leo again, not after giving away her freedom for his. A sharp pang filled her heart. He would never know what she did to save him.

"My lady. Please." Desperation laced Leo's voice.

Faye's heart stuttered. She couldn't help herself. Taking in a shuddering breath, she nodded.

Leo led her to the dance floor, where the crowds cleared the way, forming a circle around them. Faye trembled as she stood in his arms, waiting for the music to begin. Then, with slow, quiet strings, they danced.

Faye's shoes clinked softly against the wood, and Leo's movements were gentle. Faye could almost imagine that the past three years were but a dream, that everything that had happened was all just a nightmare. She closed her eyes and took in this moment, this time in Leo's arms. The last few minutes they would ever have together.

When Leo came to visit her kingdom, everything in Faye's life changed. Pathos no longer haunted her steps. No longer filled her mind. Leo showed her a whole new perspective on life and made her feel alive. His vibrant, outgoing personality was like a light amidst the darkness. Nighttime garden walks were filled with talks of a bright future where half-bloods like her would be accepted in his kingdom. They had grown closer and closer together until one night he had asked her to meet him in the garden.

Faye had waited until midnight. Leo never came. The next morning, she discovered that he had left in the middle of the night. He had abandoned her, right when Faye had thought her life would finally change for the better.

The thought jarred her out of her reverie. She opened her eyes. This wasn't right. None of it was. Leo no longer loved her. He never had. She was holding on to the thread of a memory she should have let go the moment he left without a goodbye. And yet, Faye couldn't find it within herself to release the warmth that filled her chest with his every smile, every laugh.

But Leo wasn't smiling now. Nor was he laughing. Instead, his lips were pressed into a flat line and his eyes were focused a million miles away. Cold crept into the hollow space in her chest.

A tear escaped down her cheek and she turned her head, hoping to hide it before Leo could notice. But he did notice. He brought their dance to a halt and stroked the tear away.

"Please, why are you crying?" His words were gentle, his voice strained.

Faye looked up at him, and suddenly she wanted to tell him everything. About the curse, about Pathos, about the Midnight King ... about her love for him. It burned inside her like a flame—a flame she never wanted to wither or die.

She opened her mouth to speak, but she couldn't. Not because of the curse. No, this time it was because the words were stuck in her throat. It was ironic. After being trapped in a curse to keep her from speaking of Pathos to Leo, now that she was free of it, she didn't even have the courage to whisper Pathos' name.

Another tear escaped. Faye stepped away and curtsied low.

"I'm sorry," she choked. "But I ..."

Turning, she fled into the crowd, dodging between swaying skirts and flying coattails. When she looked back, she saw that he didn't chase her this time. He stood in the middle of the dance floor, hands reaching out. And somehow, that was even worse than if he had pursued her.

"You made the right choice."

The cold in Faye's chest deepened, skirting down into her bones. She looked up at the clock that hung above the ballroom door. The hour hand ticked closer and closer to midnight.

Pathos stepped up next to her. His crisp suit and polished mask told Faye that he had dressed up for the occasion. A blood-red cape with a high collar was draped about his shoulders and a gold chain kept the cape in place. He reached out with a gloved hand.

"Come, Faye. It is time for us to dance."

Faye placed her hand in his and let him lead her across the floor in a fast-paced dance. He stalked around her with each step, looming over her like a wolf over his prey. Or an angel over his ward. Faye couldn't tell which Pathos was anymore. She spun around him, her deep-gold skirts tangling around her legs. She stamped her feet, feeling the pain jar up her legs. She spun until she grew dizzy. Tilting her head up, she danced until she was drowning amidst a sea of faces.

Dance after dance, he led her across the floor, never letting her too far out of his reach. Leo danced with Delphine several times, and once, he tried to dance close enough to speak. But Pathos whirled her away. Faye caught Delphine's eye. Her eyes were wide with fear as she stared at Pathos.

When the musicians paused to rest, Pathos finally let her go. Faye stumbled backwards, then righted herself. She drew herself up as tall as she could, even as a heavy weight pressed against her shoulders. These were her final hours above ground. She wouldn't let those final hours be weighed down by fear.

Pathos left Faye's side, disappearing into the crowd. Faye watched him leave. Never had she felt so alone as this moment.

A clock chimed the hour. *Eleven*. Faye's heart fluttered. Only one hour left. One hour until she left this world and paid her debt.

"Excuse me, mademoiselle. May I speak with you?" The voice was deep. Gentle. A voice that Faye knew all too well.

Faye froze, not daring to believe. If she turned around, he might disappear, and it might all have been a dream. But if she didn't turn around, he might leave, and she would never be able to see if it were true. If her father really was here.

With tears stinging her eyes, Faye turned. And met the deep, deep brown eyes of her father, shaded by a simple black mask.

"Papa?" It was just a whisper. A quiet, desperate whisper.

"Faye."

Her name. *He said my name!* He knew exactly who she was. Faye reached out with a trembling hand. He took it in his own. Rough, dry palms. Warm fingers. He was real. Faye let out a desperate cry. He was very, very real.

With a suppressed sob, Papa pulled Faye into his arms. She melted against him, soaking in his warmth, his smell, his steady heartbeat. Everything about him was just as she remembered, only he was a little shorter. Or she was a little taller. Whichever it was, Faye didn't care. The overwhelming scents of tobacco and cologne, the smells of her childhood, filled her nose and Faye breathed in deep.

She trembled so hard she feared she would fall to the floor. Papa's arms tightened around her, and he placed a whiskery kiss on her forehead.

"I knew you were alive. I knew you were. Oh, my sweet, sweet girl!" Hot tears splashed onto Faye's hair as he spoke.

Faye felt tears of her own soaking her cheeks.

"Papa," she cried. "Papa, I love you! I love you. I love you."

"I know. I love you, *ma belle*. I love you too."

Burying her face in his chest, Faye dragged in deep, shuddering breaths as she sobbed. For a moment, Faye was seized with fear. Finally, she had been reunited with her father. Finally, she was here in Papa's arms, something she never thought would ever happen again. This moment, this tiny pocket of time, was all she had left.

What if she stayed? What if she pulled off her slippers right here, right now, and smashed them on the ballroom floor?

Faye bit the inside of her cheek. She stiffened her muscles to keep from shaking. No. If she stayed, *she* would become the monster. She would have her father, but she would have lost her world.

Pulling back, she brushed the tears from her cheeks. Her hand knocked against the butterfly mask she wore.

"Papa, I have to go." She gripped his arms tight, digging the memory of his clothes into her skin. "I have to leave. For Mama and Colette and Desi and Adalie and the others, I have to go but I don't want to say goodbye. I don't want to say goodbye!"

"I don't understand." Papa cupped her face in his hands. "Why do you have to leave? Where are your sisters? Your mother? Are they safe?"

"No!" Faye ripped from his grasp, even as her heart broke to do it. "No one's safe. But I can't tell you more. There's no time. I'm sorry, Papa. I'm so sorry."

Papa rubbed a hand along his chin, ruffling the close-cropped beard that lined his jaw. "Faye ... don't leave."

A hand landed on Faye's shoulder. She looked up to see Pathos standing beside her. All the color drained from Papa's face and he stumbled back.

"You ..." he began.

"Yes." Pathos' voice was flat. "Me." He turned to Faye. "Come, Faye. It's time to say goodbye."

Faye turned to Papa and drank in the sight of him one last time. The way his brown-and-grey hair shone in the light. His heart-shaped face she had inherited. The way his lips curved up at the ends. Lips that had kissed scraped knees and whispered stories. His broad shoulders and gentle hands. Hands that had wiped away tears and cradled her, keeping her safe.

Pathos steered her away, toward the doors of the ballroom. Faye kept her eyes locked on Papa until he was swallowed by the dancers. When they had reached the doors, Pathos pulled Faye aside, into the shadows. He reached out and stroked her cheek with the backs of his fingers, just beneath her mask.

"I'm sorry. But I couldn't let you get attached. Then you would never leave, and your sisters would be trapped."

Faye nodded and wiped away the last of her tears. "I know."

Pathos watched her, something strange in his dark eyes. "Do you love me, Faye?" he asked in a quiet voice.

The question caught her off guard. She stared up at the wolf mask, unsure of what to say. She didn't hate him. She never could. But love? It was a strong word.

Faye let her gaze rove over the crowd. She caught sight of Leo. He was standing alone in the opposite corner, watching her. She wasn't even sure what love was anymore.

Pathos stiffened, as if sensing her thoughts. Hurt shone in his dark eyes. "You still love him."

"No." Faye shook her head. "No, not anymore."

"All these years, and I thought you'd moved on."

"Pathos—"

"Go to him."

Faye's protest died on her lips. She stared at Pathos, unable to speak. Unable to think.

"Go to him." His voice was raw. "Say your goodbyes. Then come straight to me."

Faye hesitated. She waited for him to tell her that it was all a joke. For him to drag her away. Instead, he stepped back and gestured toward Leo. Leo, who stood waiting for her. Leo, whom she had once vowed to never speak to again. Yet she found her heart succumbing to what once was, hoping for something that could have been.

Lifting her skirts, Faye ran across the room. Leo raced to meet her. She pushed between women in wide dresses and men with leering masks. She struggled past a laughing matron holding a cup she was close to spilling, past a large gentleman bending to pick up a lady's handkerchief, past two girls giggling as they whispered behind their fans.

They finally met, breathless, before the wide double doors. Leo looked down at her, grey eyes shining behind his mask. He reached out as if to touch her, then dropped his hand. Faye's chest tightened with desperation. She had so many things to say, so many things to confess. If only this were not their last goodbye.

"Come with me," he said in a low voice.

Placing her hand on his elbow, she watched as he signaled for the orchestra to start playing once more. Then he led her to large glass doors on the side of the room that led out onto a balcony.

Cold wind blew across her neck and arms, making her shiver. The moon hung heavy and full high in the sky, surrounded by a field of stars that winked in the inky blackness. Faye let go of Leo's arm and leaned against the railing, right next to a trellis of roses. She sighed as a wind blew through her hair. She soaked in the sight of the moon, wanting to print it into her memory forever.

"It's beautiful," she said softly.

Leo came up to her side and leaned against the balcony. He nodded as the wind tossed his short hair across his forehead. "Indeed it is, Faye."

Faye gasped and reached up to her mask. It was still in place. How could he know? She stumbled backwards into the trellis. Rose thorns pricked into her back. Leo grabbed her elbow and steadied her before she could fall.

"H-how ... when ...?" Her heart was beating so loudly that she could hardly hear the music flowing through the open doors.

Carefully, Leo grasped the edge of her mask and lifted it. Faye wanted to raise her hands, to cover her face, but she couldn't. He pulled in a gasp, his eyes searching, taking in every detail of her.

Tears slipped down her cheeks as she stared up at him, her heart aching. "How did you find out?"

Leo tucked a strand of loose hair behind her ear, letting his fingertips brush her cheek. A smile tugged at his lips. "I saw you hugging your father. It was then that I knew, you had to be Faye de la Rou, the missing princess of Revayr."

"Oh, Leo," she choked.

Unable to get any more words past her throat, she buried her face in her palms. He must hate her. He should hate her. She hadn't told him anything, all this time. Everyone thought her dead, and yet here she was, before the man who had once whispered in her ear that he would stand by her forever.

Warm arms wrapped around her and pulled her close. Faye curled her arms into herself. No. This was wrong. All of it was wrong. He shouldn't be hugging her. He should be casting her aside like he had done three years ago. She was a half-blood. A monster.

Faye wrestled from his grasp and threw herself against the balcony railing. She leaned over and looked down at the courtyard below, pulling in deep gasps of air.

"No," she whispered. "No, this isn't right."

"What isn't right? Faye, I know what's happened. It was the Midnight King. He cursed you and your sisters. He took you away from your family. Don't you want to be free?"

Faye bit back a cry as pain twisted in her chest.

"You don't understand." She shook her head as tears spilled down her cheeks.

"What don't I understand?" Leo leaned against the railing. Concern filled his gentle gaze.

"Don't you see?" she growled with savage ferocity. "*I* was the one who cursed my sisters! *I* was the one who dragged them down into the dark and trapped them forever. It wasn't the Midnight King. It wasn't Pathos. It was *me!*"

Leo was silent. He stared at her—expression unreadable. Faye waited for him to push her away in disgust. To tell her that she got what she deserved.

Instead, Leo took her back into his arms. He held her close, resting his chin on her hair.

"That's a lie. Don't believe that for one second. It was the Midnight King who did this to you and your family." He sighed. "I love you, Faye."

Pain, sharp and swift, filled her chest. Leo was blind to the truth. If he really knew what she'd done, if he knew who she really was on the inside, then he wouldn't be standing here, looking at her with unadulterated love. And that hurt more than him abandoning her ever had.

The horrible irony of the moment twisted like a knife to Faye's gut. If she hadn't changed the deal, if she had kept up her hopes, then she and her sisters would be free. They would all be free to return home. Every one of her sisters, her mother, the courtiers.

But now, they would get to go home, and Faye would be trapped in the Underworld. Alone. Forgotten.

Just as you deserve, she snarled at herself.

Once again, Faye jerked from his hold. She turned her back on Leo and covered her face with her hands. In the distance, a clock chimed. Faye pulled in a breath as the magic tugged at her spine. She turned and looked Leo in the eye.

"Listen," she said, her words rushed. "I need to say something before it's too late."

"Faye —" he started.

"Just listen!" She dashed the tears from her cheeks and pulled at the last of her courage. "This is my last goodbye, Leo. I can't tell you where I am going, or what is going to happen, but this is the end for me. Soon, I'll no longer be free, and I will no longer be able to see you, or anyone, again." Faye swallowed and more hot tears touched her cheeks. "You have been the brightest spot in my life. You always made me feel warm inside. You ..." she choked, then pressed on. She had to say it. She couldn't leave him without him knowing.

"You showed me what it means to live." She stepped closer, until they were almost nose to nose. She lowered her voice to a whisper. "I love you, my dear Lionheart."

Reaching up on her toes, Faye kissed him. It was a gentle, soft kiss, just a brush of the lips. For that split second, she hoped the moment would never end. And deep down, a part of her could almost believe everything would turn out for the better.

She pulled away, out of his arms, and fled the balcony.

Pathos stood waiting for her by the balcony doors. He said nothing about her missing mask, nor about the kiss. Instead, he held out his arm. Without a word, she slipped her arm into his. Together, they left the ballroom behind.

Pathos led her through the halls at a run. His grip on her wrist was tight, and her shoes threatened to slip from her feet. Heart pounding in her throat, Faye struggled to keep up.

Turning, he took a flight of stairs and brought them to a stop in what looked like an empty sitting room. Pathos pushed her toward the fireplace.

"Get in!" he barked.

Faye fell to her knees and she pushed through the flames. The warmth scorched her cheeks. Her right foot slipped on a charred log and the slipper dropped into the ash as she pushed the back of the fireplace open. She reached for it.

"Leave it." Pathos whirled toward the door.

Shouts came from outside. Her papa's strained voice. Leo's desperate cries. Faye looked back, heart pounding in her ears. If she could see them just once before—

"Do you want them to be trapped with everyone else?" Pathos' voice was thick with desperation. "Get in! Now!"

Struggling through the flames, Faye pushed herself into the tunnel that led to her Underworld tomb.

Chapter Twenty-Two – Leo

Leo watched as Faye ran out the balcony doors. He should run after her. Tell her that he loved her. But he stood frozen to the ground, unable to move. For so long, he'd thought Faye to be dead. And yet, she was right there. Alive. Breathing. Crying.

Trapped. All this time she had been right in front of him and he'd been too blind to see it. And before he found the courage to speak, she was gone.

And when they kissed … everything inside Leo tingled, but at the same time, the moment his lips touched hers, it was as if his life was sucked from his body.

An empty place in his chest grew, caving into his ribcage. The fatigue that had gnawed at Leo all night grew, and the world tilted. He threw out a hand to balance himself. This was getting ridiculous.

"Blast it all," he muttered under his breath.

Gathering his courage, Leo bolted for the balcony doors. Once back in the ballroom, he searched the crowd. Faye and the masked man were nowhere to be seen. Instead, Leo spied King Raoul stumbling toward the ballroom doors, clearly distressed by the way his shoulders slumped and his mouth hung open. Leo caught up with him.

"They've gone out of the ballroom, haven't they?" Leo asked.

Raoul nodded, his face pale and his eyes red. He firmed his jaw. "I'll gut that monster."

Leo cracked his knuckles. "We'll have to catch him first."

Together, they ran for the doors.

Jack met them outside. The guard jogged to keep up with Leo's pace and pointed up one of the grand staircases.

"They went that way!"

Leo took the stairs two at a time, heart pounding hard against his ribs. His feet beat against the polished stone floors, keeping in time with a single thought that circled through his head. *Don't let her go. Don't let her go.*

The last time, he had been the one to walk away. Last time, he had whispered promises only to break her heart.

This time would be different. This time, he would stop her. He would tell her how much he loved her, how he had never meant to leave, how if he could turn back time, he would have done it differently. How he would at least have said goodbye.

Everywhere Leo looked, the halls were empty.

"Faye!" Raoul shouted, his voice strained with desperation. "Faye!"

"Faye!" Leo joined him, hoping beyond hope that he would hear a reply.

Since she had followed the masked man willingly, there was a good chance she wouldn't respond to their cries. Still, he shouted until his throat was raw. Shouted until he was sure his voice traveled throughout the entire castle.

Jack sprinted ahead and paused at a fork in the hall. "I suggest we split up, Your Highness."

Leo slowed to a halt next to Jack. "Right. You go that way." He pointed to the right. "I'll check the left."

Raoul turned and looked back, his chest heaving with each labored breath. "I'll check the rooms here."

Nodding, Leo rushed down the left hall. Frustration mounted as, with each door he pushed open, the room beyond was empty. When he reached the end of the hall, he found the last door already open. Leo leaned inside—his movements cautious. Nothing but a fireplace.

Something glinted in the firelight. Leo squinted. It was … a slipper? A glass slipper. Leo's heart jolted. He darted forward and landed hard on his knees. Scooping up the shoe, he glanced at the roaring fire. It was the only room with a lit fire. Did that mean something?

He reached out toward the flames. The fire hissed and crackled, and the heat dug into his palm. Hissing, he jerked back.

He waited for a sign, for something that would tell him where they went. A small part of him searched for the taste of magic. Leo almost laughed at the thought. What would Father say, knowing that Leo could somehow sense magic? He could hear him now. *The crown prince of Eura does* not *sense magic!*

But the prince of Eura was many things his father hated.

Gripping the slipper in his fist, Leo stood. He searched the room carefully, picking up the pillows off plush chairs, feeling the shelves of the bookcase against the wall, and lifting the corners of the worn blue rug.

"Looking for something?"

Leo froze at the sound of the voice. It was unfamiliar, and yet, he had heard it before. Slowly, Leo turned. The masked man stood in the doorway of the room. The firelight played along the grooves of his wolf mask, deepening the red of his cape, making him look like a creature from a night tale. Leo gripped the slipper tight, the only weapon he had in reach.

"Where is Faye?" he barked.

The man cocked his head. "Why do you care what happens to a half-breed?"

"I'm not my father." Leo moved one step closer. "Where is she? What have you done with her?"

"Done? I have done nothing." The man seemed to float as he entered the room. "She made the choice to leave you. I gave her the opportunity to stay."

Leo lifted the shoe as he stalked closer, ready to break it and use the shards to carve the man into pieces. He grabbed the man's collar and jerked him close.

"Where is she?" he roared.

The man didn't flinch. "Break that shoe and you'll sever all ties Faye has to this world."

Leo dropped his arm and stepped back, the anger roaring through him twisting with fear.

Straightening his jacket, the man puffed out his chest. "You want to find her? Go to the disgraced Countess Leroux. When you find her, ask her how her husband and son died. She will tell you everything you need to know, my lord."

Giving Leo a mock bow, the man pushed past Leo and made his way to the fireplace. Leo grabbed for him, but the man was too quick. He slipped from Leo's grasp and plunged into the flames.

Leo staggered back in horror. The flames leaped high, threatening to escape the fireplace. After several moments, they disappeared, as if a wind had blown in and snuffed them out, leaving behind nothing but glowing embers.

∽

The next morning, King Raoul could not be consoled. He paced the castle, shouting for someone, anyone, to find his daughter. Scrambling to obey, his men rode out the castle gates.

Father had exploded when he heard what Raoul was up to. Leo skipped breakfast and headed to the stables with Jack to avoid his father's temper. Mounting his grey gelding, he rode out into the city with Raoul's men.

It was all a waste of time. Leo had told Raoul last night of the masked man's words, but Raoul refused to believe it. Leo shook his head as he rode at a fast trot. He wouldn't question the methods of a man driven mad with grief and desperation. Instead, he needed to focus on finding out who this elusive Countess Leroux was.

Whenever he reached a group of women, he would slow and ask them if they knew a Countess Leroux. Most would become petrified and bob curtsies. Others would titter and whisper together. The less enchanted would simply tell him no and continue on their way.

Beside Leo, Jack shook his head. "We need a better way of finding this woman. Do you know anything else about her? Anything at all?"

Leo shook his head. "Nothing. All the man said was to ask her how her husband and son died."

Jack grimaced. "Not the most pleasant subject."

Leo spied a group of maids making their way to the market. He steered his horse toward them and jumped from the saddle.

"Excuse me!" he called.

The girls turned and gasped. They all bobbed curtsies and kept their gazes on the ground.

"Do any of you know a Countess Leroux?"

Confusion flashed over the faces and Leo sighed. Yet another miss. He was about to turn away when a girl with blond braids pushed through the crowd. She squinted at Leo with suspicion in her sharp eyes.

"I know a Madame Leroux. What do you want with her?"

Excitement buzzed through Leo's veins. "Tell me, my lady, where I can find her, and I will pay you handsomely."

The girl blushed. "Begging your pardon, prince, but I'm not so poor as to want to tell you about my friend for gold. I don't trust no man who goes around asking what about Madame Leroux and her family, Your Highness, sir, if you know what I mean." She shifted, looking uncomfortable.

Leo nodded, even though her speech was somewhat confusing. "I understand, miss. I can assure you I am no dastard. I simply wish to speak to her about an urgent matter."

The maid scrutinized him for several moments, then nodded, as if confirming that he was true to his word. She pointed up the street. "Just go up that road yonder and take a left at the cheese seller's stall. When you reach the manors and houses of them rich folk, look for a cottage with a row of sunflowers by a green door. It's not easy to miss. That's where she lives."

"Thank you, so very much. You have done your prince a great service." Leo pulled several gold coins from his pocket and dropped them into the woman's hand.

She curtsied her eyes wide. "Lights bless you, Your Highness, sir!"

Giving her a nod, Leo jumped up into the saddle and urged his horse into a fast trot toward the lower town, with Jack following close behind.

As he rode, Leo caught a glimpse of a man hefting a giant wheel of cheese into the back of a cart. Just beyond him was a street that led out of the market. Leo steered his horse to the left, leaving the market behind.

Manors with picket fences and lush gardens sprawled out before Leo. With any luck, this countess or whatever she was would be close by.

With a snort, his horse threw its head back and came to a clattering stop. Leo leaned forward, clutching its mane to keep from falling. *What in blazes?*

"Come on, Ghost." Leo rubbed his horse's neck. "I've got to find Madame Leroux."

"Are you looking for me, my prince?"

Leo startled and looked down. A woman dressed in dark-green silk stood in the road, her hand raised as if to stop him. Her other hand rested on a panther-headed walking stick. Next to Leo's horse, her skin was almost as dark as the night sky.

Dismounting, Leo gave her a small bow. When he looked up, he was startled by how catlike her eyes were. They were a pale, glowing green with slitted pupils. She pinned him with that predatory stare, eyes narrowed.

Leo swallowed. "Are you Countess Leroux?"

The woman lifted one perfect black brow. "I am."

"I was told by a man in a wolf mask to ask you a question. One that would help me find Princess Faye de la Rou."

Madame Leroux closed her eyes and leaned against her cane. She let out a breath, then looked back up at Leo. "And what is your question?"

Leo was almost afraid to say it. He dropped his gaze to his boots. "How did your husband and son die?"

All emotion left her face and she straightened. "Follow me."

Turning, Madame Leroux started off across the street at a slow pace, leaning heavily against her walking stick. Leo watched her with some trepidation. For all he knew, she could be an Enchantress. His heart leapt at the thought. Could she, perhaps, be the descendant of the White Lady?

Jack came to Leo's side and nodded to the woman before them.

"Is that her?"

"It is." Leo watched her take small, shuffling steps. "She seems weak, and yet at the same time, I wouldn't want to cross her."

Jack nodded, then squinted. "Whoever she is, be cautious. If that masked man told you to find her, they could be in league."

Nodding, Leo started after her. He wasn't entirely sure if this woman could be in league with the Midnight King, but he still couldn't deny the … *unhumanness* of her. While he wasn't about to put his full trust in her, she was the only lead he had.

She passed through a gate into the yard of a small stone house that was decorated with a row of brilliant yellow sunflowers along the walls and a green door, just as the maid had said. The same house, Leo realized, at which he had first seen Faye.

It seemed so long ago now. Now that the pieces were coming together in Leo's mind, he felt like a colossal idiot. How did he not see it? How had he not noticed when she had been looking right at him, laundry spilled at her feet?

Because you weren't looking, Leo thought to himself. Not really.

Madame Leroux looked back at him and gave him a sad smile. "Faye did most of the gardening. She loves flowers."

Leo's heart leapt into his throat. "S-she is very skilled, madame."

Madame Leroux nodded. "Yes. Yes, she is."

She pushed the door open as Leo and Jack tied their horses to the gate. They followed her inside and Leo paused in the doorway to take it in.

The house was small, the inside made of dark wood. Shelves lined the walls of the sitting room, and an open doorway led to the kitchen. A clock hung on the wall above the fireplace next to a painting of Madame Leroux's family. Leo noted the handsome man with light-brown skin and a warm smile who stood next to a much younger-looking Madame Leroux, her eyes alight with pride. Two girls and a young boy, all of which were an even mix of their parents, were framed between their parents. Both the older girl and the boy had their mother's unsettling eyes.

While the furnishings were extravagant, fit only for someone of rank, they were well worn, giving the home a cozy feel. A heavy wool blanket was draped over the back of a dark-green couch. No doubt Madame Leroux brought most of these items from Revayr with her.

"Please, sit anywhere you like." Madame Leroux disappeared into the kitchen.

Leo and Jack shared a look. Jack positioned himself next to the fireplace while Leo took the stuffed chair next to the nearby. A small, framed painting sat on the mantel next to a vase of flowers. Leo stood once more and reached out to pick it up.

"Tea?"

Leo startled and shoved his hands into his trouser pockets. He took them out again when Jack raised his eyebrows. "Yes, thank you."

Madame Leroux cocked her head as steam rose from the teapot she held. Once more, her piercing eyes bored into his. "Please, sit."

Leo sat in the chair once again. Carefully, she made her way across the room and poured tea into tiny china teacups. Picking up a cup by its saucer, she held it out to Leo.

"Now, before we begin, I must tell you where I come from." She looked him in the eye. "Pandalia."

Leo choked on his tea. "Pan-what?"

"Pandalia, for I am a Faerie."

Leo caught his teacup just before it went crashing down onto the hearth. Jack took a step forward, his hand on his sword. Cold filled Leo's stomach.

"If my father found out …"

Madame Leroux batted her thick eyelashes. "You wouldn't tell on a poor, harmless woman, would you?"

"But … Fae … you're dangerous."

She smiled, showing pointed teeth. "My dear boy, anyone can be a danger to someone else. It's all about how you choose to act." She straightened and cleared her throat. "Now, I have a question of my own. What do you know about Faye and the Midnight King?"

Leo curled his hands into fists. "I know everything. How he cursed her and her sisters and lured her away. But what I don't understand is why. Or where she is."

Madame lifted her chin. "Then you know about the slippers."

"The slippers? What …" He glanced at Jack, then remembered.

The glass slipper he had picked up from the fireplace. It was resting in his saddlebag. Leo resisted the urge to run out and grab it.

Madame's lips curled in a smug smile. "I see. So, you don't know everything." She sipped her tea, watching him over the rim.

Leo shuddered. He was glad that Jack was in the room. Otherwise, Leo would have felt completely defenseless against this infuriating Faerie. While he didn't think all magicfolk evil as his father did, Leo knew enough to be cautious. This Faerie wasn't the friendly, warm type like Queen Arjean.

"Tell me about the slippers."

Madame Leroux leaned forward. "Before I tell you anything, I want you to promise me something, Prince Lionheart."

"And what is that?" Leo gripped the armrests of the chair, ready to leave this blasted house at a moment's notice.

"Promise me that if I help you find your princess, that you will set things right for the Fae. That you will let us live in peace, without fear of death or imprisonment. Do this for us, and I will help you."

Leo stared at the woman. What could he say to that? He wasn't the king of Eura. He was only the crown prince. He couldn't change the rules. He couldn't break down years of hatred and spite and anger. It was impossible. He had been begging for his father to acknowledge the Fae for years with no results.

"I can't promise that."

Madame Leroux's gaze turned hard and she stood. "Then you have no business being here." She shuffled toward the door, cane pounding against the wood floor.

Leo jumped to his feet. "Wait! You still haven't answered my question about your husband and son."

The Faerie froze. Leo's heart pounded in his ears.

Madame Leroux looked back over her shoulder. "My husband and son were murdered by a madman who tried to steal my daughters," she growled. "But instead of fighting for justice, my king threw me from my own country and shunned me from his court."

Something about her story seemed familiar. Something he couldn't quite place.

Jack emerged from the shadows of the fireplace. He stared at the Faerie with wide eyes.

"You're Aurore. The Faerie who was accused of murdering her family and banished from Revayr. King Raoul never heard your pleas for help, because the Grand Duke banished you before you could reach him."

Leo raised his eyebrows at Jack, surprised. He shrugged in return.

Madame frowned and hunched her shoulders. "Yes. That's right. But that doesn't change anything. If you aren't willing to help my kind, then I don't see why I should bother helping you."

She reached for the door handle. Leo took a step forward and held out his hand as if to stop her. Pulling in a breath through his nose, Leo clenched his jaw. He would give the Faerie what she wanted. A promise. That was all he could give.

"Wait."

Aurore curled her fingers into a fist.

"I promise. I promise to fight for the Fae for however long it takes. I can't promise to change the rules, as I am not the one who wears the crown. My father is adamant in his decisions. But I can promise to fight for the law to change."

She spun toward him, expression fierce. "You swear this?"

Leo closed his eyes. If he agreed to this, he would be turning his back on everything his father believed in. But really, would that be so wrong? Father wanted all magicfolk dead. While he never expressly said those words, Leo knew it to be true. The hangings. The ridicule. The banishments. The wings nailed as trophies to the city walls. He'd known for years that what he did was wrong. While Father could turn a blind eye, Leo could not. With a firm jaw, he opened his eyes and nodded.

"I swear."

Aurore's full lips turned up in not-so-wicked smile. "The slippers are the key. Break them, and the princesses will be free."

Leo frowned. He looked to Jack. Then back at Aurore. "You mean to tell me that all this time, Faye could have broken the slippers and been free?"

"Yes. But I suspect she had her reasons for staying. After all, she does have eleven sisters, and who knows what the Midnight King's done to them."

A sinking feeling filled Leo's gut. "Give a prisoner one key to their own shackles, and if they love a fellow prisoner enough, they'll stay chained."

"Exactly." Aurore winced as she sat on the couch. "But I suspect the slippers are also what lets you into the Underworld. Faye wore them each night we went to the masquerade balls. She tried to hide them, but I noticed. No one would wear them willingly unless they had no other choice."

Leo turned to Jack. "Get the shoe."

Jack nodded. "Right away, Your Highness."

He crossed the room in three quick strides. When the door closed behind him, Leo turned back to Aurore.

"So, all I have to do is put on the shoe and it will take me to the Underworld?" Leo grimaced at the thought. Would he even be able to put the shoe on? His feet weren't exactly small.

Aurore shrugged. "I have no idea. I wouldn't advise wearing it, though. That was what got the princesses in this mess in the first place. However, if you're going to seek out the Underworld, you'll need protection."

"What kind of protection?" Leo squinted his eyes. She wasn't going to cast some kind of magic on him, was she?

She held up a hand. "Wait here a moment." Turning, she limped away into the recesses of the house.

For a moment, Leo tapped his fingers against the end table. To think, he'd be going down to the Underworld. The legendary world of horrors itself. But as his mind began to run wild with possibilities, the familiar tapping of Aurore's cane returned.

"Here we are," Aurore said, coming back into the room. She held a drape of fabric across her arm. "This is my cloak, so it might be a bit small, but if we …" She trailed off as she held the shimmering black fabric up and shook it. The hem lengthened until it trailed on the floor.

"There we are." She held it out.

Leo took it and threw it about his shoulders. It sat uncomfortably tight across his back. Madame Leroux hummed and brushed her fingers across the shoulders. The cloak widened until it settled into a better position, and the hem lengthened again.

She nodded and stepped back. "There. That should do it."

Leo frowned. "What do I need a cloak for?"

She smiled. "It makes you invisible. That way you can sneak in."

"Oh. I see." Leo didn't see. But he was grateful for the gift, nonetheless.

Madame Leroux reached into her belt and pulled out a dagger, wrapped in a thick scabbard. She held it out. "You'll also need this. It's a relic I picked up on my search to avenge my husband's and son's deaths."

Taking it, Leo spun it between his hands. The pommel was adorned with carvings, but no gems. He pulled the blade out an inch. The whole thing was made of gold, except for the leather wrap around the grip.

"A gold dagger?"

Aurore flashed sharp teeth. "Gold is the only thing that can kill the Midnight King."

Leo snapped the blade back into the scabbard and tied the straps around his waist. Then, the door opened, and Jack rushed inside with the slipper. Gingerly, Leo took the slipper from Jack, turning to Aurore. "What do I do now?"

Aurore removed a small gold pocket watch from her pocket. Its tiny hands ticked quietly in the room, joining the louder clock hanging on the wall. She eyed it a moment, then snapped it shut. "Now, you wait."

Chapter Twenty-Three – Faye

Faye yanked off her glass slipper as she ran, and held it high over her head, ready to smash it into the steps. All of the anger building inside her dulled, twisting into something else. Something colder, darker.

She paused, then lowered her arm. It wouldn't do to break it in a fit of anger.

Looking back, Faye waited for Pathos to appear. He had been right behind her, but now he was nowhere to be seen. She sat and leaned against the wall and its painting of golden trees. Closing her eyes, she took a moment to breathe. A moment to still her rapidly beating heart and the nervous energy that surged through her limbs.

Everything trembled. Faye dug her hands into her hair and leaned forward, gasping for each lungful of air. Each one was stuttering, stilted. Her knees pressed painfully into her ribcage. This was it. This was the last time she would walk down these steps. The last time she would see these trees.

What would she do once her sisters were gone, and she was trapped here, forever? The thought shot a spike of fear through her that stole her breath away. In only a few hours, she would be separated from her family, from her sisters, locked in an eternal tomb.

I will save my sisters. My mother, she thought firmly. She was doing this for Colette, Desi, and Adalie. For Estelle, Genevieve, Kamille, and Linette. For Helaine, Jenine, Margaux, and Belle. For all of her sisters that she had dragged down into the dark three years ago. It was time that they were set free. Time that they got to live the lives they deserved.

Boots pounded on the steps and Faye bolted to her feet. Pathos clattered to a stop beside her. He was breathing hard, and his cape swirled around him like a herald of death. Its crimson color took on a blood-red hue in the darkened stairwell. He paused, staring at the shoe resting on the step where she had dropped it.

A heavy silence cloaked them. Pathos bent and picked up the slipper. He held it out to her, shoulders hunched. Faye dropped her gaze and took the shoe. The glass was cold in her grip.

"So, what now?" Faye asked, her throat tight.

Pathos stepped down so that they were at eye level. "Now is the time that you choose, my lady."

He reached out and brushed a loose strand of hair behind her ear. Gentle. Cold.

"The only way for you to truly begin to live is to cast off your half-blood. You can become an Undead. Painless. Perfect."

Perfect. A word that had always haunted Faye. She would never be perfect. Not in her half-blood mongrel state. Pathos was right. If she gave up her mongrel blood, if she embraced becoming an Undead, she would no longer have to feel the weight that pressed against her shoulders. Or the dagger constantly twisting her heart, knowing that she was leaving Leo behind. She could become free. Free of everything.

"But what about my sisters?"

"While you go through the ceremony of becoming an Undead, everyone will be distracted. I'll lead your sisters out. They'll go free."

Pathos wasn't giving her a choice. Still, it was a simple one. "Fine. But you better keep your word."

Pathos let out a sigh, as if a heavy weight had lifted from his shoulders. "You're making the right choice."

Faye knew she should feel happy. Relieved. But all she felt was a deep, aching pain lodged in her chest.

As she walked, the horrible gold ball gown shifted and changed. Color bled from the fabric until all that was left was a hint of gold among brilliant white, with a long silky train and layers of lace that shone gold in the light. Faye shuddered as a new pair of shoes surrounded her feet, made of pure diamond. She held out her hand as drops of diamond fell from one of the trees. They gathered to form a simple white colombina mask. With shaking fingers, she held it up to her face. It stuck to her skin, cold and heavy.

The magic pulled her on faster, and she raced down the steps through the gold, silver, and diamond forests, then on through the tunnel. Pathos followed at a slower pace.

When they reached the beach, Faye counted the boats. His five brothers stood in their usual row, waiting for her sisters. Pathos marched ahead, shoes crunching the crushed diamond shore.

Faye slowed to a crawl, rubbing her damp palms onto her skirt.

Her sisters were all dressed in gold tonight, each with a mask that matched her own. Faye's stomach churned at the sight. It was a cruel joke. With each golden skirt, Pathos was reminding her exactly who was in charge.

Faye steeled her nerves. She had to do this. For them.

Pathos held out his hand, his eyes glittering behind his empty mask. "Come, my lady."

Faye swallowed and placed her hand in his. Gripping her glass slipper tight, she climbed into the boat.

He rowed her across the lake, then lifted her out of the boat and onto the shore. As soon as he placed her on her feet, Faye rushed across the shore to Adalie's side. If this was to be the last time she saw her sisters, then she didn't care what punishment Phagos, Nosos, or any of the other brothers decided to dole out on her. They couldn't touch her.

Not while she was the favored of Pathos. Grabbing Adalie's arm, she pulled her sister close and hugged her tight.

"This is it," she whispered. "This is your last night here."

Adalie trembled in her arms. "Pathos told us he's going to help us escape. That you're staying behind. Why, Faye? Why not come with us?"

Faye bit her lip but didn't reply. What could she possibly say to that? There was nothing she could tell her sister to make her understand.

"Make sure you find Margaux and Belle. Keep them safe."

Adalie nodded and leaned back, wiping a tear from her cheek. "I know. I'll take care of them. Pathos said he's going to bring us up in Revayr, back in the ballroom."

Relief flooded into Faye's veins and she relaxed a little. "Good. That's good."

Faye pulled Adalie in for one last hug. She squeezed her eyes shut to keep the tears at bay.

"You don't have to stay."

"I do."

"No, Faye." Adalie pushed back. She grabbed Faye's hands. "Please. Colette told us what you said. How this is your fault. But I don't care. I don't. I just want you to come home. Come home with us."

Something in Faye's heart broke. Could they really have forgiven her? Truly? It wasn't possible. How could they forgive the person who so willingly destroyed their lives?

Faye firmed her lips. "You have to stay strong, dear sister. You can do this. Make sure you tell Papa that I … that I'm dead." She swallowed. "If he really knew …"

Adalie nodded, her eyes tight. "He would die from despair."

Phagos came up behind Adalie and grabbed her shoulder. He looked at Faye with cold eyes. "Enough talking. Get moving, both of you."

Taking a step back, she kept her grip on Adalie's hand for as long as she could before Phagos jerked Adalie away. Tears pricked her eyes as she watched them leave. She should have told Adalie that she loved her. That she was sorry. She should have said goodbye.

One by one, her sisters filed into the black forest. They looked back at Faye but said nothing.

Faye bit the inside of her cheek and strangled the glass slipper in her hand.

"Come, my lady." Pathos held out his arm to her.

Faye looped her arm into his. Together, they followed their siblings into the forest.

∞

Faye was surprised by the amount of people that inhabited the Underworld. Guests crowded not only the walls of the Midnight King's ballroom, but also the halls and the courtyard. Could she even call them guests? Each one was identical in dress—black, with a simple volto mask hiding their identities. Were they the courtiers that had fallen with her and her sisters?

Faye caught a glimpse of gold out of the corner of her eye. Heart pounding, she whirled around. But instead of seeing her mother's brilliant wings, she saw instead a sea of black masks, staring, as if waiting for her to fall so they could devour her whole.

Faye pushed through the crowd of undead, searching for a brilliant scarlet dress. When she didn't see one, she whirled on Pathos, who was always two steps behind her.

"Where is she? Where is Colette?"

Pathos shrugged. "I must prepare. You may say your goodbyes while you wait."

"But what about your rule?" Faye swallowed at the memory of her feet moving of their own accord.

"This is the one exception. Don't you want to tell them goodbye?"

Faye watched him go. She fiddled with the shoe in her hands, not sure what to do with it. As she searched the crowd, Faye spotted a bright red dress and Colette's flame-bird mask. Her sister stood near the entrance, tall and straight. Belle clung to her skirts—her tiny face turned up in sorrow. Faye struggled through the crowd of pressing bodies.

"Colette," Faye said softly. "May I speak with you?"

Nodding, Colette pulled Belle away. "Go on," she said. "Go and find Desideria."

Instead of obeying, Belle threw her arms around Faye. "Please come with us!" she cried.

Faye hugged her back and kissed her brown hair. "Shh! We mustn't let the others know," she whispered. "Only Pathos knows that you're leaving. Can you be quiet for me?"

Belle scrunched up her nose but nodded.

Desi made her way through the crowd and pulled Belle away. "Come along," she murmured.

When both had left, Faye turned back to Colette and gripped her hands, careful to not squeeze her right hand too hard. "I need you to promise me something."

Colette stiffened and yanked out of Faye's grip. Despite her brilliant attire, she might as well have been a pillar of ice. She stared coldly at Faye.

"I can't promise you anything."

"It's just one thing, Colette. One thing is all I ask, before you leave."

Colette looked down at her hands. "What do you want?"

Faye bit her lip. She wanted to wrap Colette in her arms. She had never been a warm person, but she had never cut Faye off either. She had been their protector, their leader, the one they could all lean on and trust. Now, she was cold, and—Faye could barely stand the thought—distant.

Taking her sister's hands in hers once more, Faye squeezed them tight. She looked into Colette's blue eyes. "I want you to find happiness. Promise me that you'll try."

Colette's mouth twitched. "Don't stay behind and maybe I'll find a way."

Faye reached out to wrap Colette in a hug, but Colette moved out of reach. Turning, she made to leave, but hesitated. After several moments, her gaze softened. In that one small glimpse, Faye caught sight of heavy vulnerability. It hit her so hard she fought to breathe.

Her sister, her strong, unmovable sister, was just as scared as she. Faye almost took a step closer but stopped herself. Colette always hated goodbyes. So, Colette turned away and pushed through the crowd. Soon, she was swallowed by the press of bodies, out of sight.

Faye watched her go and a lump formed in her throat. Those were the last words she would ever speak to Colette. Their last moments together, and Faye didn't even have the heart to say she loved her. Another sister she had let down. Another moment wasted. The thought was more painful than Faye could bear.

But, in just a few minutes, every ache, every pain, every hurt would soon become a distant memory.

Chapter Twenty-Four – Leo

Leo jerked up in his seat as the mantel clock chimed. The carved metal hands pointed to the number twelve.

"Midnight," he whispered.

He stared at the fireplace, waiting to see a shimmering light, or perhaps the back fall away, but nothing happened. The seconds ticked by and Leo frowned. Pushing to his feet, he looked at Madame Leroux, who stood with her back to him, gazing out the window. Jack was asleep on the couch, his sword resting in his lap.

"Did it not work?" he asked as he glanced at the fireplace. The moonlight silhouetted her small figure, making her look more like a statue than a living being. "Madame?"

Madame Leroux turned from the window, her shoulders sagging with a quiet sigh. "The portal is open now, as long as you have the slipper. But it will close any time now." She limped to his side, her stick thumping loudly on the wood floor. "Just crawl inside and push the back open. Hurry."

Leo knelt on the hearth and stared at the brick wall. This whole thing was ridiculous. Imagine he, a crown prince, crawling through the ashes of a peasant's fireplace, all to chase after the word of a masked man and a disgraced Faerie. A wonderful, horrible, act of rebellion. A thrill raced down his spine.

"Is there a problem, my prince?" Madame asked from where she stood.

"No, none at all." Leo gave her a wide grin as he wiped his sweaty palms on his trousers. "Just … admiring your ashes."

Madame quirked an eyebrow. "I see. And do you find our ashes to your liking?"

Leo didn't miss the sarcasm in her voice. He let out a weak laugh. "Yes, they are very, well, ashy."

Madame sighed and rolled her eyes. "Do I have to send your friend here instead?"

She gestured to Jack, who still slept. Surprisingly, he hadn't jumped up and volunteered to come in Leo's place yet. Most likely Madame had put some kind of Faerie spell on him to keep him asleep.

"No, that won't be necessary." Leo steeled his muscles and bent over to crawl inside the fireplace. If Faye, a princess could do it, so could he.

The cloak tangled around his legs as he crawled forward on one hand, the other tucked to his chest to keep the slipper safe. Reaching out, he pushed the back of the fireplace. The cool stones gave under the slight pressure. Then, Leo tumbled forward into a dark hole.

He fell down several stone steps before he was able to throw out his arms and dig in his heels. The slipper slipped from his hand and bounced away. Each time it hit the next step, Leo cringed, expecting it to break. But, mercifully, it didn't.

Pain flared in his elbows and knees. He groaned and sat up. Whoever thought it was a good idea to put a set of stairs in a portal instead of a tunnel was an idiot.

Picking up the slipper, Leo stood and adjusted Madame Leroux's cape around his shoulders. Although he could still see himself beneath the cape, he hoped that the Faerie had been right, and it would hide him from the eyes of others.

Leo trotted down the steps, taking in the odd masonry. Frescoes were painted on the walls, a golden forest on one side, and a silver forest on the other. The trees had bark that shimmered like real chunks of gold caught in sunlight, and beautiful blooms hung heavy on their branches. Leo reached out to touch the wall, but stumbled when his hand went right through. He froze as his foot landed on not stone but soft, loamy earth. The trees were no longer a painting, but were an actual forest, stretching as far as the eye could see.

Is this real? He couldn't be certain. To his eyes it was just a painting on a very solid wall, and yet he couldn't deny what he felt beneath his boots.

Hesitantly, he made his way to the nearest tree. The tips of his fingers skimmed against smooth, cold bark. He reached up and plucked one of the golden blooms from the tree. It lay like a glittering jewel in his hand. The petals were soft and curved out like a rose, tiny filaments peeking out from the center. They pulsed with a gentle glow. Almost like a heartbeat. Leo brushed his finger across them, and he came away with his skin coated in gold dust.

"Amazing," he whispered.

A sneeze echoed up to him and he froze. Footsteps clattered on the steps above him. He sucked in a breath and shoved the flower into his pocket, then pressed himself against the stairwell. Slowly, a tiny girl came into view, dressed in a simple golden gown. A white silk mask hid the top half of her face from view, but it couldn't hide her trembling chin and the whimpers that escaped her throat.

Leo held his breath. It was one of the twelve princesses, possibly the youngest. She clattered by him, glass slippers peeking out from underneath her skirts. She slipped and he winced, and he almost reached out to her. But he held back. If he announced his presence to her too soon, she might bring him unwanted attention. The princess righted herself and continued on.

Once she passed him, Leo followed, moving as quietly as his boots allowed. Twice on the way down, his foot slipped, and he held in a curse as the tiny princess looked back, fear shining in her brown eyes. When they finally reached the bottom step, Leo hung back, letting her get a head start.

Shuddering, Leo pulled the cape tighter. To think, for the past several nights, he had been dancing with Faye without even realizing it. All the while, wondering where Faye and her sisters had gone. What a fool he had been. A blind, rotten fool who couldn't see what was right under his nose.

The tiny princess led him through a tunnel that opened up to a beach of glittering white sand, a lake stretching out before them. The water in the lake was still, not a single ripple disturbing its surface. Six black boats of obsidian lined the shore, a young man dressed in black and wearing a mask standing in each.

The girl made her way to the first boat, where a man in a dragon mask stood waiting, long horns curling up from his cloak. One of the older sisters stood beside the boat, holding out her hand. Leo tried to remember which she was. Linette? No. Helaine?

"Come along, Margaux," the sister said in a soft voice.

Margaux took her hand and clambered awkwardly into the boat. She sat, her gold skirts poofing around her like a cloud. The older sister looked back a moment, brows furrowed.

Leo wrapped the cloak tighter around himself. Had she seen anything? His heart pounded in his ears.

"Genevieve!" Margaux whispered, her voice strained.

Turning, Genevieve lifted her skirts and stepped into the boat. Leo followed on her heels. His boots crunched sand and Genevieve whipped around. Leo scrambled to a stop. She was so close, her nose inches away from his chest, brown eyes wide.

"Get in the boat." The dragon-man's voice was deep.

Genevieve turned and placed her other foot in the boat.

As Dragon-Man used his pole to push the boat into the water, Leo stepped inside as carefully as he could, just narrowly missing Margaux's tiny feet. The cloak brushed against Margaux's arm and Leo bit back a curse.

Margaux gasped and shuddered. She looked around with quick, jerky movements, her eyes wide. Leo crouched on a small bench and leaned against the bow. The iron lantern swayed, sending up a loud creak.

Margaux squeaked and whipped around. She leaned forward and reached out to the bench Leo sat on. Leo froze.

"Sit still!" Dragon-Man barked.

Margaux hesitated, then turned back around. "I thought I heard something."

She and Genevieve shared a look. Dragon-Man remained silent. He turned away and pushed the boat farther across the lake.

As they slid over the smooth, glassy surface, Leo remained tense. Fear curled in his gut. His heart pounded in his ears as he watched the sisters.

Genevieve leaned forward until her forehead almost touched Margaux's. "You heard it, too?"

Leo could hardly hear her whisper. Margaux nodded. Genevieve looked up to where Leo was sitting.

"Something's in the boat with us."

Margaux's mouth dropped open. She shivered. "Is it a ghost?"

"I don't think so. Whatever it is, it has magic."

Leo gripped the edges of the cloak close about his legs to keep from giving even more of himself away. If they found out, then the masked man would find out, putting him and the girls in danger. And all Leo had to protect them with was a tiny, gold dagger. There was no way he could fight off an Enchanter and protect the girls at the same time.

Still, he reached underneath the cloak to his belt and gripped his dagger tightly with sweaty fingers.

Leo searched the faces of the princesses, but with their masks, it was hard to tell who was who. He guessed that since Margaux rode in the boat with him, the next boat over held Belle and two others. The eldest had to be Desideria, but the middle girl, he couldn't remember. The fourth boat only held one occupant. The fifth, two. And the last …

He jolted upright and the boat rocked. Dragon-Man spun around.

"Sit still, both of you," he growled.

Genevieve and Margaux paled. Leo stared at the boat farthest from him. It slowed as it hit the sand first and the masked man jumped out. When he turned to help the girl exit, Leo spotted a glint of silver.

The wolf man. Anger stirred inside Leo and he had to fight the urge to jump from his boat.

There was a girl with him, dressed in white. Her light-brown hair hung down her back, shining golden in the half-light. That had to be … His heart skipped a beat.

Faye ran across the beach, away from the man in the wolf mask toward a girl dressed in gold. They embraced, holding each other as if they would never let go. Leo's throat tightened. The other girl had to be Adalie, Faye's twin. Leo never knew Adalie as well as he knew Faye.

The boat rocked as it scraped the sand. Dragon-Man dropped the pole into the boat. He jumped into the water, sending up a splash that soaked Margaux's dress, making it wilt. She gasped and sat there, dripping, arms akimbo. Genevieve leaned forward and placed a finger on her sister's lips. Her eyes were wide. She shook her head.

Dragon-Man stalked across the beach, away from them.

"Come on," Genevieve whispered. "I'll help you out."

Genevieve climbed from the boat, then lifted Margaux and placed her on the dry sand. Hand in hand, they followed after Dragon-Man. Another of the masked men approached Dragon-Man.

"Why is she wet?" the young man growled from behind a snarling tiger mask.

"They were talking. Their voices drive me mad."

"If Pathos hears you've mistreated any of the girls tonight …"

"What, he'll hang me? He already snapped my neck. You need to not be so paranoid, Ekdikeo. One day, Pathos will get killed by his foolish ambitions and I will be the Midnight King."

"Nosos!" Ekdikeo's voice was filled with horror.

Nosos pushed past and stormed toward the wood. Leo's heart throbbed in his throat. He couldn't be sure if it was excitement or fear. The dragon-masked brother, Nosos, was plotting against the Midnight King. Either Nosos felt possessive of the sisters, or he was trying to gain the crown for himself. Leo wasn't sure if he liked either option.

Ekdikeo watched Nosos leave, then turned to Genevieve and Margaux. The girls gripped Margaux's skirt and wrung it between their small fists.

"Gen," Ekid barked. "Leave it. She'll dry on the way."

Rising, Genevieve took Margaux's hand. The two hurried up the shore and were the last in line. Leo followed closely, passing by a series of trees that looked like a piece of art, black and gnarled, with brilliant purple leaves. Leo shook his head. This place was beautiful, but something crackled in the air. It scraped along his shoulders, irritating his skin. A deep magic that threatened to carve its way into Leo's bones.

Tiny blue lights bobbed and swam through the air, following Leo as he hurried after the princesses and masked monsters. Whispers touched his ears, words he couldn't understand. Leo gripped his hood to keep it from falling. Gut twisting, he fought off a shudder as the magic grew stronger with each step. It was hard to believe the princesses had survived down here so long. Leo felt as if he were suffocating with each step that led him deeper into this rotten kingdom.

Chapter Twenty-Five – Leo

The path ahead opened to a bare rocky cliff. Beyond the trees, a stone bridge arched across a wide chasm ending at the foot of a castle hewn from dull gray stone. Tattered flags hung from the castle's spires, each one black, the insignia faded. Archways shaded the bridge at intervals, two giant, ugly gargoyles sitting atop each, an iron lantern hanging between their feet.

Leo shuddered. It all looked to be an invention of the Enchanter inside, a pitiful attempt at trying to make the Underworld as alluring as possible.

One of the gargoyles snapped its wings and Leo jumped biting back a yell. Red eyes blinked open, gazing straight at him. Leo froze. His grip tightening on the dagger's handle. Could gargoyles see through magic?

"Come on, Belle, hurry up!" Genevieve called—her tone desperate.

"I can't go any farther. My feet hurt," Belle whimpered.

The tiniest princess flopped to the ground, right underneath the gargoyles. She pried off her slippers, and Leo winced. Her tiny feet were mottled with purple-and-yellow bruises, some of which looked like they didn't come from dancing. Belle tentatively touched a blister on her right foot. She bit her lip, a sob escaping her throat.

Genevieve made to go after her, but Ekdikeo grabbed her arm and jerked her away. Another one of the smaller princesses paused and walked back to her sister's side. Margaux. She knelt and pulled Belle close.

The gargoyles' eyes shifted to the girls, but they didn't move from their perches, even as hunger shone within the polished obsidian.

After most of the group moved far enough away—just out of earshot—Leo hurried to the sisters' sides. Kneeling beside them, he threw off his hood. Both princesses shrieked, and Belle fell hard on her seat. She pointed a stiff finger at him.

"Floating head!" she squealed.

"Shh!" Leo held out a hand and shot a glance up at the gargoyles. "Please, don't make a scene."

Belle clutched her sister tight. "Wh-who are you?"

He tried to give them a gentle smile, but the sounds of the gargoyles slavering put his teeth on edge. "I am Prince Lionheart ap Owen of Eura. We used to all be friends three years ago. Before you all disappeared."

Margaux rolled her eyes. "Oh, you're *that* prince."

Leo frowned. "What do you mean?"

She sighed. "Faye was *in love* with you. Then you went away and she got hurt." She wrinkled her nose. "Disgusting."

Leo's cheeks reddened and he cleared his throat. "Ah. Well, yes. We were … very close. But I'm not here to discuss the past. I'm here to free you. All of you."

The princesses stared at him in silence, eyes wide, mouths agape. Belle slowly peeled away from Margaux and peered up at him, hope and suspicion shining in her eyes.

"Pathos already promised we get to go free."

Leo frowned at that. "Pathos?"

Belle pointed toward the castle. "Yes. He's the Midnight King and dances with Faye. The one with the wolf mask."

Anger stirred inside Leo. All this time, the Midnight King had been in *Leo's* castle, dancing in *Leo's* ballroom. He ground his teeth together and fought to keep his tone calm.

"Do you really think Pathos will keep his promise?" Leo asked as the princesses drew closer together. "I can tell you, he won't. Trusting a monster like him is lunacy. I'm here now, and that means I'm going to rescue you. I just need you to help me get into the castle first."

Margaux rose to her knees. "We'll help you. But only if you promise us something."

"Anything."

She bit her lip and blinked hard, tears shining in her deep brown eyes. "Don't let them take hurt my sister"

He recoiled, a shudder rippling across his skin. "What?"

"You don't know?"

Leo shook his head. "What are you talking about?"

Belle's blue eyes widened. "They're going to kill Faye."

∞

The castle's doors opened wide, as if waiting to swallow them whole. Leo pressed forward, rushing inside just before the doors creaked shut.

"You should hide on the dais, near the Midnight King's throne. That way, when he comes out, you can kill him," Margaux whispered in a matter-of-fact tone, her dark brows scrunched in determination.

Leo frowned. It was odd how she spoke of Pathos and Midnight King, almost as if they were two different people. Was it just a habit of hers, or was there something else going on?

"Are you going to kill him?" Belle asked, looking up at him with wide eyes.

Leo swallowed, suddenly feeling the weight of duty. "I'll do what I must."

Leo had hunted wolves before, and that was with a bow and arrows, but nothing this big. Killing a person—even if he was a twisted Enchanter—would be very different. He reached into his belt and touched the hilt of the dagger. Hopefully, Aurore was correct, and it would be enough.

The girls led him along the nightmarish castle corridors. Statues lined the halls everywhere, their dead eyes staring out, their stone faces grim. Leo's skin crawled at the sight of them. Something about them wasn't right. As if they were more than just statues.

They passed by one, a woman in rags with the face of an angel. A child clung to her legs, and she hunched over in a protective stance. The mother's head seemed to turn as he passed by, her mouth open in a cry of distress. Then, they arrived at the ballroom.

In the center of the ballroom, the Midnight King's brothers gathered, the princesses at their sides. Crowds of masked men and women hovered on the edges of the dance floor.

A dais rose at the end of the ballroom, and on it stood a single throne, molded from iron with wicked points that speared upwards in a fan, like a crown. Though the throne was empty, Leo guessed it wouldn't be for long.

A girl dressed in white pushed her way through the crowd. Her shoulders were hunched, her movements stilted. To Leo, she looked almost like a doll made of porcelain. Fragile. Breakable.

"Faye," he breathed.

There she was, watching her sisters, lingering just out of reach. Just like she did at his own masquerades. She stood tall, her shoulders thrown back, her head high. Yet her lips were pressed together tight, and her chin trembled, as if she were choking back tears.

Leo wanted to run up to her, to sweep her in his arms and carry her away from this wretched place, but all he could do was stand there and stare, his throat tight. She didn't deserve this. None of them did.

A shadow peeled away from the darkness shrouding the corners of the room, coalescing into the shape of a man. The man in the wolf mask. Pathos. He gripped Faye's shoulder with long fingers and loomed over her as if to whisper in her ear. She nodded.

Leo stared at Faye, in the grip of that monstrous man, drinking in her petite form, her long, caramel-colored hair, her smooth pale skin. And underneath the mask, two deep chocolate eyes that always took his breath away. The need to speak to her rose inside of him. Just a small moment. A minute, a second, to tell her that he was here. Here for her.

Leo stepped as close as he dared, just out of reach, but not close enough. Never close enough. He could hear her breathy sigh. See the constricting of her throat. The shaking in her hands.

"I'm here," he whispered.

Faye stiffened and her eyes widened. Leo quickly backed away, regret tightening his throat. He shouldn't have said anything. What if Pathos had heard him?

Silence fell over the room like night. Everyone turned toward the dais as Pathos climbed the steps. The monster lifted an iron crown of spikes and placed it on his head. And, the moment he turned around, the crowd fell to its knees.

Black mist poured from his hands and surrounded him in a cloud of smoke. Fear curled around Leo's chest. Now he understood why Margaux spoke of Pathos and the Midnight King as two very different entities. The atmosphere shifted the moment the crown touched Pathos's head and cold crept into Leo's bones.

Now, everything made sense.

The Midnight King sat on his throne.

"Faye de la Rou." His voice echoed throughout the room, deep and commanding.

Faye stepped forward, head high. Pausing before Pathos, she dropped into a graceful curtsy, neck curved, head bowed. The Midnight King's voice rang out once more.

"Dance."

Faye stood poised. Still. A soft melody floated through the air, and she began to dance. Leo had no idea that he could become enchanted all over again. Faye floated across the dance floor as if her feet didn't even touch the ground. Leo could imagine wings, large and white, sprouting from her back and carrying her away.

And yet, her lips trembled. Her hands shook. As if she were clinging to the last threads of her life. The fear in Leo's chest cinched tighter. His beloved Faye was taking her last dance in front of a monster.

Threads of black and gold appeared on the dance floor, glowing in the wake of her steps. Leo watched, entranced. The threads intersected, forming a deliberate pattern. He glanced back up at Pathos. Gripping his throne's armrests, Pathos leaned forward, intent.

Then, Leo felt it. A sense of breaking. The spell over this place was unweaving, thread by thread. The air snapped like a handful of tense strings being cut one by one. A sluggishness filled his bones. A yawn choked his throat, but he pushed it back. Brushing a hand along his arm, he fought back a shudder.

The White Lady's curse was breaking, and the Midnight King was using Faye to do it.

Gripping the dagger in his belt, Leo inched toward the dais. He would stop this curse before the Midnight King and his brothers escaped. Because the moment that the last thread snapped, the world above would burn.

Chapter Twenty-Six – Faye

A small smile tugged at Faye's lips. This was what she had been waiting for. The chance to say her goodbyes in her own way. In the Revayrian way. Standing, she turned and strode to the middle of the ballroom. Her sisters backed away, forming a ring around her. The ghostlike courtiers watching.

I deserve this. I deserve this.

The thought echoed through Faye's head as she danced. She deserved her fate. Never anything else. After all, this had all been her fault. If she hadn't listened to the voice calling her, if she hadn't run away, her sisters never would have followed. And they wouldn't all be in this mess.

She glanced to where Adalie stood, her face twisted in pain. Faye's throat tightened and her hands trembled. She didn't want to leave them like this. But what choice did she have? It was the only way. They all deserved the chance to live. Especially little Belle and Margaux and Jenine. They were but children and knew nothing of what life was really like beyond glass slippers and masquerades.

Faye closed her eyes to block out her sisters' faces. She lifted her hands above her head, striking a solemn, yet triumphant pose. With her bare toes pointed, she slid across the floor, moving in a weaving pattern. It was an ancient dance, a wild dance, one that, with one misstep, could ruin the whole purpose.

With each foot placement, she created an unseen picture, an ancient symbol that represented life, love, and sorrow. Mama had painted it on the dance floor back home, teaching its steps to her and her sisters, warning them that this dance was magic. And magic was something they should never take lightly.

Faye tucked her arms close and spun. She had been a naïve child. Her mother warned her against magic, and what did she do? Follow the boy with magic in his eyes and danger in his smile. She spun harder, tucking one leg up while she twirled on her toes, before planting her foot and spinning again. She would not make that same mistake again. At least with this magic, her sisters would never forget her.

With one last pirouette, Faye raced across the drawn pattern, no longer dancing, but running now. Lines spiderwebbed across the floor, glowing faintly. The pattern appeared before her eyes. She paused at the pattern's edge and panted, her ribs aching. With one last flourish, she performed a dancer's curtsy—arms in front, one leg extended, head bowed.

The room filled with deafening silence. Tears glistened on each of her sisters' faces. One by one, they copied the bow, turning toward her. Faye fought back tears as love for her family swelled in her heart. Pain gripped her chest and it deepened with every breath.

Pathos stood and the lines dissipated. He held out his hand.

"Come."

Faye's mouth dried and she trembled. She took in a deep breath and stepped toward the dais. With one last look at her sisters, she climbed up the steps.

Each one was harder than before. Faye wanted to scream, to run. The last thing she wanted was to die and be brought back a monster. But it had to be done. She placed her foot on the next step, her bare toes digging into the cool stone.

I deserve this.

Step.

I deserve this.

Step.

I deserve this.

I deserve this.

She stopped before Pathos, her gaze on the floor. He towered over her, his shadowy form stretching out, as if to swallow the whole room. He placed a hand on her shoulder, and she shivered at the cold that spread across her skin.

"Kneel."

Faye fell to her knees. She peered up as Pathos reached for his belt. Gripping the bone hilt of his dagger, he pulled it free, revealing a dark, rust-red blade. Like blood. His masked face turned toward her, and she quickly dropped her gaze.

This was it. This would be her last moment as Faye. As herself. She looked back at her sisters, locking gazes with Colette. Her sister stood tall, clutching Desi's hand. Faye tried to give her a smile, but her lips were numb.

Closing her eyes, Faye waited, holding fast to the image of her sisters. At least they'd be the last thing she saw before she died.

Her heart thudded against her ribcage, beating out her death dirge.

Pathos jerked her head back, his cold fingers wrapped in her hair. He leaned close. So close his hot breath spread across her cheek.

"You made the right choice."

I made the right choice.

There was a pause, and then she felt it. Pathos' dagger pierced her neck.

And stopped.

Faye snapped her eyes open. Pathos's arm trembled. Inch by inch, the blade lifted, as if some force was pushing back. And before she could blink, Leo was there, a golden dagger clenched in his fist as he struggled to push Pathos back. Faye stared at him, open-mouthed. How had he gotten here? And how had he just … appeared?

Leo grunted and looked back at her, grey eyes pinched with effort. "Run!"

It took a moment for Faye to register his words. But then, chaos erupted. Shouts from the monsters. Her sisters pulling her away, dragging her down the dais and toward the ballroom doors. Pathos' brothers chased after them, Nosos in the lead.

Faye paused and looked back. Leo was struggling with Pathos. She should go back. She should help him.

"Faye, come on!" Adalie's voice was clogged with fear.

She couldn't let him do this. Not when he had done nothing to deserve death.

The comb! Faye reached into her hair and plucked out the golden comb Pathos had given to her. She would stab Pathos's arm, only hurt him. Not kill him. She could never kill him.

Dodging Nosos's outstretched hands, she ran toward the dais.

"You will never escape this!" he shouted after her. "You *will* die, Faye de la Rou!"

Faye spotted Leo's cloak, lying where he had appeared. She dove for it and grabbed the corner, just as someone's hand snaked around her ankle. Scrabbling, she snagged the edge and jerked it toward herself, before twisting around. Nosos lunged at her, fingers digging into her ankle bones. With a burst of energy, she lashed out with her free foot. Her heel slammed into his shoulder. Releasing a grunt, Nosos stumbled but didn't let go.

Just as she aimed for his neck with the comb, a rumble shook the floor. Faye whipped around toward the dais in time to see Leo fly backwards. With a dull thud, he landed on his back and slid across the polished floor. Pathos had his hands outstretched, the darkness oozing from his skin growing deeper.

Light glinting on the muzzle of his mask, Pathos laughed.

Chapter Twenty-Seven – Leo

The Midnight King's laughter scraped against Leo's ears. Cold seeped into his skin. It dug deep into his bones until Leo was sure he would never feel warmth again. The darkness that surrounded Pathos spread across the dais and pushed down to Leo, quiet as a whisper. Cutting him off from everyone else. Leo scrambled back and his grip on the dagger slipped.

"Prince Lionheart ap Owen," Pathos rumbled.

His words were a whisper and a shout, a boom of thunder and the quiet flash of lightning. It wrapped around Leo, pinning him to the ground. Floating on silent feet, Pathos descended the dais steps.

Pausing before Leo, he reached up with charred fingers for the wolf mask. Leo stared, transfixed, as he gripped the edges and peeled it away.

The Midnight King was a dead man. And yet his chest moved with breath. The fear that had gripped Leo strengthened at the sight of his face.

He was the same age as Leo, with black hair pinned down by an iron crown of pointed spikes. His eyes two chunks of darkness. High cheekbones accentuated his gaunt face. Rotting skin wrapped his bones in a tight embrace. His lips turned up in a ghastly smile. The darkness surrounding them dissipated, until a tall, thin man stood before Leo.

Pathos gave Leo a low bow as he tossed his mask to the floor. "Welcome, White Lord."

Leo glanced back at Pathos' brothers, who stood around Leo in a ring. The brother in the deep-red dragon mask

217

pinned Faye to the ground, her arm twisted behind her back. Leo tightened his sweaty grip on the dagger.

"Why do you call me that?"

The Midnight King's unhinged grin grew even wider. "What, did your father never tell you? I expect not, seeing as how he hates magic and all."

"Tell me what? I don't understand," Leo barked. His fear deepened, digging its claws into his rapidly beating heart.

"Your mother was the daughter of the White Lady."

Leo laughed. It was a wild, barking laugh. The laugh of a madman. Perhaps Leo had gone mad. As mad as the monster before him. "Daughter of the White Lady? You really expect me to believe that?"

The Midnight King was no longer smiling. "If I was lying, then how do you explain your magic?"

"M-magic?" Leo's laughter grew deeper. He hunched over, clutching his stomach. Just because he could feel magic didn't mean he *was* magic.

Right?

"I … I've never used magic, not once in my life!"

Even as Leo spoke, doubt crept in. He had never thought of it before, but was it not normal for a Human to feel magic? No one spoke of it because feeling magic was too close to being magical, right?

But, what about the time when his hands had glowed in the castle courtyard? The only word he could use to explain it was magic. And yet, it couldn't be true. Father hated magic. He hated anything to do with magic. It was against his nature to even consider marrying anyone of Enchanter blood. Hadn't Father been telling Leo over and over that he could never marry Faye because of her magic blood?

But then, why else would he hate magic, if it weren't for his magical wife dying, leaving him all alone?

The thought hit Leo like a kick to the stomach. His laughter died.

"No," he said to himself as he straightened, muscles shaking. "No, it can't be true."

"Oh, but it is, my lord, it is. You see, back before the war, Everland was friendly with the kingdom of Eura. And the White Lady had a daughter. A pretty little thing that caught King Richard's eye when he was a young lad. They were soon married and had a son, a little boy they named Lionheart.

"But when you and I were just babes, the White Lady declared war on my father. She thought that what he was doing was wrong. She could never understand the need for immortality. This war lasted for years, and your mother decided it was her duty to join the fight." Pathos grinned again. "She died not three months after joining her mother. See, she hadn't gained the power of the White Lady yet. She was vulnerable. My father snapped her like a twig and left her to rot."

Anger burned inside Leo's chest. He raised the dagger, ready to stick it into Pathos' chest. "You lie!"

"If I'm lying, then why is it I can do this?" He reached out a hand and closed his fist, as if grabbing hold of something.

Pressure built inside Leo's chest. Pathos drew his fist toward his chest and the pressure inside Leo grew. Something inside Leo pressed against his skin. Leo gasped as pain streaked through his ribs. The dagger fell from his numb fingers, hitting the floor with a clang.

"No!" Faye's scream cut through the air. "No, Pathos, please! Please, you're hurting him!"

Leo couldn't breathe. His lungs burned as he struggled to for air. The world spun. The pain grew more and more intense with every tug of Pathos' hands. With a horrifying ripping sound that sent a scream up Leo's throat, a thread of light burst from Leo's chest and spun toward Pathos.

Faye's screams pounded against Leo's ears. Leo fell to his knees as the light spun from his chest. Every nerve, every vein, screamed for relief as his limbs shook.

None of this should be possible.

None of this should be possible.

Leo was a Human. A simple prince with a very unprincely attitude. He cared for those of magic blood. But he could never *be* one.

It's so simple. Pathos' voice burned through Leo's head. *If I take this, you will no longer be an Enchanter. You'll just be Human. Isn't that what you want?*

Was it what he wanted? To be a simple Human, to no longer feel his father's anger and disappointment? To have his father be proud of him at last?

But he had given that up the moment he chose to believe that Faye and her sisters were still alive. That the Midnight King was real.

I'm offering you a second chance.

"A second chance." An ache filled Leo much deeper than the burning pain. A second chance of winning his father's love. Of winning his father's respect. A second chance to be the prince that he was meant to be.

With one last tug, the light pulled from Leo's chest and flew into Pathos. Leo collapsed onto the stone. He sucked in ragged gasps. The warmth that had always filled his chest was gone.

Pathos spread his arms as the light sank into his skin. Darkness and light twisted together like living snakes around him, pulsing like a heartbeat. Pathos stepped over Leo and made his way to Faye's side. Nosos stood and backed away. Leo could only watch as Pathos placed a hand on Faye's cheek.

"My lady," he murmured in his rumbling voice.

Tears stained Faye's cheeks. "Why?" she choked.

"I had to. I took the burden of his magic on myself so that he can live a normal life. So that others won't hate him and call him filthy for being a half-blood like you. I did it to save him from himself."

Faye struggled to rise, and Pathos helped her with gentle movements. Anger burned in Leo's gut. He shouldn't even be allowed to touch Faye, not after everything he had put her through.

"G-get ... away ..." Leo wheezed, barely able to get the words past his numb lips.

Faye's deep brown eyes settled on Leo. She reached out as if to touch him, even though they were separated by several feet, only to pull back. She looked to her sisters who huddled together like a flock of swans, each one frozen with an expression of horror or anguish on their faces.

"It's time, my lady." Pathos helped Faye stand.

"Let them go first. I don't want them to see."

Pathos nodded and gestured to Nosos. Nosos and the other brothers herded the princesses from the ballroom. The moment the doors slammed shut behind them, Pathos turned to Faye and pulled out his dagger once more.

"I always keep my promises, Faye. You know this. Your sisters will be set free as a sign of good faith. And after you die, the others will go. I swear this."

Faye nodded and closed her eyes. "Be quick."

Pathos pulled her close and pressed his dagger to Faye's throat.

Leo tensed. What should he do? Faye remained still, compliant. Leo dug his fingers into the floor. He pulled himself forward. His limbs burned with each movement. His heart ached to see her like this. Defeated. Hopeless.

A small whimper escaped her lips, as she murmured the words, "I'm sorry."

Pulling himself closer, he reached for his fallen dagger. "Please, don't hurt her."

Pathos pressed his cheek to Faye's. A deep sadness pulled at his face.

"Oh, I won't hurt her, I'll only be freeing her." His arm snaked tighter around her waist. "Freeing her from all the hurt and pain. Isn't that what you want?"

Faye blinked, sending more tears to stain her cheeks. Leo stared at her. Why was she not fighting back? Why was she agreeing to this?

"Faye?" Leo hated how his voice shook. "Faye, you can be free. You can leave."

She looked away, lips trembling, eyelids closing over those brilliant brown eyes. Leo inched closer. Pathos dug the dagger into her skin. A grimace crossed her lips, but she didn't cry out. Leo froze.

He couldn't believe it. She had fought so hard, only to welcome death. Why? Did she not want to be free? He couldn't fathom the thought. For so long she had been a prisoner. But now that Leo had finally come to set things right, to set her free, she just … stood there.

"Do … do you want this?" he whispered, his throat thick.

Faye looked him in the eye. She licked her lips. Her mouth opened, then closed. With a shudder, she sagged against Pathos.

"I deserve this."

Pathos' arm jerked. Crimson flooded down Faye's neck. Leo yanked his burning limbs upright, screaming.

But it was too late.

Faye's body hit the floor—her eyes lifeless.

Chapter Twenty-Eight – Leo

"No!" Leo's shout echoed through the room. In his head. Pounding with his heart. Over and over.

He lunged forward, feet barely touching the floor, muscles burning. He fell beside her. Gathered her into his arms.

He placed his hand over her neck. Warm blood oozed between his fingers. Faye took in shallow, gargling gasps. She reached up and pulled his hand away. Her eyes, wide and wild, locked onto his and he could imagine her voice.

I deserve this. Those horrible, terrible words tore at his heart. He pressed a kiss to her forehead, even as he felt her soul slip away.

It was over. Leo pulled her close. Buried his face in her hair. A wild cry wrenched from his throat. He hadn't fought hard enough. Hadn't done enough. She was dead and it was his fault. All his fault. He could have saved her. And yet he had been the coward who had let this curmudgeon take her life.

Tears slipped down Leo's cheeks and he didn't care that Pathos was watching. Let him think he was weak for loving. Leo placed his hand over the cut, applying pressure, even though it was far too late.

"Oh, Faye," he cried.

She had been wrong. So wrong. She didn't deserve this. She never had. No matter what she believed, she had never done anything to deserve her fate.

Now she was gone. All because she believed that lie.

Pathos picked up his mask and situated it onto his face. Raising his arms, he tilted his face toward the ceiling. A

223

brilliant mix of light and dark poured from his skin and across the dance floor. The symbols lit up—their colors so bright Leo had to shield his eyes. The ground rumbled and dust fell from the ceiling. Leo hunched over Faye's body to protect her from the falling debris.

A loud groan and crack came from outside, accompanied by the princesses' screams. Pathos lowered his arms. He marched to Leo's side and knelt. Black eyes pierced Leo with a tired sympathy. He reached out and grasped Leo's shoulder tight.

"The seal is broken. The fight is over. You've lost, White Lord."

Leo growled and slammed his fist into Pathos' mask.

Pathos howled and fell back. A crack ran up the side of the mask. Leo shook out his aching fist. Fighting against stiff muscles, he rose and gripped Pathos by the collar. He shook the man.

"Bring her back!"

Pathos hacked a laugh. "You know I can't do that."

"Was this your plan all along? To kill her and leave her broken body here? To cast her off like a doll? To escape this place and rule the world?"

"No!" Pathos wriggled in Leo's grip. "In order to open the seal, the magic needed a blood sacrifice. Faye's blood has been spilt, but you can still bring her back to life."

"How?" Leo tightened his grip until Pathos choked.

"A kiss." He strained to speak. "Only true love's kiss can break this spell."

Leo made to let Pathos go, but the monster continued to speak.

"However, if it's anything less than true love, she'll remain dead forever." A gruesome smile stretched his lips, showing crooked teeth. "How deep does your love for her *really* go?"

Leo threw Pathos to the ground. Scooping up Faye's body, he staggered for the door. Pathos' wild laughter followed him, and a chunk of the ceiling fell between them.

True love's kiss. It was only something that happened in folktales, not real life. Leo wasn't ready to believe the monster who had just slit Faye's throat. Still, a wild, ridiculous hope flared to life in his hollow chest. And any hope was better than none.

No one followed them. Leo clutched Faye tight to his chest, limbs numb with shock. If Pathos or his brothers weren't pursuing, did that mean he didn't need Faye or Leo anymore? Nausea churned in Leo's stomach. He was tired of playing games with Enchanters.

As soon as Leo exited the castle, he was met by Colette's wild shriek. She and her sisters were grouped together in the courtyard, far away from the crumbling walls. Pathos' brothers surrounded them, blocking off their escape.

Colette gripped Leo's arm. Tremors shook her as the corners of her eyes pinched with pain and she clasped her bandaged hand over her mouth, unable to look away from Faye's limp body.

"Pathos," Leo spat.

Her face shifted from horror to raw anger. She gripped her fan so tight her knuckles popped.

"Wait here. Don't let the others see her."

Turning, Colette marched back toward the group.

"Nosos!" she commanded. "Let us through. Your brother got what he wanted."

Nosos stepped forward to block her way. "The Midnight King may keep his promises, but I am under no obligation to keep them." He gripped her arm. "You girls are going to stay with us."

Leo took a step closer, ready to intervene. But Colette held up a hand. She flipped her fan so that the handle was pressed against Nosos' throat.

"Let us leave or you'll get stuck like the pig you are." Her voice was a deep, icy growl.

Nosos laughed. Colette didn't hesitate. Swinging her arm back, she slammed her fan into his throat. He fell, choking as blood spurted. Pulling off one of her slippers, Colette pointed its heel at the others.

"Anyone else want to go back on their brother's word?"

The brothers backed away. Colette motioned for her sisters to follow her.

"Hurry. We must leave this place."

She ushered her sisters toward the bridge and Leo followed, Faye pressed against his chest. As he ran across the trembling courtyard, he looked back. The brothers were kneeling around Nosos. Leo's heart jumped when he saw Nosos' leg twitch.

It was just his imagination. Nosos couldn't still be alive after what Colette had done.

Only gold can kill the Midnight King. Madame Leroux's words echoed through his mind. Leo cursed. He had left the golden dagger in the ballroom.

When they reached the bridge, Leo was surprised to see the gargoyles missing. He hurried to catch up with Colette.

"Where did they go?"

She glanced up at the bridge's arches, her jaw tight. "I don't know. But I would feel better if they were here."

Leo couldn't help but agree. They hurried across the bridge and through the woods. Every step Leo took, the weight of Faye's body grew heavier in his arms.

The thought circled over and over in his mind. Faye's body. Warm blood on his hands. On his shirt. A tremor worked its way into his hands and up his arms. He pushed the thoughts aside. Right now, his greatest concern was getting the remaining princesses to safety. It was what Faye would have wanted.

When they emerged from the trees, Colette took the lead, ushering them to the boats. She stepped inside one of the obsidian crafts and waved to Leo.

"Get in. We'll place her on the bottom."

Leo climbed in after her and gently placed Faye's body in the hollow bottom of the boat. Faye's head lulled to the side, and her eyes were closed. If it weren't for the gash in her neck and the blood staining her dress, Leo would have been able to imagine that she was sleeping.

As Colette reached for the pole to send the boat into the water, Leo stopped her by placing a hand over hers.

"I'll do it. You see to the others."

She nodded and stepped from the boat. Colette hurried along the beach to her sisters, ordering them each into different boats. Leo jumped out and hurried to the remaining crafts. Colette had three sisters in each boat, which left two behind for anyone to potentially follow them. Leo stepped up to each of the remaining ones and shoved them into the water, making sure they were too far out for anyone to retrieve.

Once the sisters were shoving off, Leo and Colette piled into Faye's boat. Leo picked up the pole and pushed them into the water. They slid across the lake's smooth surface.

"Once we reach the tunnels, I'm smashing these horrible things," Colette grumbled as she readjusted her feet in her glass slippers.

"Why can't you break them now? That will end the curse, won't it?"

"Yes, but the lake's shores are made of crushed diamond. It would be painful to walk on."

Her words brought to mind the glass slipper he had kept in his pocket. His cloak was lost in the ballroom as well the slipper. A small thought raced through his mind. If Faye's slippers weren't broken, would she still be trapped?

Colette sat on the bench, stiff, her hands clenched in her lap. She kept her gaze pointedly away from Faye's body. Though she maintained a stone exterior, Leo could see the hurt hiding underneath in the way her shoulders shook.

"It's alright to cry," he said softly.

She pulled her shoulders back and looked him in the eye. Her words were savage. Harsh. "I won't cry. Not until my sister is alive and the Midnight King's head is on a stake."

Chapter Twenty-Nine – Leo

Colette was the first to break her slippers. She smashed them against the tunnel floor, thousands of glass fragments spinning across the shaking ground. A groan sounded from above and Leo tensed as a spidering crack snaked across the ceiling.

"Hurry." Colette gestured to the others. "Break them and go!"

One by one, the princesses slammed their slippers into the ground. They shot tear-stained glances toward Faye's body cradled in Leo's arms, but none of them said a word. Once the slippers were destroyed, they dashed up the shaking steps. Leo should have felt something with each break. He should have felt the severing of magic. Instead, a deep, cold hollow filled his chest where his magic had once been.

His magic. Leo couldn't help but laugh at the thought. Not more than a day ago he had believed himself to be Human. Now, he wasn't even sure what he was.

Leo waited until they all had passed before following. One of the sisters looked back. Adalie. The ache in Leo's chest grew. She looked so much like Faye.

"May ... may I walk with you?" she whispered, her voice tremulous.

Leo's throat tightened and he gave her a nod. With a trembling hand, Adalie gripped Leo's arm. And they hurried up the steps together.

Anger and guilt twisted together inside Leo. Faye could have walked away with them. Instead, she had chosen death. Because she thought she wasn't worth saving.

Didn't she know that she was worth everything?

Didn't she realize that she was loved? That she was needed and wanted by her family?

Her family. Leo hadn't even been able to save the queen or the courtiers. They remained trapped in the darkness, unable to go free. What was he going to say to King Raoul when he found out that his daughter was dead, when Leo could have saved her? Raoul would hate him.

He squared his shoulders and continued up the steps. If they hated him, so be it. He didn't deserve any less. After all, he had been on the ground, frozen like a dolt, and Pathos had—

Leo shook the thought away. He couldn't bear to relive that moment. The only thing he could do in this moment was hope. Hope that Pathos hadn't lied, and a simple kiss could bring Faye back to life.

Something in the air shifted around Leo. He looked back at the stairs behind him. Nothing. Nothing but darkness. Then, with a groan, the stairs split as a rumble shook the ground. Screams filled the stairwell. Leo's heart jumped into his throat as he shifted to keep Adalie from falling.

"Open the door!" Colette shouted above the noise.

Light spilled down from above. The princesses surged forward, shoving and pushing until they all tumbled through the opening. Leo hefted Faye's body through, into the ashes of a fireplace. Behind him, Adalie screamed.

Leo twisted around just in time to see the step beneath Adalie's feet crumble. Leo reached out and grabbed her hand. Only, he wasn't holding onto anything else. He toppled forward after her. Strong fingers gripped Leo's wrist.

"I've got you, my prince," Madame Leroux's voice grunted in his ear.

He turned to see Madame silhouetted in the fireplace. She knelt in the ash, her green eyes glowing in the half light. Behind her, Colette was gripping Madame's waist to keep her from falling. And just behind them stood a very shocked and worried-looking Jack.

Madame reached out her other hand.

"Bring her to me."

Leo heaved Adalie up with all his might. Her bare toes scrambled at the crumbling rock and her fingernails dug into his skin. Finding purchase, she lunged upward. Madame grabbed Adalie's upper arm and hauled her through the opening and into the fireplace.

Madame gripped Leo's other hand and dragged him up and into the ashes. Leo coughed as he inhaled grains of wood.

Jack hoisted Leo to his feet.

"Are you alright, Your Highness?" he asked, a slight tremor in his voice.

Leo nodded. He glanced at his shirt, at the blood that stained the front. "I'll be fine."

"What happened? What's going on here? Are they …" Jack's mouth moved but no words came.

Leo swallowed the pain. "Yes."

Jack pressed his lips together as he stepped back, allowing Leo to see Faye's body lying on the couch. Adalie cupped Faye's cheeks in her shaking hands and stared with wide, blank eyes, as if waiting for Faye to rise and laugh like this had all been a joke. Part of Leo wished she would. Anything to stop him from reliving the scene of her death over and over.

A heavy silence filled the room as Leo stumbled on shaky legs to the couch. He collapsed and pressed his forehead into the hard wood edge.

A rustle of fabric and the thump of a cane filled the silence.

"What happened?" Madame rasped beside Leo.

Adalie shivered as if she were cold. Desi ushered Margaux, Belle, and Jenine from the room and down the hall.

"When will Faye wake up?" Jenine whispered.

Desi shushed her and a door clicked shut.

Leo shifted and kept his gaze on the floor. If he looked at Faye now, he would fall apart. Lifting his hands, he stared at the blood, and his throat grew tight.

"I couldn't save her," he said, his voice wavering. "I couldn't ... I wasn't able to defeat the Midnight King. That beast is still alive and Faye ..."

Adalie began to shake. She gripped Faye's shoulders and shook her. "Wake up. Wake up!"

Colette and Estelle rushed to Adalie's side and wrenched her away. Screaming, she thrashed against them, stiff fingers reaching for Faye. The girls fell to the floor in a heap as Adalie screamed, tears streaming down her cheeks. Estelle held her tight as they both shook with sobs, and Colette stroked Adalie's hair.

Genevieve spoke up from where she stood behind the couch, brown eyes brimming with tears. "Isn't there anything we can do?"

"I don't know." Madame shook her head. "I'm afraid she's gone."

Leo turned his back on the room and slammed the side of his fist into the fireplace mantel. Pain rattled up his bones. That small, ridiculous, mad spark of hope flared in his chest like a dying ember.

"Pathos." Leo spat the name. He rushed toward Madame. "The Midnight King, he said something, something about true love's kiss."

Madame stumbled back, as if struck.

Leo grabbed her arm and his desperation almost tipped her over. "Madame, please, will it bring her back? Is there a chance?"

She shook her head and placed a hand over her eyes. "Oh, my dear Faye, forgive me, please, forgive me."

Gripping her shoulders, Leo shook her. "Faerie! Can we use true love's kiss to bring her back?"

"I don't know!" Madame jerked from Leo's grip and leaned on her cane. "I've only ever heard it used in folktales before. It's not Fae magic."

He turned to Jack, who stood next to the door. Desperation clutched him by the throat. "J ... Jack? You know more about—about magic."

Pain crossed Jack's face and he shook his head. "I wish I knew, Your Highness, I really do. But ..."

Leo's mind raced. He gripped his hair as he stared at Faye's limp body. Pathos' voice echoed in Leo's head, over and over.

True love's kiss will bring her back.

But did Faye love Leo? Or had she given her heart to Pathos? Did it matter if Leo loved her more than the air in his lungs?

He had to try. If he didn't try, then he would never be able to face Faye's sisters for the rest of his life. Lunging across the room, Leo knelt by the couch.

"My prince, wait!" Madame Leroux cried.

Leo leaned forward and touched his lips to Faye's. They were cold and unyielding. He squeezed his eyes shut and prayed for her life to be restored. That this strange magic would somehow bring his Faye back.

The cold in his chest intensified, spread, until it felt as if ice were forming inside the hollow of his chest. Faye's lips moved beneath his. Leo snapped his eyes open and jerked back. Faye was staring back at him, her brown eyes dull. She blinked, slow and heavy. She gasped in a rattling, raspy breath.

But the gash in her neck remained.

Leo sat back, his heart thudding hard against his ribs. *What in all of Eura ...?*

"Faye?" The word barely passed Leo's lips.

"Faye?" Genevieve rushed to Leo's side. When her eyes landed on Faye, she gasped and covered her mouth with her hands.

Panic rose in Leo's chest. Her skin was cold. Her lips blue. The gash still gaped open on her neck. The kiss had worked. The magic had brought breath back. And yet it worked in all the wrong ways. Faye was alive.

But Undead.

Chapter Thirty – Faye

Something was wrong. What, Faye couldn't tell. She stared at her sisters, standing around her in a huddle, their eyes wide. Leo knelt on the floor, his face twisted in anguish. And in the corner, Madame Leroux's eyes were wide with shock.

Leo hung his head a moment, jaw working. He looked up, swallowed and reached out a hand. Faye glanced down at it and frowned. What was he trying to do?

"Are … Faye, do you feel alright?"

"Feel?" She didn't *feel* anything.

Faye touched the side of her face. Her skin was cold. Was that normal? She couldn't remember.

"What happened?" she asked, rubbing her forehead. Her mind was empty of all but impressions of memories. Something had happened. Something she couldn't stop. Something she deserved.

Adalie rushed forward. Her eyes were wild and tears stained her cheeks. She gripped Faye's face in her clammy hands. "You were dead! But you're alive now, only … you're not alive …" She pulled Faye into a rough hug, fingers digging into Faye's skin as if she were too afraid to let go.

"I …" Faye gasped, her breath ragged in her throat.

She lifted a hand and touched her neck. It was wet. She pulled her hand away—her fingers covered in red. Faye stared at it, not quite comprehending. She was bleeding. And yet, she felt no pain. No fear. No anger. No sadness.

Just … nothing.

She closed her eyes. The memories came back slowly, of Pathos holding her. Of the overwhelming despair and guilt that had weighed her down so much that she gave up. Even as Leo tried to save her.

But it is what I deserved. I never deserved to live. Not after what I'd done.

Opening her eyes, she pushed away from Adalie and Leo, moving as far back on the couch as she could.

"Stay away from me," she said.

Faye.

The Midnight King. He was calling. Everything inside Faye jumped at the voice, willing her forward. She must answer.

Faye pushed to her feet and wobbled. Adalie let out a small cry and grasped her hand. Madame Leroux marched forward and pushed her back onto the couch. Faye struggled to free herself from the woman's grip, but her limbs didn't seem to want to work properly.

"Why ..." Leo scrambled to his feet and gave Madame Leroux a lost look.

"You have brought her back as an Undead!" Madame's voice was harsh, and her pale eyes flashed. "That beast lied to us. We can't let her live this way."

Leo stumbled back and Adalie let out a wail. Faye watched them. So that was why she had blood on her neck. She was alive. But not. She was like Pathos now. Exactly what he wanted.

"You're not suggesting we kill her?" Leo's voice was filled with disbelief.

"Of course not!" Madame twisted her hands together.

"My lord, the Midnight King planned this." A man Faye had never seen before spoke from near the door.

Colette rose from the floor, pushed past Leo, and looked Madame in the eye. "How do we bring her back whole?"

Madame shook her head. "I'm afraid that is up to Faye now ..."

Faye drowned out their voices as Pathos called her again.

Set us free, Faye. Bring us to your home.

I'm coming, Master.

Struggling to her feet once more, Faye pushed past Madame Leroux and staggered to the fireplace. She fell to her knees on the hearth. Someone tugged at her sleeve, holding her back. Faye looked behind her to see Adalie. Her twin's eyes were wide, tears staining her cheeks.

"Please, Faye, don't go back. Please, stay with us! We'll fix you, I promise!"

Faye shook her off and turned back to the fireplace. "I'm not going back." Not yet.

"Then what are you doing? Pathos and the others are dead. They must have died. The castle was crumbling, they were killed!"

Killed. Faye paused and frowned. Could they be killed? If they were killed, had she something to do with it? She trembled.

Master, did I kill you?

No, my lady. You only wounded them for a moment. Come, set us free and your transgressions will be forgiven.

Yes, Master. Faye extended her hand to touch the back wall of the fireplace.

"No!" Madame Leroux's cry filled the air like a panther's roar.

Adalie tugged on Faye again, harder. Colette was there, clutching at her dress. They were all pulling. Tugging. Trying to stop her. To keep her from touching the wall.

Faye strained against warm fingers that dug into her cold flesh. Strips of fire eating away at her skin. Her fingertips were mere inches away. She wrested herself from their touch.

"Faye, don't." Leo's quiet voice punched through the pleas and cries of her sisters.

Faye faltered. Twitched her neck in his direction. There was something about him that made her want to stop. To turn away.

"Please. Come back to us." His grey eyes sparkled with tears that splashed onto his freckled cheeks. He held out a hand, beckoning.

Suddenly, Faye wanted to take his hand. She wanted him to hold her. To tell her everything was okay, that he forgave her for what she had done. Her sisters were here, away from the Midnight King, away from the balls and the monsters. They were safe, just as she always wanted. She reached for him.

No, Faye! Open the portal!

Faye dropped her hand. Turned away. She could not disobey Master.

She touched the wall. Madame Leroux let out a wail.

Adalie and Colette yanked her back.

Faye smiled. A broken, disjointed smile.

The back wall of the fireplace rumbled open, revealing the dark passageway. Someone appeared from the darkness and crawled out into the light. Faye scrambled back. He stood and brushed off the front of his suit. He looked up—the moonlight slanted against the curved horns of his bull mask. That masked face turned toward Adalie.

"Hello, my dear."

Adalie screamed and gripped Colette, who stood frozen. Faye picked herself up and backed away. One by one, the Midnight King's brothers emerged until all five of them stood in the room.

Madame Leroux positioned herself in front of the girls, Leo at one side and the guard on the other. Faye looked on. She frowned. Why did they resist? There was no point in resisting the Midnight King.

"Stay away," Madame Leroux shouted, a warning in her voice.

"Faye!" Adalie didn't reach out anymore. Instead, she watched Faye with pain in her eyes.

For a split moment, Faye could almost believe she felt something. The hollow ache that empty love leaves behind. But then it was gone, and she kept her eyes trained on the floor. She was where she belonged now.

The brothers moved away from the fireplace, forcing everyone to crowd closer. Nosos elbowed through the crowd and planted himself in front of the door, just as Estelle bolted for it. She bumped into Nosos' chest and scrambled back.

Darkness oozed from the portal. It rose and coalesced until it took on the form of a man wearing an iron crown. Pathos paused before the fireplace. His wolf mask glinted deep silver in the dim light. He turned to Faye and placed a hand on her cheek. Cold spread through her veins.

"Well done, my lady."

Faye lowered her gaze. She did only as she was bidden. She didn't deserve the praise.

Pathos leaned close and pressed his forehead to hers. "At last," he whispered. "You are mine."

An odd ache filled Faye's chest. She curled her fingers into the fabric of her bodice, trying to tear the ache horrible feeling away. She didn't want to feel it. It was that same ache she had felt the moment before Pathos had sliced her neck. She didn't want to feel. Not anymore.

This is what you deserve. Her own voice echoed through her mind, harsh. Grating. *You deserve the pain. The hurt.*

Pathos gripped her hand in his, pulling her attention back to the room. He gazed at her sisters, one by one, until he settled on Madame Leroux. The darkness around him seemed to grow deeper.

"Tonight, there will be one last ball. Tonight, the princesses of Revayr will dance with the princes of the Underworld." He moved farther into the room until he stood right in front of Leo.

Leo glared at him, his hand a fist.

"You honestly fell for the bait? Though, I don't blame you. There is just something about Faye that would lure away even the best of us. If only true love's kiss were more than just a folktale."

Leo made to lunge at Pathos, but the guard held him back.

Pathos stepped away and addressed the room.

"Tonight, Prince Lionheart, King Richard, and King Raoul will die, and I will take the throne."

Gasps echoed through the room.

"No!" Colette shouted, her pale cheeks flushing red. "You can't do this!"

Faye watched it all, that dull ache throbbing where her heart had once been.

He looked back at Faye. "And Faye and I shall rule Revayr. A new Revayr, a better Revayr. All the world will never forget the name of Everland."

Adalie reached out to Faye. Faye shook her head.

Phagos laughed, loud and harsh. "This is going to be fun."

Chapter Thirty-One – Leo

Faye was gone. Pathos swept her away the moment he and his brothers had emerged from the fireplace. Then, the dozens of gargoyles that had guarded the bridge followed behind and took them all captive.

And even though Leo and Jack fought hard against the monsters, Leo was still weak from his lost magic. The magic Pathos ripped away.

He snorted at the thought. All this time, he'd had magic. Maybe even magic strong enough to free the princesses, but he didn't even know. And it was too late to change things now.

Now, those monstrous creatures were roaming around outside the house, with Pathos's brothers, Daimon and Poneros, guarding outside the door. Leo paced the cramped sitting room.

"What do we do now?" he asked Madame Leroux who sat on the couch with her two daughters, Bonnie and Delphine.

Madame shook her head. "I don't know."

Colette rose from the floor where she and Estelle had been cradling Adalie. Adalie's screams had quieted to a heartbreaking silence.

"We escape." Colette walked over to the kitchen's open doorway. "There's a back door. We can escape over the wall."

"How?" Estelle asked, voice shaking. "There are gargoyles everywhere."

"If Your Highness would allow me, I could try to distract them," Jack said, stepping away from the fireplace, his hand on his empty scabbard.

Colette's jaw hardened. "No, leave that to me."

She made for the door, but Leo grabbed her arm.

"What are you doing? Are you trying to get yourself killed?"

Eyes as hard as stone, she gripped his wrist with her uninjured hand. Her fingers were cold as ice. "I suggest you unhand me, monsieur."

Leo let go but didn't back away. "You'll get hurt. Or worse."

"I've spent the past three years locked away in the Underworld surrounded by monsters. I think I know how to handle myself."

Turning on her heel, Colette marched toward the door. Leo looked back at Madame Leroux and Jack.

"We're just going to let her go?"

Madame shrugged. "I think you'll find that there's much more to Princess Colette than meets the eye."

"I'll go with her." Jack marched through the room and out the door.

Leo hurried into the kitchen and peered through the windows, but it was too dark to see anything. Silence filled the house. Leo's breath fogged the window and his heart pounded in his ears as he waited for a sign.

Frost spread across the glass. Cold penetrated deeper into Leo's bones. He shuddered and pulled back. Ever since his magic had been ripped away, it seemed as if he were slowly turning to ice on the inside.

Leo watched as the frost spread farther, taking over the glass. Was this his doing? Was this because of what Pathos had done? He rubbed his arms as the cold seeped deeper into his bones.

The door opened and Colette leaned heavily against the door frame. Leo rushed forward but stopped when she held up a hand.

"I'm alright," she gasped. "But we don't have much time."

Straightening, Colette marched back into the living room. "Estelle, go and bring Desi and the others out here. Madame, the way is clear. Do you know anywhere we can go to escape Eura?"

"The woman with the green umbrella."

Colette's brows wrinkled. Leo scratched the back of his head.

"I'm sorry, the what?"

"My daughters know whom I speak of." Madame looked down at Delphine, who traded a secret-laden glance with her mother.

"Excellent." Leo clapped his hands together. "Shall we get going?"

Estelle emerged from the back of the house with the others following. Delphine jumped to her feet. She took Bonnie's hand.

"Come on. Follow me and be quiet." Delphine led the way through the kitchen and out the open door. Leo hesitated, staying behind. He looked back at Madame.

"Will you be alright on your own?"

Madame gave Leo her unsettling grin. "Don't worry about me, my prince. I am more than capable of caring for myself."

Giving her a nod, Leo followed the others out into the back garden. When he stepped onto the wet grass, the whispers of the sisters filled the air like rustling leaves. Colette and Desi stood opposite of each other, their fingers interlocked. Colette had removed the bandage from her hand, allowing Leo to see the raw flesh where her ring finger was supposed to be. Even though it looked painful, Colette's expression remained focused.

Disgust at himself filled him at the sight. Pathos knew that leaving behind evidence of Colette's death would send Leo searching again. It was the push he needed to fall right into the madman's trap.

Belle stepped into their cupped hands and gripped the ivy that covered the stone wall. With a grunt, she pulled herself up on top of the wall. Swinging her legs around, she dropped out of sight.

"Is there anyone on the other side yet?" Leo asked in a whisper. He didn't feel right about the small girl going over alone.

"Estelle, the Leroux girls, and Jack have gone over," Desi replied as she lined the sisters up according to age.

The tension in Leo's chest eased a little at that. If Jack was with them, then they would be safe.

Margaux went over next, then Jenine. Leo checked the night shadows for glowing red eyes as he paced behind the sisters. The garden was eerily quiet. No rustling of wings, no deep growls. Just what had Colette done? Leo eyed the eldest sister. She looked exhausted and her arms trembled. Leo could only guess she gave them all a right hook.

Linette scrambled over next, followed by Kamille.

The Midnight King's brothers' voices were muffled. Cart wheels rattled against stone. Leo stiffened. He strained his ears to listen.

Something shifted in the grass. Leo searched the shadows. He found a dark lump moving against the even darker ground. It sniffed and growled.

Turning, Leo ran back toward the girls. All of the princesses except Colette, Desi, and Adalie were over.

"Hurry!" he hissed. "The gargoyles are waking!"

Colette moved as if to run back, but Leo pushed her toward the wall. "No time. Hurry!"

A growl emanated from the darkness. Leo cupped his hands and bent his knees. Adalie pressed her slippered foot into his hands. She gripped the stone wall's ivy and began to climb as Leo lifted her higher. His muscles strained with her weight.

Something flashed by and Adalie screamed. She slammed against the wall and fell back. Lunging, Leo tried to catch her, but she slipped out of his grasp and hit the grass.

Two glowing, red eyes appeared as the gargoyle pounced. Leo gripped his left fist and punched the beast's face. Pain ricocheted through his bones on impact. The gargoyle let out a shrill screech, wings flailing as it fell backwards.

Shouts came from inside. Desi gripped her hair in panic.

"What do we do?" she cried.

Leo gestured for the wall. "Keep going. I'll see if I can hold them off."

"No!" Colette held out a hand. "We must distract them from the others. They need time to escape or risk getting caught."

Fear gripped Leo's heart and he paused a moment to listen. There was no sound from the other side of the wall. He couldn't risk looking back. Instead, he inched toward the gargoyle that circled Desi. Adalie sat frozen, inches away from the door, light from the windows shining in her wide eyes.

Leo rushed at the gargoyle—arms spread. With a snarl, the creature jumped at Leo, snapping its teeth. Its jaws slammed shut right next to Leo's hand. He jerked back with a hiss—eyes locked on the beast's massive claws. Just beyond, Colette and Desi yanked Adalie to her feet and the three bolted for the door.

It flew open just as Colette reached for the handle. But Daimon stood silhouetted against the light, the fangs on his mask glittering white. The moment Daimon's foot touched the grass, the gargoyle calmed and slunk back into the shadows.

"Get inside," he growled.

The girls scurried inside. Leo followed at a slower pace, tense. He could knock the impertinence from the masked boy, but it would be foolish to try. Who knew how many gargoyles waited in the darkness, and Leo had no gold weapons to fight back with.

Swallowing his anger, Leo walked into the house. The gargoyles followed, red eyes glowing in the dark, stone bellies sliding through the grass.

"Where are the others?" Daimon shouted as he slammed the door shut. He stalked into the sitting room and shoved Colette's shoulder. "What did you do with them?"

Colette glared at him but said nothing. Leo placed himself in front of her and the others.

"I would leave the ladies alone if I were you." Leo kept his voice cool.

Madame came to Leo's side, her green eyes flashing. She snarled at Daimon, flashing wickedly sharp teeth.

Daimon took a step back, then puffed his chest out. He pointed behind Leo. "Tell me, or I'll kill the small one. Don't think I won't."

"Kill her and I'll snap your neck." Leo took a step closer. He towered a head taller than the boy.

Daimon growled, a wild, feral sound. Quick as a snake, his long, bony fingers wrapped around Leo's throat. He pushed Leo backwards, slamming him to the floor. Sparks exploded in Leo's vision. He fought for breath as pain spread through the back of his skull. He scrabbled at the boy's fingers. Daimon was strong, stronger than Leo had thought possible.

"Tell me where they are!" he screamed, his fingers squeezing tighter, digging into Leo's veins. "Tell me or I'll kill him!"

"No!" Madame reached for Daimon with clawed fingers. Daimon threw up a hand and darkness wrapped around Madame, pinning her in place.

"Tell me!" Daimon twitched, his free hand turning black.

"If you kill him without the Midnight King's consent, you'll be the next to die." Colette's icy tone cut through the tension of the room. The air seemed to grow colder with each breath. "I'll not say where they are to anyone but Pathos himself."

Leo's vision was tunneling. He tried to speak. Tried to tell Colette to leave him. To run. They could escape while they had the chance. Leo searched the blurry faces for Colette. Instead, he saw a pillar of white. Was it snow? Ice? Light?

"Fine." Daimon's voice came from far away. "You'll go to the Midnight King. But don't think we won't send gargoyles looking."

The noose around Leo's throat lessened. He gasped and lunged upwards. His forehead cracked against Daimon's mask. Daimon howled and fell back. Leo wrapped his hand around the boy's throat.

"Leo, don't," Colette said, calm.

It took more effort than Leo cared to admit to release his hold on Daimon. The room spun as the masked monster struggled for air. Daimon wriggled from Leo's hold and scrambled away.

Exhaustion hit Leo and he dropped his pounding head into his hands. He'd almost killed a man. It didn't matter how much the Enchanter deserved it—the thought still shook Leo to his core. He'd almost killed a man. And some small twisted part of him knew he'd do it again.

Desi knelt next to Leo, her dark-brown hair falling in front of her face. Hesitantly, she put a hand on his shoulder.

"Are you alright?" she whispered.

Leo inched away from her touch.

"I'm fine," he rasped.

The front door opened and Poneros stepped inside. His rat mask looked especially gruesome in the lantern light. Grabbing the back of Daimon's jacket, Poneros jerked his brother to his feet and yanked him outside. When he came back, Leo struggled to his feet.

"Get in the carriage," Poneros barked.

Colette took Adalie's hand and together they made their way outside. Leo and Desi followed, just behind Madame Leroux.

"I could have killed him," Leo spoke past his closing throat.

"I know," Desi whispered back. "But to what end?"

To what end? Leo didn't care. Just as long as the Midnight King and his demon brothers got exactly what they deserved.

Chapter Thirty-Two – Faye

Faye had no idea what Pathos planned. But whatever it was, he moved with the confidence of a man who knew he would win.

Pathos' brothers jeered at King Richard as they chained him to his own throne. Each link was the size of Faye's hand, crafted of magic. King Richard struggled against them, his face red.

"You'll pay for this!" he cried. "You and all your filthy kind!"

Quick as a snake, Pathos swooped toward King Richard and grabbed him by the throat, sending the throne back on two legs. The king choked as Pathos leaned in close.

"The only crimes committed were your persecution and vile disregard for my kind, while you yourself married an Enchantress." Pathos' grip tightened and Richard twitched, gasping for air. "You are a hypocrite and a fool. You deserve more than death."

Shoving away, Pathos stalked across the dais to where Faye stood. She stared at Richard. He heaved for breath as the brothers continued to wrap him in chains. His head slumped forward, and his shoulders sagged in defeat.

Faye wrapped her arms around herself, unsure of how to feel. King Richard had persecuted her kind for years. The evidence of his crimes littered the castle and streets. And each time he could have stopped his atrocities, he turned a blind eye. Execution seemed a fitting end.

Faye knew she should feel some sort of regret. After all, this was Leo's father. But they had nothing in common.

Where Leo was kind, his father was cruel. Where Leo smiled, his father remained callous. She wouldn't be sad to see the king die.

"I will try to be merciful, for your sake," Pathos said, placed a hand on Faye's shoulder. "But the king must die. Only then will our kind live in freedom."

"Kill him in any manner you wish," Faye replied. "I don't care."

Just as the brothers finished chaining Richard to his throne, the ballroom doors flew open. Gargoyles stalked inside, pushing before them a crowd of courtiers, servants, and guards. The people, the *Humans*, quivered in fear and bumped against each other like a herd of sheep. Faye looked between them and Pathos. Beside her, Pathos watched, all emotion hidden.

Once they reached the center of the room, Pathos held out his hand.

"Kneel."

The crowd fell to the floor in a huddle. They were frightened sheep, the whole lot of them. Ready to bow and scrape to any new power that would grant them life. Faye curled her lip, disgusted.

Poneros entered and bowed to Pathos. Then, rising, he turned and dragged someone into the room, a small crowd following. Faye's breath hitched in her throat. Colette, Desi, Adalie, and Madame Leroux were marched inside, each with their hands bound. Next, Leo followed in Poneros' grip.

Faye took an involuntary step forward. Pathos gripped her arm.

"Don't worry, my lady. Your sisters won't be harmed."

They were shoved into the crowd. Leo pushed forward— his eyes trained on the dais.

"Father!" he called.

He made to run up onto the dais, but a gargoyle snapped its teeth at him. He fell back into the crowd, his eyes blazing.

"Stay back, son." Richard's voice trembled and sweat beaded his brow. "Don't do anything to make him angry."

"Listen to your father, boy," Pathos said as he removed his mask and tossed it to the floor. A wicked smile pulled at his lips. "You wouldn't want to make me angry."

Pathos' face had changed. His skin no longer hung from his face, and his cheeks weren't quite so hollow. Instead of cold marble, his eyes were more like pieces of the night sky, a deep, depthless black, with the faintest light swirling inside. Even as she watched, Faye could see Leo's stolen power stitching his face back together.

It was strange, seeing him almost Human. And yet, he still held a deadlike aspect. As if instead of being whole, he was just the ghost of a man.

Below, Leo glared up at Pathos but remained silent. His gaze turned instead to Faye and softened. Faye glanced to her bare feet, the empty place in her chest growing.

She didn't need his empathy. She didn't need his love. What was past was past. She was done with her old life, with the pain and hurting and sadness. None of that could touch her now. Even if that meant sacrificing the only emotion she longed to feel.

"Welcome, my friends," Pathos boomed to the crowd below. His voice sent a chill through Faye's veins. "You are all here tonight to witness the fall of your old king and the rise of a new one."

Pathos gestured to King Richard. The chains around him clinked and tightened.

"This man will be executed for his crimes against the magicfolk. For too long he has hunted us, murdered us just for being who we are. But no more! No longer will we bow to this king's whims! For tonight, the magic will rule, and the Humans will bow or face death."

Richard released a cry of pain as the links snaked tighter. Leo lunged forward once more.

251

"This is ridiculous! You kill him, you enslave the Humans, and you will get an uprising. We will fight back, no matter the cost. Both magic and Human blood will spill." Leo stood firm, even as Poneros tried to pull him back.

Pathos laughed. "You count yourself as one of them, when you yourself are an Enchanter?"

The crowd around Leo shrank back. Only Madame and Faye's sisters stood firm. As well as one other figure. Faye clutched her skirts. Papa.

He had his arm wrapped around Adalie and his cheeks were stained with tears. He looked up at Faye, his eyes begging her to join him. To come home. Only, she couldn't come home. She no longer belonged with the living.

"All of you are getting exactly what you deserve," Pathos spit as he paced the stage. His voice boomed and hissed across the room like angry sea waves, pummeling into Faye's core. "The filth of Humans will be wiped from existence, as well as any Faerie, Changeling, Half-blood, or Witch who stands in my way. You will all burn!"

Lifting his hands, he stretched them toward the ballroom floor. Symbols glowed across it, and the ground began to shake. The people screamed and scrambled away from the symbols as if the light burned their feet. Each one was a perfect circle filled with jagged lines. Faye's chest tightened. She had seen these symbols before.

Papa stood firm against the chaos. He held his daughters tight. Madame stood with him—her gaze locked on Faye.

This was wrong. They were among the crowd. Standing against Pathos. But they should be standing with her. If they didn't, then …

Pathos meant to kill them. He meant to open the floor and send them all into the Underworld. Not again. Not again.

Whirling around, Faye grabbed hold of Pathos' arm. "You always keep your promises," she gasped. "Always! I held up my end of the deal. Now you hold up yours."

Pathos jerked from her grip. "What are you talking about?"

"You mean to send them back to the Underworld. My sisters! You promised that they would be safe. You promised that everyone—*everyone*—would be allowed to go free, including my mother." Panic bubbled past the numbness and the cold, filling her limbs with an aching fire.

Pathos' lips curled into a snarl. "I already kept my promise. I let your other sisters go, didn't I? They'll be free. But they," he pointed a rigid finger at her family, "have defied me. They stand against us. Either they join us or die."

Faye looked down at her family. At her sisters, her father, Madame. She couldn't let them die. Not when she had fought so hard, so long to free them, to keep them safe.

His gaze softened and he placed a hand on her cheek. "They won't die. They'll be safe in the Underworld. Away from the chaos and the fights. Don't you want your family safe?"

The panic burning in her chest weakened. Yes, they would be safe and out of the way if they went to the Underworld. When Pathos took over, they wouldn't be harmed. But her other sisters were still out there. Faye pulled away and gripped her hair. The floor shook and she stumbled back.

King Richard caught her eye. Then closed his eyes as his face paled. He seemed to no longer be breathing. Whether he was dead or alive she couldn't tell, but the chains dug deep into his skin. She could imagine them cinching tighter, tighter, until his bones cracked, until blood poured from his mouth. It was what he deserved.

But was it what she wanted? Did she want the world to burn? All she ever wanted was to be free. No part of Pathos' plan was even close to freedom. Could she stand by, quiet and meek, while everything descended into chaos?

"No." It was just a whisper. But she had said it.

"What?" Pathos looked down at her, a dangerous glint she had never seen before shining in his eyes.

Faye shrank away. "Please, Pathos, let them go. They haven't done anything wrong. Keep your promise. Let them go!"

Pathos loomed, his shadow blocking the light.

Her voice was weak, trembling, but she held her ground. "Let my family go."

Pathos remained silent. He stared at her, brows knitted, eyes narrowed. Cold filled Faye's veins as she waited, waited for him to answer.

Rearing back, Pathos slapped her cheek.

Faye stumbled back. Shock rippled through her. She placed a hand on her stinging face.

Pathos had never, *ever* slapped her before. He had never hurt her. That was the one thing she could always trust. And yet, he had …

Grinding her teeth together, Faye gathered her courage. She dropped her hand. Curled her fingers into a fist as Pathos walked away.

The ground shook and a loud crack filled the air. Faye stumbled and fell to her knees. Even as her world shook and pain filled her cheek, she knew. At last, she knew.

From this moment on, she would no longer belong to Pathos.

Chapter Thirty-Three – Leo

The symbols burned through Leo's boots as he stared at Pathos and Faye. Her face, once so expressionless, was now twisted with shock. She held her cheek as Pathos walked away. In the distance, a clock chimed. Leo froze, listening.

Twelve chimes. Midnight.

The ground began to shake. Around him, the crowd lost their footing. Colette grabbed hold of his sleeve as she tried not to fall. Before him, the gargoyles took flight. Leo bolted.

He charged toward the stage and his father's throne. The chains that bound his father filled his vision—they were tightening, ever tightening. Soon, Father would be crushed. Leo bolted up the steps and knelt before the throne.

"Father!" He gasped for breath. "How do I fix this?"

Father shook his head. His eyes widened and he wheezed, "Look out!"

Hands gripped Leo's arms. Leo lunged forward and gripped the golden cord that hung from his father's belt. The hands yanked him back and the cord snapped.

Leo struggled against Daimon's arms, taking a quick glance around. Faye was frozen on the dais, staring at the ballroom floor. Pathos stood with arms outstretched, brows knitted in concentration. The symbols on the floor were splitting.

Whipping around, Leo wrapped the cord around Daimon's neck. Daimon choked as the gold seared into his skin. The brother fell to his knees, his snake mask hiding his expression. Leo gritted his teeth and cinched the cord tighter. With one last jerk of the limbs, Daimon fell.

Leo kept hold of the cord, his own wrists still bound. He gripped it tight in his fist. No time to think about what he'd done. He had to save his father.

Rushing toward the throne, Leo fell to his knees. He tugged at the chains, but they continued to tighten, link by link. Leo banged his fist against the armrest. There had to be a way to stop it.

"Father, I don't know what to do," Leo choked. "How do I fix this?"

Tears swam in Father's eyes.

"I'm sorry," he gasped. "I never knew—"

The chains cinched tighter. Leo gripped them in his fists. He pulled at them, anger surging, filling the cold place in his chest.

"Why didn't you tell me? Why didn't you tell me what I am?" The words came out a desperate shout.

"Your mother … she told me your magic would be the key … if he ever found out …"

He knew. Leo fought back a hysterical laugh. Father knew all this time that Leo's magic could open the Underworld. All this time he knew Leo was an Enchanter. Not Human. Leo had never been Human.

The ground rocked and screams filled the air. Faye jumped from the stage and ran toward the ever-widening hole. Leo's lungs froze as he watched three courtiers slip and fall into the darkness.

No time. As much as it pained him, Leo turned his focus to Pathos. Both light and darkness streamed from the Midnight King as he concentrated on the chaos.

There was only one way to stop this madness.

Kill Pathos. Take his power back.

With a yell, Leo ran toward Pathos, the golden cord locked in his grip. Pathos twisted to the side—his eyes wide. Ekdikeo burst from the darkness and slammed into Leo. They toppled off the dais and onto the floor. Leo tucked his arms close as he rolled. Planting his hands on the trembling ground, he pushed to his feet.

Ekdikeo crouched. With careful steps he circled Leo as a short, black blade flicked from his sleeve into his hand. Every muscle in Leo's body tensed as he prepared for attack. He was virtually defenseless against the brother with only a golden cord. It was a stroke of luck that the cords were woven from real gold.

Leo gripped the cord in his bound hands. Like a prowling tiger, Ekidikeo continued to circle. In the distance to Leo's right, a crack split the floor. Leo's mind raced. If he could just get Ekidikeo with his back to the crevice …

With a growl, the brother lunged. Leo dodged out of the way of the knife, slicing the bonds that held his wrists together against the blade, and threw out his right arm. Before Ekidikeo could react, he slammed into Leo's arm and Leo dragged him to the ground. They slid toward the hole as the floor bucked and groaned.

The ground dipped. Fear gripped Leo's chest and his heart squeezed. He scrambled for a handhold. A smaller crack opened, inches away from his face. Gritting his teeth, he gripped the edge. Wrenching pain shot through his hand and up his arm as he jerked to a halt. The wood bit into his skin, the splinters digging into his fingers.

A roar filled the air as Ekdikeo slid past Leo. Strong fingers latched onto Leo's leg. The pain in his hand strengthened as Ekidikeo's added weight dragged him down. He kicked Ekidikeo's mask. A loud crack filled the air as his tiger mask fractured. With a wild shriek, the brother's grasp slipped, and he fell through the ever-widening hole, disappearing into darkness.

Wood groaned as the floor cracked around Leo, caving in a wide circle. Leo grunted as he pulled himself up. Pain lanced through his fingers. His muscles shook.

Dropping the cord, Leo gripped his purchase with both hands. With a wild yell, he heaved himself up and onto the last of the floor that hadn't buckled. He rolled away from the hole—hands tucked to his chest.

When he looked back, his breath left his lungs. The middle of the ballroom floor had completely caved in, forming a jagged circle that looked like a hungry mouth.

Don't look. Don't look. If he looked, the pain would worsen. If he kept his eyes trained on Pathos, he wouldn't have to see the damage done.

Pushing himself up with his elbows, Leo staggered to his feet. He stumbled toward the dais. Pathos' gaze flicked to Leo, then away. He backed toward the edge of the dais.

"Oh, no you don't," Leo growled.

He wouldn't let Pathos get away. Not this time.

Leo raced across the floor and leaped up the steps onto the dais. Lowering his head, he rammed into Pathos. They both tumbled to the floor. Using his elbows, Leo pushed himself into a sitting position. In a blur of black, Pathos charged. Before Pathos could make contact, Leo turned to the side. Sharp pain filled his shoulder the moment Pathos's forehead connected.

Pathos hissed and gripped his head. Leo balled his hand into a fist and slammed it into the Midnight King's cheek.

"Don't you *ever* hurt Faye again!" he roared.

Pathos spat blood. He snarled, showing crooked teeth. "Faye is mine! She will always be mine!"

Leo looked back at the ballroom floor and for a moment, his heart stopped beating. There, at the edge of the hole, Faye lay on her stomach, reaching into the void, Desi gripping her legs.

"Then why don't you save her?" Leo shouted over the noise. "Why don't you stop this madness before she gets herself killed?"

Pathos turned to where Leo was looking. His eyes widened.

"No!"

Leo smashed his elbow into Pathos' temple. Like a rag-doll, Pathos crumpled. But when Leo reached for the monster, his body turned to smoke.

All around Leo, the world darkened. Something collided into him from behind. Strong arms gripped him around the chest as he toppled to the floor. He reached out, searching for something, anything to use as a weapon. The arms released him, only to be replaced by hands around his throat. Pathos' laughter grated in his ear.

The cold in Leo's chest strengthened to the point he felt like his ribs might crack. It bit down deep into his bones and stiffened his muscles. His lungs burned as he fought for breath. His eyelids fluttered.

No! Need to stay awake. Save Faye. Save Father. Get … magic … His thoughts faded and turned to wet sand. His head felt heavy. Pathos' arm ground against the bones in his neck.

Warmth. He needed warmth. A desolate winter was raging in his body and he had to find the fire.

Reaching out, he felt the source of heat. It curled around his fingers, as familiar as an old friend. As a part of himself.

Leo's eyes snapped open. Light spilled from Pathos' chest and into Leo's shaking hand.

The magic inside him began to wake.

Chapter Thirty-Four – Faye

This can't be happening. The thought circled Faye's head as she stared at the crumbling ballroom floor. At the people screaming, running, fighting to get away.

She was suddenly back in her home castle. Music, loud and cheerful, rang through the ballroom. Brilliant gowns of different colors and sleek black tailcoats flared as men and women danced. Laughter, bright and golden, filled the air.

She stood at the edge of the room, Pathos clinging to her hand. The floor began to glow with brilliant symbols.

The floor shook.

A fissure opened and before she knew it, everyone was slipping, falling, reaching.

Reaching, scrabbling for solid ground. Splinters digging under her nails.

Falling, falling, falling into the black. Faye couldn't breathe. She shook, limbs numb, terrible, horrible fear clawing its way under her skin. Pushing against the barrier of her hollow chest. Not again. *Heavens above, please, never again.*

Adalie's scream reverberated across the room, *Leo's* ballroom, and pierced Faye's chest. She shook herself awake from the memories. Below, the floor had buckled and Adalie slid across the polished wood. Right for the open gash that yawned like a hungry tomb.

"Adalie!" Faye screamed as she bolted across the dais and onto the ballroom floor.

Courtiers, guards, and servants spilled across the floor and into the widening cracks like discarded ragdolls. One

261

of the courtiers flew across the abyss and slammed into the opposite side. A large shaft of wood impaled him through the chest. His dying scream echoed through Faye's mind.

Adalie scrambled for a handhold, fingers scratching divots into the floor. Faye dove and grabbed her wrist just as she slipped through the jagged hole. In a flash of gold, Colette was next to her, taking hold of Adalie's other wrist.

"Pull!" she screamed.

Planting her elbows on the floor, she pulled. The world continued to shake, and Faye's grip slipped. She found herself slipping down. Splinters of wood dug into her upper arms as she scrabbled for a foothold.

"I've got you!" Desi cried over the screams and ominous groans of wood and stone.

"On three," Colette ground out.

Faye nodded as sweat slicked her palms. She readjusted her grip on Adalie's wrist. Adalie latched eyes with Faye as she dug her nails into Faye's wrist.

"Don't let go!"

"I won't, I promise," Faye said between pants. Her ribs were digging into the floor and the muscles in her arms screamed.

"One," Colette began.

Faye squeezed her fingers tight.

"Two!"

Taking in a deep breath, she steeled her muscles.

"Three!"

With a yell, Faye and Colette pulled just as a shock rippled through the floor. The room rocked backwards and Adalie flew from the hole, slamming into Faye. The girls slid across the floor toward the dais. Colette's back hit the dais steps first, then Desi. Faye collided into Colette's stomach, seconds before Adalie collided with Faye's legs. They lay there in a tangled pile of limbs and skirts, breathing heavily.

Faye squirmed around until her nose was inches from Colette's. Fear shone in her sister's eyes.

"Are you alright?" Faye gasped.

Colette's eyes widened and she shoved Faye's chest. "Move!"

Turning, Faye looked up to see a monstrous black panther stalking toward them. Adalie screamed as it charged. The panther slid to a stop inches away, nails digging furrows into the floor.

"Hush, child!" the panther growled in a deep, feminine voice. Its glowing green eyes pinned Faye to the floor. "It is I, Aurore Leroux."

"Madame!" Faye placed a hand over her hollow chest. "You ... you're ..."

"Yes, I am a Pandalian Faerie. Quick, we haven't the time. On my back, now!"

"Come on, Desi, Adalie, Faye." Colette shoved her way out of the pile and struggled to her feet.

Desi helped Adalie to her feet and Adalie stumbled to the panther's side.

Faye shook her head. "No, Adalie, Desi, you two go." She looked up to where Leo was struggling with Pathos. "I've got to help Leo."

Desi gave her a worried look but nodded. She climbed up behind Adalie and Madame bolted for the open doors. Faye looked to Colette.

"Are you with me, sister?"

Colette nodded—her blue eyes bright. "Always."

Gripping Colette's hand, Faye rushed for the dais. She didn't know what she was going to do, or how, but she had to stop Pathos, one way or another.

An explosion of white filled Faye's vision. She lost her grip on Colette's hand and flew backwards. Her spine hit the floor and her teeth clacked together. A ringing filled her ears.

Spots danced in Faye's vision. She shook her head as a deafening silence pressed in. She searched the floor for signs of Colette but saw nothing. The room was empty but for Leo, Pathos, Phagos, and Poneros. Like broken puppets, the two brothers were staggering to their feet where they had been grappling with Human guards, limbs hanging at crooked angles.

And there, standing on the dais in the center of the glow, was Leo. His skin, his eyes, his hair, everything glowed a brilliant white. The sight of it stole Faye's breath away as she shielded her eyes.

Glow dimming, Leo burst across the dais and tackled Phagos. The brother fell like a toppled tree. After several moments of struggling, Leo stabbed Phagos in the chest with something long. With a wild scream, Phagos burst into a cloud of obsidian ash. When Leo turned away, Faye spied Madame's cane clutched in his fist. Only, it wasn't a cane, but a long, thin blade made of gold.

Poneros drew his own blade. With long strides, he approached Leo, confidence in the set of his shoulders. Leo remained calm, his eyes two burning white suns, his movements quick and sharp. Their blades met with a loud screech of metal against metal.

Leo fought with a wild ferocity, beating down on Poneros' dagger with heavy strokes. With a final stroke, the dagger flew from Poneros' hand. The saber flashed and Poneros' head tumbled from his shoulders. As his body crumpled, it too turned to black ash.

The rumbling came to a stop. Faye staggered to her feet. Only she, Leo, Pathos and King Richard were left in the room. Pathos picked himself up from the dais. He gripped the back of Richard's throne. The king was slumped forward in his seat, no longer struggling. Leo held up his sword.

"Let him go," he growled, his voice echoing, turning to music.

Faye's chest ached and she shivered as she stared at the slumped body of the king. There was no doubt in her mind that he was dead. Leo's jaw clenched and his hand trembled.

Pathos' eyes were wide and wild. "You want your precious father? Then take him!"

The chains slackened and the king's body tumbled from the throne. He rolled down the steps. Leo dropped the sword and rushed to his father's side. Faye looked down at the sword. Then up at Pathos.

She had only one chance. One chance to end this. The only way to save them all, the only way for all of this to end, was for Pathos to die.

The thought hurt more than Faye expected.

For three years, *he* had held her and her sisters prisoner. *He* had given her the shoes. *He* had betrayed her and threatened to kill her sisters after she had trusted him for so long.

And yet, he had been there for her when Leo left. He had always been kind. And hadn't *she* been the one to curse her sisters? Hadn't *she* been the one to lure her sisters into the trap? The one that caused the floor to open and all of the courtiers, guests, and even Mama to fall into the darkness of the Underworld?

Shadows surrounded Faye, cloaking, crushing. They dug beneath her skin and filled her veins. They curled inside her hollow chest and locked her bones in place.

All of this was her fault. Everything that had happened was because of her. Because she had been selfish, self-centered, and blind. Everything that had happened to her, everything that had happened to her family, she deserved. And she deserved much, much worse.

Faye brought her hand up to the jagged gash in her neck. She felt the cold flesh, the dried blood. She was dead. And yet she still lived. The thoughts still plagued her mind. The anger, the hate, the frustration still raged inside her, pounding against the fragile walls that kept them at bay.

Would it be better to live? Better to feel again?

No. What has happened is exactly what you deserve. In fact, you should die, fully, and rid this world of the burden you create.

The hollow place in Faye's chest widened. It stretched so tight she felt her ribs crack. Faye doubled over in pain.

Just give in. Give in, and it will all be over. Give in to the darkness, and you can be at peace.

All she had to do was give in to the darkness and she would no longer have to fight. No longer have to feel weary. She could rest. Finally rest.

Faye felt the splintered wood beneath her feet. Felt the rough fabric of her dress. And beyond the dark, she could see Leo glowing softly as he cradled his father's body.

Leo hadn't given up. Even when Pathos had ripped his power away. Even when his father was chained, he hadn't given up on her, or himself.

If he could live despite his losses, perhaps she could keep going just a moment longer. Just long enough to right her wrongs.

Faye took a staggering step forward. Then another. Another. The golden blade gleamed despite the darkness. Faye reached for it. The cold pommel bit into her skin.

As she made her way toward Pathos, one staggering step at a time, the voices whispered, shouted, screamed inside her. The darkness snagged at her arms and tugged at her clothes. It dug its shiny claws into her hair. Pulling. Tugging. Jerking. Dragging. All trying to keep her back.

Faye ducked her head and plowed onward. She slapped a hand over her ear as the voices grew louder.

Selfish. Stupid. Ugly. Worthless. Unlovable. Coward. Traitor.

Tears touched Faye's cheeks. She gasped in a shuddering breath. Could the Undead cry? They burned her eyes and skin as if they were tiny pieces of coal. Through the blur, she could see Pathos.

He was waiting for her on the dais. His arms hung at his sides and his face twisted into a pained expression.

"Faye," he said. Soft. Quiet.

Faye placed one bare foot on the first step. Then the next.

"Faye."

She reached the dais.

"Faye, don't. Please, I never meant to hurt you."

She halted an arm's length away. Looking up into his eyes, she gripped the saber tight. So tight the panther head's tiny metal fangs pricked her palm.

"Did you ever love me?" Faye choked past her closing throat.

"What kind of question is that? You know the answer."

The hollow in her chest deepened. Faye's shoulders fell. "What you think is love, it's not real."

Pathos clenched his jaw. His dark eyes narrowed with pain. "Why ..." He choked on his words. "Why can't you love me?"

"I did." Faye looked down at the blade. "But I can't. Not anymore."

Faye lunged. The blade slid into Pathos' body, right between his ribs. Pathos gasped and staggered back. Faye released the blade, her hands shaking.

Pathos fell to his knees. He reached down and pulled the blade from his chest. Crimson blood stained the front of his white shirt. He looked up, hurt burning in his dark, dark eyes.

"It's over, Pathos," Faye whispered. "I can't belong to the darkness anymore."

Pathos' breath rattled in his chest. Stumbling, he dropped to the floor, mouth gaping as he fought for breath.

Faye hesitated. Should she hold him? Should she walk away? How was she supposed to act, when the man who had hurt her for so long, and yet protected her with a fierce loyalty, lay dying at her feet? She clutched at her chest, her thoughts racing. Pain, deep and penetrating, gripped her.

"You … you are bound with me," Pathos choked. "I die … you … die."

Faye looked down at her dress. Blood was oozing from a wound that shouldn't be there. The world blurred and Faye collapsed to the floor.

"Faye!"

Warm hands held her tight. Light pierced the darkness. Faye looked up into Leo's beautiful grey eyes, shining with a brilliant light that sent warmth into her frozen bones. Tears stained his cheeks, and yet determination hardened his jaw, his shoulders, his light.

"Faye, please! Please, you need to let go of Pathos. Please, I need you to live!"

Choose life. She could let go of the shadows, let go of the past and step into the light. The possibility was there, right in front of her. All she had to do was reach out and touch it. Take it in her hand and allow life to stitch her back together.

Faye reached up and touched Leo's cheek. Felt the stubble on his cheek. The soft red hair on his temple. Closing her eyes, Faye curled in close to him, soaking in his warmth.

"I choose life," she sighed.

The ground shook. Strong arms lifted Faye. Leo held her close to his chest as he raced for the open door, skirting around the holes in the floor. Faye looked over his shoulder at Pathos' body. She stiffened. Someone else was there.

Nosos crawled across the ballroom floor like some form of twisted goblin toward Pathos. Gripping Pathos' shirt, he dragged his brother's body across the floor toward the hole. He paused and looked up, red dragon mask in place. Then, tipped back, he fell into the darkness, pulling Pathos down with him.

Chapter Thirty-Five – Faye

"Put me down!" Faye gripped Leo's shoulder tight as she stared at the hole.

In her chest, her heart began to beat, one painful stutter at a time. Her neck burned and she reached up to find the skin stitching itself back together.

Leo placed Faye gently on her feet. Stumbling, she searched the room for any sign of a golden dress or yellow hair. For a sign among the bodies that Colette was here. That she had survived.

Through all the chaos, Faye had forgotten about Colette. And now, the thought crushed her. But no matter where she looked, she saw no sign of her sister.

Faye's breath hitched in her throat. She raced for one of the cracks in the floor, her feet sliding across the polished wood as the tremors shook the ground. Arms flailing, she slid to a stop right on the edge. Her body tipped forward as she stared down into the darkness.

"Colette!" she screamed into the darkness. "Colette!"

Leo grabbed her around the waist and pulled her away. Faye struggled in his grasp, pushing at his hands.

"No, let me go! Colette!"

"We can't stay here. The castle is falling to pieces!"

As if to prove his point, a chunk of the ceiling crumbled and fell, slamming into the dais. Faye's heart seized in her chest as she spied King Richard lying at the bottom of the steps.

"What about your father?"

"He's dead." Steel lined Leo's words. He tugged on Faye again. "Come on, or we'll both be buried."

All the fight left Faye's limbs. She allowed him to drag her from the room and out into the castle entryway. Dust and mortar fell like snow, clinging to Faye's skin and eyelashes. It stung her eyes. She coughed and held a hand over her head.

Debris dug into her feet as they dodged a falling chunk of pillar. The castle groaned and the suits of armor toppled. The entrance to the castle stood open, though Faye wasn't sure how long that would last.

"Faye! Leo!" Desi's voice cut through the rumbling. A dark figure appeared in the doorway, silhouetted against the brilliant red fire burning behind her.

The doorway groaned. Faye looked up, her heart in her throat. She froze. If she ran under it, and it collapsed …

Leo tugged on Faye's hand. "Come on! We've got to go now!"

Faye stumbled. Leo dragged her across the threshold. With a loud snap, the frame buckled and collapsed. Debris sprayed outward, slamming into Faye's back. She covered her head and hunched over.

Madame's strong hands gripped Faye's shoulders. She pulled Faye to her feet. Without a word, they raced down the steps and across the crumbling courtyard. When they stepped onto the street, it was like a different world. The ground was steady. The houses were still intact.

Faye turned to see Leo facing the castle, head tilted back as he watched the destruction. Slowly, Faye came to his side. She wrapped her arm around his and laid her head on his shoulder.

"I'm sorry about your father," she whispered.

Leo's jaw clenched. He rubbed a hand across his cheek, then shook his head, eyes tight with pain.

"Come on. We've got to find your sisters." His voice was thick. Broken.

Turning, he walked away, shoulders stiff, head lowered. When he reached the castle steps, he kicked at chunks of the castle wall, sending them skittering across the courtyard. Faye bit her lip as a pang of sorrow filled her heart. Had she said something wrong?

Picking through the wreckage, Desi and Adalie approached, hesitant. They paused an arm's length away. Guilt and sorrow layered in Faye's chest and throat. Reaching out, she pulled them both into a hug. A *real* hug. No longer were they controlled by the Midnight King's rules. No longer did they have to fear. She allowed herself to relax, even though her legs still trembled.

They were free. They were finally, completely free.

Desi brushed the dark-brown hair from her face and looked into Faye's eyes.

"Where's Colette?"

∽

Outside, the city was in an uproar. The people panicked, packing their things and running away. Faye shuddered as she watched a family piling into their cart. Her breath fogged Madame's window and the ticking of the clock echoed in the muffled silence. Farther up the street, a house burned with brilliant flames.

Word had spread that the castle was in ruins and King Richard was dead. Somehow, the citizens had also learned that Leo was an Enchanter. They blamed him for his father's death. They said that he had been in league with the Midnight King, plotting to kill the king and take back the country for the magicfolk.

Numbness crawled across Faye's skin, threatening to pull her down into that darkness once again. She wrapped her arms around herself. So many things were different now. And yet so much was the same.

All this time, Madame Leroux had been a Faerie and Leo an Enchanter. Not only an Enchanter, but the White Lord, ruler of Everland. Or, at least, what was once Everland.

Mama, Papa, and Colette were missing. And Faye couldn't be sure if Pathos was even dead.

It was one small comfort knowing the rest of her sisters had escaped the city, guided by the woman with the green umbrella, whoever that was, and Jack. They and Madame's daughters were hidden away at a safe house.

Around her, Madame's sitting room was dark, the only light coming from the flickering fire in the fireplace. She was alone—all the others crowded in the kitchen at Madame's table drinking tea.

She had failed. She had failed because she had been so worried about herself. So selfish and self-centered she couldn't think beyond her own wants.

Tears burned her eyes, but she pushed them back. She was done crying. Done feeling sorry for herself. Now was the time to act. And this time, she wouldn't fail. This time, she would save her family, even if it meant making a deal with Nosos.

Her skin crawled at the thought. The memory of him dragging Pathos away resurfaced and Faye rubbed her arms. Something deep inside her told her that Pathos still lived. But she prayed to the heavens that her blow had killed him.

Faye retreated into the kitchen and took the seat next to Adalie, who sat at the end of the table.

"What do we do now?" she asked, turning to Madame who was resting at the head of the table.

Madame looked vulnerable without her panther-headed cane. But Faye knew better now. Faye could see the Faerie burning beneath the surface. How Madame's green eyes were too bright, her accent too perfect. Faye had met many Pandalian Fae in her life when she lived in Revayr. How could she have forgotten what they looked like?

Desi rose from the her chair, her movements stilted. She clenched her shaking fingers together. "I guess that means … that means …"

Madame leaned forward and placed a comforting hand on her arm. "It seems you, my dear, are queen of Revayr now."

Desi's lips twisted, as if she were holding back a sob. Faye came to her side and wrapped her in a tight hug. It felt good to be able to touch her sisters again. She propped her chin on her sister's shoulder.

"It'll only be for a little while. Just until we find Mama and Papa and Colette. There has to be a way down there."

"But our slippers were shattered. We're no longer bound to the curse." Adalie curled her feet up underneath her chair. "That was our only way in."

"No." Faye pulled away from Desi. "Not all our slippers were broken. I left one behind in the Underworld. And the other …" She turned to Leo.

He sat next to the kitchen fireplace, arms resting on his knees. A faraway look filled his eyes, as if he wished to be anywhere else but here. Trapped in his own skin. Faye's heart pinched at the sight. Not only did he lose his father, but also his kingdom and his people's trust. And who knew how many of those servants and guards had been his friends?

She knew exactly how that felt.

Kneeling next to his side, Faye placed a hand on his shoulder. "Leo?"

He blinked. Slow. Looked up at her. His smile was wooden. "Yes, Faye?"

"The slipper that fell from my foot. What did you do?"

"I broke it." His voice held none of the warmth she remembered.

"What about the other? Do any of you remember what happened to it?"

He shook his head. Desi and Adalie murmured their denial.

Faye nodded, her chin firm. "Then we still have a way."

"But the curse is broken, my dear. It died with you. I don't think that slipper will do you any good." Though Madame's voice was gentle, her words still stung.

Faye slumped to the floor. She was right. With the curse broken, all the slipper was now was a fancy piece of glass. Faye dropped her head into her hands.

"We need to go home." Adalie was quiet. "We've got to follow our sisters."

Of course. How could Faye have forgotten? She pulled her hair back from her face. Their sisters would soon be smuggled out of Eura, back to their kingdom. Once they got there, they would need Desi and Adalie to care for them. Faye pushed herself up to her feet.

"Alright then. We'll go home. But we'll all go together." She looked down at Leo. "Including you."

He frowned. "Me?"

"You can't stay here," Desi said. "You need to come with us."

"And leave my kingdom without a ruler? What kind of prince would I be if I did that?"

"I don't think they want you." Faye winced at her own words. But they were true.

With the Fae and the Humans rioting, no one would accept an Enchanter leader. If there was one thing the Fae and Humans could unite on, it was their hatred for Enchanters.

Hurt filled Leo's eyes. He hung his head. "You're right. They don't."

"I'll send you through the underground network," Madame said. "We'll make our way to the graveyard tomorrow. We'll need to hurry, though, so that you can travel with your sisters."

Faye held out her hand to Leo. "What do you say? Are you coming with us?"

When he looked up at her, Faye could see just how lost he felt. He was a prince without a kingdom, born of a race hated by all. All of which he had no control over. Leo was broken, just as she was, and Faye wasn't sure if she could help him put himself back together again.

After several moments of hesitation, Leo reached up and took her hand.

"We'll get through this. We'll just have to take it one step at a time." She spoke the words as firmly as she could, hoping that someday, she would believe them herself. "Today, we run. We go home. But tomorrow, we fight, until we can get back everything we lost to Pathos. No matter the cost."

Leo nodded. He rose to his feet and gripped her hand tight, his fingers warm against her cold ones.

"No matter the cost."

Epilogue – Aurore

Aurore's nerves ached with each step she took. She leaned heavily on her new cane as she walked, a gift from Faye to replace the loss of her old one.

The girls were safe now, on their way to Revayr with the help of her dear friend Etain. She was the only Faerie Aurore had ever known with the ability to find and use old portals. The princesses would be safe in her hands. Of that, Aurore was sure.

Still, her hands shook, and her heart wouldn't stop its incessant fluttering. The letter clenched in her hand crinkled as she lifted it once more. Nocturne's beautiful handwriting was written across the envelope. For such pretty words, they held a dire message. One that Aurore couldn't wrap her mind around.

Delphine's clear, beautiful voice poured from the open windows of their home. Bonnie's laughter rang from the back garden. Sounds so sweet, Aurore's heart ached.

Many of the Humans had abandoned the city and now only a few Fae remained who had come out of hiding. She knew they would be safe for only so long before the Titanians threatened to hang them along with the Humans.

She pushed open the door and paused a moment, resting her aching body. Delphine's singing softened before dying away. She crept to the front of the house, a shaky smile on her lips.

"Mama? Are you alright?"

Aurore nodded and shut the door. "I'm alright."

"Faye and the others, they're gone now? Etain took them away?"

Easing her way into the armchair, Madame nodded. "All are off on their way to Revayr, including the prince."

"Crown Prince Lionheart." Delphine frowned. "Who would have known he was an Enchanter?"

"He never did those horrible things. You know this, don't you?" Madame couldn't keep the reprimand from her tone. She didn't want her daughter believing the lies and gossip spreading across the city.

Delphine nodded quickly. "Of course, Mama." She shuddered and wrapped her arms around herself.

Madame reached out and brushed the backs of her fingers across her daughter's soft cheek. She watched the way her dark eyes were fixed on the floor and her leg moved with nervous energy. "What's on your mind? You can tell me."

Delphine peered up from under her lashes. "What will we do now? The seamstress's shop was destroyed and there's nowhere for me to find work and—"

"Don't worry yourself, my dear. I've brought some good news home with me." She held up the crinkled letter. "Your Aunt Nocturne's invited us to stay with her."

Delphine's eyes lit with excitement and she sat up taller. "We're going back to Draconia? Oh, Mama, I love it there! Bonnie will be so excited! I know she doesn't remember much but we'll get to see cousin Artorus and maybe he'll even let us fly around!"

Aurore laughed as her daughter's excitement grew. "Go on, go and tell Bonnie. We need to pack right away. We'll be leaving tonight."

Jumping to her feet, Delphine rushed through the house and out to the back garden, shouting all the way. "Bonnie! Bonnie, pack your things! We're going to Draconia!"

As soon as her daughter left, Aurore smoothed the letter out on her knee.

I fear the Night Woman has escaped into the wild once more. I've heard whispers of how she was able to break free of Everland before it became Underworld. But I never believed the rumors to be true. Not until I started to dream again. Oh, my dear sister, I haven't had dreams like this since we escaped.

Andromeda is coming back. I can feel it in my bones. She means to continue what she started. And I fear that means coming after me and my son next.

Aurore crumpled the letter, stood, and threw it into the fire. She watched the paper curl as it was consumed by the flames.

Andromeda was coming. Somehow, she had escaped the curse that kept her sons trapped. No doubt she had broken free the moment the Midnight King had touched the ground with his feet.

Poor Nocturne always had the worst of it when they had been in Andromeda's clutches. And while Nocturne was a Draconian and Aurore a Pandalian, they were as close as sisters. They were the family each other needed to survive.

Aurore picked up the small, old painting and took in the details she had memorized long ago. In it, two young women with midnight skin—one with shimmering green scales patterned across her skin and two large, black wings, the other with ebony curls and catlike green eyes—stood next to each other, their smiles wide. Behind them stood a woman with a different kind of magic. Her skin was pale as ivory, a sharp contrast to her deep-black hair. Her smile showed teeth like knives and her long black nails were curved like talons.

The last time Aurore heard, Andromeda was dead. But now, it seemed death had not taken her. And now, nothing could stop her from taking what was never hers.

Acknowledgments

This is my first attempt at writing acknowledgements, and I want to include a whole passel of people in here, but since I don't want to write an entire book of thank yous, I'll keep this brief.

First, I'd like to thank my mom for her unending support and belief in me. What a lucky kid I am to have a mom who doesn't think being an author is insane.

And of course, thanks, Tony, for finally coming around to the idea and making sure that I'm financially taken care of. I know you care about us step-kids, even if you don't know how to show it.

A big, fat THANK YOU to Keturah, because you promised to murder me if I didn't put your name in the acknowledgements. There, happy? But, really, thank you for bringing me junk food and patting me on the head whenever I announced I was throwing in the towel.

This brainchild of mine would be nowhere near as cool as it is today if it hadn't been for the mighty sword wielded by the coolest, sweetest, most enthusiastic and awesomest Content Editor in the world. Lydia Jane Craft, you've earned a billion gold stars for your efforts.

Another big, illustrious thank you to Kendra E. Ardnek, Wyn Owens, and all the members of Arista's Band of Fairytale Retellers. You people rock, and without the Tattered Slippers challenge, *Curse of the Midnight King* would never have happened. I *will* read all of your amazing books one day. I promise!

I feel like I should throw in a thank you to Eliana, Sofia, and Netanya, my twin separated by a year. The fact that you

281

guys haven't grown tired of me talking nonstop about my book by now is really saying a lot. Love ya, sistahs.

Kyle, I feel I owe you a huge hug and a gazillion-million-trillion thank yous. Without you, I wouldn't have had the strength to push forward. Thank you for talking me off the literal ledge more than once. Everyone deserves a friend like you.

Rachel Richardson, you get a thank you for being my friend of I-don't-remember-how-many-years. Your enthusiasm to see me published is the best thing a gal can ask for. You're still my bestie for life!

Thank you to Kelly McWilliams and all of your encouragement and gentle nudging to help me make this book better. Your support and advice mean the world to me! Thank you to entire team of #FaithPitch, and to Tessa Emily Hall for taking a chance on me. Without you guys, I wouldn't be here today.

Thank you to Elaina Lee for this beautiful cover! You did an amazing job!

Phoenix, thank you for all of your last-minute help and your encouragement! You officially have bragging rights of reading this book in almost every stage it's gone through. You rock, and I hope that someday you'll reach your writing goals as well!

And thank you, you amazing person who decided to pick up my book and read it all the way to the acknowledgements. Yes, I'm talking to you. You rock!

Now comes the greatest, humblest thank you of all. Thank you, God, for the gift and for moving the pieces of my life in all the right directions, even when I couldn't see it, to get me here. Thank you for being You.